DEAD GIRLS TALKING

DEAD GIRLS TALKING

MEGAN COOLEY PETERSON

HOLIDAY HOUSE · NEW YORK

1 3 5 7 9 10 8 6 4 2

Library of Congress Cataloging-in-Publication Data

Names: Peterson, Megan Cooley, author.
Title: Dead girls talking / Megan Cooley Peterson.
Description: First edition. | New York : Holiday House, 2024. | Audience:
    Ages 14 and up. | Audience: Grades 10-12. | Summary: Bettina Holland,
    known for being the daughter of The Smiley Face Killer, confronts her
    past and questions her beliefs about her father's guilt when a series of
    copycat murders emerge, as she teams up with Eugenia, the mortician's
    daughter, to unmask a murderer closer to home than she ever imagined.
Identifiers: LCCN 2023023545 | ISBN 9780823457014 (hardcover)
Subjects: CYAC: Murder—Fiction. | Fathers and daughters—Fiction.
    Mystery and detective stories. | LCGFT: Detective and mystery fiction.
    Novels.
Classification: LCC PZ7.1.P456 De 2024 | DDC [Fic]—dc23
LC record available at https://lccn.loc.gov/2023023545

ISBN: 978-0-8234-5701-4 (hardcover)

For my mom. I miss you.

"SMILEY FACE KILLER" SENTENCED TO LIFE

WILMINGTON, N.C.—Convicted murderer Trapper McGrath has been sentenced to life in prison without the possibility of parole.

"Justice has been served today," said prosecutor Jack Ledbetter outside the courthouse. "I hope Prudence's family can finally find some peace."

McGrath, 28, was convicted for the June 2009 murder of his wife, Prudence McGrath, 23. The couple's 6-year-old child was at home at the time of the killing and made the grisly discovery.

Dubbed the "Smiley Face Killer," McGrath fatally stabbed his wife three times in the chest. After killing her, McGrath carved her mouth into a permanent smile, earning him his moniker.

Several key pieces of evidence convinced the jury, including a threatening note the defendant wrote to his wife. McGrath's fingerprints were found on the murder weapon, which had been dumped in some bushes near the family's home, and his clothing contained traces of the victim's blood.

"This sentence can't bring our daughter back," said Wells Walker Holland, the victim's father. "But I can rest easier knowing this animal will spend the rest of his life behind bars."

CHAPTER
One

It's been nearly six months since I visited my father in prison.

Six months since I heard the clanking metal.

Six months since I smelled the stale desperation mixed with cheap deodorant.

Every six months—no more, no less. Two court-ordered visits a year.

I was with my mother the day he killed her, and my testimony helped convict him. I had a memory of him from that day—of the shape of him, moving down the hallway to their bedroom. I never saw her alive again after that. Only her broken body, eyes unblinking, jagged slashes on either side of her mouth.

The media quickly named my father the Smiley Face Killer.

A judge granted him visitation rights in the custody agreement between him and my grandparents—even though he's in prison for life—which is *beyond* messed up if you ask me. But no one asks *me* anything.

I never want to see him again, and I have a plan to make that happen. I stuff my letter into an envelope, address it, and add a stamp. With any luck, he'll relinquish those rights, and I won't see or think about him for the rest of my life. He usually spends our visits rehashing his tired claim of innocence anyway; he *says* he was with my grandfather the morning of Mom's murder, but Granddad was at work, and that alibi fell apart in court. It's total fucking nonsense. He needs to get a new lie.

I've got one year of high school left. I don't want to waste it on him. I can't.

"You wrote it?"

Grams steps onto the veranda. Behind her, the windows are as tall as the porch roof; Grams said when she was young they'd open them all for the breeze. I can't imagine this place without central air. It's so big—a true mansion. Huge Greek columns run up to the second story, where my grandparents' balcony faces the front yard.

I hold up the letter. "I just want it to be over, Grams. I need it to be over."

The peach sky illuminates the golden tendrils that have broken free from her chignon and frame her face. Thunder booms in the distance, but on the veranda of Magnolia House, our family's ancestral home, it's a calm spring evening. This is the same porch my mother used to ride her pink tricycle on; I saw it in a photograph once.

She sighs and looks out across the lawn. "Are you sure? He is your father, after all."

"Like I could ever forget."

I hand the letter to Grams, and she turns it over in her jeweled hands. "You're right. Enough is enough. You have a life to live, a future to plan, and that man doesn't deserve any part of it. Not after what he did." Her voice catches, same as it always does when she talks about what happened. She had twenty-three years with my mother before

2

my father decided to play God. Twenty-three years, but all she can think about is that single day. It's all I can seem to think about too. And I'm so tired of it.

I stand and hug her, the only real mother I've ever known.

She holds me tighter. "I love you to the moon," she whispers.

"And back again." I squeeze my eyes shut. Squeeze out the fear and doubt. I am safe here, in this house, in this life they have given me…as long as we all stick to our parts.

Grams steps back. "Should I mail this for you? I can post it in the morning after my yoga class." She's always been delicate with me. Watchful. Overprotective, even. *We have to be careful in raising Bettina,* I heard her tell my grandfather once (before the maid caught me eavesdropping). I think they're worried I'm going to run away with some older guy, get knocked up, and get myself killed—just like my mother did.

"No, I want to do it myself."

"You're going now?" she asks, wringing her hands. "I could get Cook to make us some strawberry lemonades. We'll enjoy the sunset."

"Now. No time like the present." I slip on my jean jacket. It belonged to my mother; I found it in the attic a few weeks ago. An aughts original. "Let's have the lemonades for breakfast."

"You're going by yourself? I'll send Hank along." Hank is our driver, and he does other odds and ends at the house, too. Painting, light yard work, chasing away journalists. (I once wondered if Grams and Hank were sweet on each other, until she introduced me to his husband at our Christmas party.)

"I'll be all right, I promise."

"At least drive there. It's getting dark." My grandmother hates the darkness. She usually won't go out after sunset.

"I'd like to walk. Don't worry, I'll come straight home."

"*Please* be careful, Bettina."

I kiss her cheek and set off down Magnolia Street (my great-great-grandparents were so rich, the town named the street after our house). Eventually, I reach shops and cafés and the video store I keep waiting to go out of business but never does. And there it is: the freestanding mailbox outside the movie theater. The original *Star Wars* is playing, same as it does every spring, and I think maybe I should buy a ticket and forget everything for a while.

Trapper McGrath
Bertie Correctional Institution
Windsor, North Carolina

I close my eyes, take deep breaths, and wait for the sidewalk to stop swimming circles around my feet.

Twenty visits in ten years, two hours per visit. I've looked my father in the eyes for a total of forty hours since the trial ended. So why does mailing him a letter make me so nervous?

"This is dumb," I mutter, and I drop the letter inside. Let the mailbox door snap closed. Try to ignore how much it sounds like the clanking of those bars.

He can rot in that place. He's not taking me with him.

I will sweep him away into the current of my past. Put an end to it. A fresh start for me—and, in a way, for the mother I never really knew. Because I *can't* keep being the girl whose father killed her mother. It makes me want to claw out of my skin.

The flashing lights of the theater's marquee paint the sidewalk in baby spotlights, and I dig through my purse for some cash. A dark theater, a cold Coke, and total anonymity. I can be anyone when I'm here. I can be *normal.*

"One, please," I tell the attendant, who sighs, puts down her glittering green phone, and rings up the ticket. My phone lights up with a text from Xavier.

Xavier: Train in 10. Meet me on the tracks.

"That'll be eight fifty," the girl says.

My heart pounds, and my palms grow slick. Grams is likely drinking bourbon on the veranda, watching the long driveway, the changing shadows, tensing each time she thinks she sees me. I should go home, play a game of cribbage with her, and finish my poem for English class.

"You want that ticket or what?" the girl asks.

"I changed my mind," I say, and she rolls her eyes. "George Lucas ruined it anyway with all his bullshit edits."

She finally looks at me for the first time and frowns. "Wait…aren't you, like, that girl from the news?"

I pretend not to hear her and take off down Market Street and around onto Carter, following the smell from the soy-oil factory. Plumes of black rise from its dirty smokestacks. The farther I go, the more cramped the houses become, almost touching each other. Beyond them, at the edge of Wolf Ridge, the Smoky Mountains heave up, peaks blanketed in pines. Electrified fences close off the quartz mines in the foothills.

My grandparents love living so close to the mountains, but they make me feel caged in. Trapped.

Xavier steps out from a boxy gray house on the corner and lights a cigarette. "Hey, Bett," he says. I lick my lips as I watch him take that first drag. His mouth curls around the cigarette, then blows a smoke ring. He joins me on the sidewalk and offers me a drag. I take it, flick my overprocessed blond hair behind my shoulders, and inhale.

"You're lucky I was already downtown," I say offhandedly, giving him back the cigarette.

"Or what? You wouldn't have come?" He smirks and walks faster. I hurry to catch up, and my long black skirt tangles with my feet. I manage to sort myself out, but Xavier keeps moving. He is always in motion, more blur than boy. "Come on, Miss Bettina," he says in an exaggerated southern drawl, not looking back. "I ain't got all day."

I started talking to Xavier Hart in detention after Christmas break, when I was in for being tardy three days in one week. He sat in the back and painted his fingernails blue. He caught me staring and tossed me the bottle. I wore that polish until it chipped completely away. Rumors follow him through the halls like flies: that he was kicked out of his last school for keeping a knife in his locker. That he drove drunk and killed his older brother. That his entire back is covered in a pentacle tattoo. (It's not. Sadly.)

Smoke trails behind Xavier as he rounds the corner. The soybean plant looms to our left, blotting out the setting sun. Ahead, the train tracks lace the ground.

He checks his phone and then stares down the tracks. "A couple minutes, tops. Come on."

We head east, away from the plant, his house, the stray dog eating a bag of garbage someone dropped in the middle of the street. If my grandfather knew what part of town I was in, he would have a stroke.

Xavier stomps out his cigarette and puts his phone into his jeans pocket. Then he hops onto the tracks, his feet balanced on a rail, and picks a dandelion. He doesn't look at me or invite me to join him.

"I'll play, since you insist," I say sarcastically as I stand next to him.

"Can you feel it?" He catches me staring at him and holds my gaze in his.

I forget to breathe, and I have to restrain myself from leaning into him. Then his eyes close and he turns away, and I remember the rules. I close my own, the heat and the pulsing buzz of the cicadas intensifying.

I *can* feel it: a vibration coming up through my feet. Weak at first but strengthening.

The train's whistle pierces my courage, and my eyes fly open. Xavier looks asleep, but his lids twitch. I stare at the light from the train engine, half a mile away, real-but-not-real at the same time.

I always leap off first. But not tonight.

The train hurtles toward us, whistle going crazy. I swear I can hear someone yelling. I blink, blink again, and it's almost here.

Xavier's arm brushes mine. "We better move!" he shouts.

I grab his wrist. "Why? You scared?" My mouth is so dry I can barely get out the words. The horn blasts, and the heat of the approaching engine practically singes my skin.

Nothing is real now: not the looming black shape growing larger by the second, not Xavier's wide eyes, not even the laugh bubbling up through my throat.

"*Shit!*" Xavier wraps an arm around me and heaves us to the side. He lands on top of me in the gravel. The train whips by, hot air billowing against us, metal on metal, violence.

"You're crazy!" he says, pushing himself off me.

I take deep breaths and raise my head to see the last train car flash past us. I am insignificant, a blip. It makes me feel better, somehow. Like maybe my problems are insignificant too.

Xavier shows me his back as the train rounds a corner.

"Are you mad?" I ask. This isn't our normal routine. The power balance is all off. My skin tingles.

He turns and leans over me. "Come on."

He takes my hand, pulling me up, across the tracks, and to the other side of a weeping willow tree. The wild grasses grow tall here, and no one sees us. Or maybe they do. That's part of the thrill, I guess. There's no one around, but there are eyes everywhere in this hick town.

"Don't be mad," I say, trying to come off flippant. My heart pounds, and I wonder if he's going to walk away from me. Instead, he backs me into the tree and presses his body into mine. Daylight couldn't pass between us.

"You think I'm mad?" he asks. His pupils are huge, turning his blue eyes black. He licks his lips and looks at my mouth.

I can't speak.

He reaches for the bottom of my skirt, pulls it up until his hand finds the skin of my thigh. He stares at me as he trails his fingers up my leg, slips a finger under my panties. I swallow, and Xavier smiles.

I slam my mouth into his. The pressure is building—louder than that train, louder than the clanking of those bars.

This is like coming alive.

He lowers me to the ground, the feel of him on top of me a comfort, a weight keeping me from blowing away. I think of the train, how it was here and then it wasn't, how if we'd stood there three seconds longer, police and flashing lights and my sobbing grandmother would be here now. Instead of us. Instead of this.

Xavier leaves a trail of kisses down my neck, and I reach for the button on his jeans. "Are you sure?" he pants. He pushes up my shirt, squeezes the fat on my hips, and part of me wants to cover myself back up.

"Yes," I whisper, wondering if he heard me.

His eyes meet mine, a silent agreement passes, and he unzips.

Then it's happening. His eyes are on mine, still, black, intense. I look away, stare at a half-drunk bottle of Mountain Dew someone left in the dirt. It's swarming with ants.

Xavier puts his cheek up next to mine. "You're amazing," he breathes.

I hold on to his back, touch his impossibly soft hair, bite my lip from the pain. He puts a sloppy kiss on the corner of my mouth, shudders, and then rolls off me. I pull up my panties and rearrange my shirt to hide my stomach. He lies on his back, eyes half closed.

I want so badly to stroke his hair, to curl up in the crook of his arm, but I don't dare. So I sit there, picking at my cuticles, my bones vibrating with the need to say something, to touch him, to ask him if he wants to go catch the next showing of *Star Wars* with me.

His phone chirps, and he sits up, resumes his aura of nonchalance. "It's the guys," he says, like it's not a big deal, like there isn't a pile of *him* in the dirt next to us. "There's a party at the cemetery coming up."

I wait for an invitation, but he keeps scrolling through his phone.

"Enjoy your stale beer," I say, "and your hangover at school."

He ignores that and points his phone's screen at me. "Someone just texted me this." It's a news article about the ten-year anniversary of Trapper's conviction. I don't share his last name anymore; my grandparents changed it to Holland, hoping people would forget about my father and his connection to me. But the murder colors this town, kept alive with gossip and whispers and conspiracies. It has legs, and I haven't figured out a way to take it out at the knees.

"I don't live in the past." I stand abruptly. "I'd rather live now."

I quickly walk away, severing whatever connection there was between us, not giving him time to ask me to stay or to pretend he's not fishing for details about my mom.

And maybe he's not. He's never once mentioned it until tonight. Still, I'm not willing to be an object of curiosity for anyone, not even him. I have to be careful who I'm friends with. One mention of my mom's death, and it's over—I cut them out.

Probably explains why I'm on my own a lot.

But then, if you never get close to anyone, you can't lose them. And everyone leaves in the end. Either by choice or by fate.

The girl is gone from the box office as I pass by the movie theater. A guy sits in her place, selling tickets to a group of junior-high girls dressed in jean shorts and high-tops. They wear purses, but awkwardly, not quite used to the accessory. Giggling at something the guy says, they collect their tickets and go inside. I remember when I had friends like that.

Grams is still on the veranda when I get home. I'm about halfway up the drive when she stands, picks up a glass, and goes inside, the door soundless as it closes her off from me.

I'm late.

At least she leaves the light on.

After that, I don't want to go inside. Instead, I head toward the one place someone will listen without judgment: the cemetery.

CHAPTER Two

The end of my street butts up against the woods. They're a shortcut to where my mom lies silently, but I won't pass through. Not even during the day.

These woods are where Wolf Ridge's first body was found.

It happened a year before my mom died. Trapper's suspected previous victim, though they could never tie him to it. No DNA, no fibers, no hair. Her name was Cherry Hobbs, and she worked at a gas station at the edge of town. Some kids found her stabbed to death—just like Mom—in the woods right before Halloween, her body heaped onto a pile of blood-soaked leaves. Poor kids thought she was a prop from the Boy Scouts' haunted house over on Birch Street.

Everyone said she was a junkie, that she slept around. That's probably the real reason her case remains unsolved.

So I stick to the roads. They're empty this time of night—except for curious eyes peering out from behind curtains, the blue light from televisions pulsating behind them. Someone is *always* watching you in Wolf Ridge. What we lack in culture, we make up for in small-mindedness.

I hold my breath as I pass the Cline house, our town's only funeral home. It's an old Victorian, white, with peeling paint. When we were kids, there was this old rhyme we used to say every Halloween:

> *If you knock*
> *On the undertaker's door,*
> *He'll lop off your head,*
> *And then come for more.*
>
> *He'll cut out your bones!*
> *And dig out your guts!*
> *Hide you in the basement*
> *With the corpses and rot!*

Tonight I make the mistake of looking.

Eugenia Cline, their daughter, sits on the porch, head bent over a book, flashlight pointed at the pages. In Wolf Ridge, women and girls are to be seen as beautiful playthings. Us Holland women never leave home without at least a swipe of lipstick and a hint of mascara. Here, if you refuse to do at least that, you're nothing.

Eugenia is unmanicured, unpainted, and unfinished. Because of that, she's always been just a little too far down the popularity food chain for me to say hello to. (Besides, she helps put makeup on the dead bodies for viewing. At least that's the rumor.)

As if she can read my thoughts, she lifts her head. Her dark, almost whiteless eyes meet mine. She doesn't smile or wave or nod. Just watches me. A chill ripples up my back, and I look away.

I turn onto Dogwood Lane. The Mount Olivet Cemetery sits at the end of the road, behind a line of magnolia trees and a black wrought iron fence. Some of the graves date back to the founding of the town in the late 1700s. The newer stones are near the back, in neater rows, with potted flowers and even a bench to sit on.

I can find my way to my mom with my eyes closed: just follow the gravel pathway as it winds west, the moonlight turning my skin a grayish blue. (I only ever come at night.) Her stone is the biggest: a marble angel with an ethereal face, her wings encircling a slender gothic headstone. MOTHER, DAUGHTER, SISTER is carved on its pedestal.

I touch the angel's face, same as always, then sit in the grass before it.

"Hi, Mom," I say, my voice a scratch. I look behind me, just in case, but only the shadows are watching.

That's one good thing about dead people—they can't eavesdrop.

"So." I clear my throat. "It happened. With this boy Xavier. He seemed nice…but then he asked about Dad."

I wonder what this conversation would be like in a normal mother-daughter relationship, not one separated by six feet of dirt. Maybe other girls don't tell their moms when they lose their virginity. But if I had *my* mom, I'd tell her every ugly thing about me.

I crane my neck up, watching the angel's face. Sometimes, when it's really late and I haven't been sleeping much—or I've snuck just a little too much from Granddad's liquor cabinet—the angel's face moves. Smiles, or grimaces.

Once a tear slipped out of her eye and dripped onto my forehead.

It had just finished raining that night, but no one will ever convince me she wasn't weeping.

"What do you think I should do?" I ask. "Give him another chance?"

Tonight, the angel's face remains lifeless.

I pluck a blade of grass and roll it between my fingers, gazing at the headstone again. I don't know why I keep coming out here, thinking Mom's going to speak eventually. I stand, shaking my head. "I'll see you later, Mom," I say, and head back down the gravel path.

As I'm exiting the cemetery, a bat swoops down in front of me. I scream. (Every so often, we get a bat inside Magnolia House—Grams and I usually shriek and cower under the furniture while Granddad chases it with a tennis racket.)

A porch light on the house across the street flips on, and I hide in the only place I can—the woods beside the cemetery. I fit my body behind a huge live oak and hold my breath as a door squeaks open.

"Anybody out there?" It's the voice of our chief of police, Carl Bigsby, who's good friends with Granddad.

I peer around the tree. Bigsby stands on his front porch wearing saggy boxer shorts and a white T-shirt. As he looks up and down the street, his wife comes out in her nightgown. She says something, and the chief raises a hand to her. Everyone in Wolf Ridge knows Bigsby puts hands on his wife—but apparently no one is allowed to talk about it, let alone punish this asshole. His wife quickly backs into the house. He spits tobacco onto the lawn and goes inside, flips off the light. I keep watching, and sure enough the curtains in his picture window spread open.

Always watching.

Behind me, the woods offer no light. But they do offer cover, so I venture deeper into them, reluctantly taking the shortcut home. Just this one time. If I don't, Creepy Chief Fuckhead will bust me for curfew-breaking. No thanks.

The woods are black. On Halloween, people sometimes smash pumpkins in here or hold séances to invoke Cherry's spirit. It's macabre to me—but to them, harmless fun.

I stay as far away from the southern edge of the woods as I can. That's where she was found.

The spring canopy blocks out most of the moonglow, so I wake up my phone, using its meager light to navigate the fallen trees, twisted roots, and old junk forgotten by generations. It smells like wet dirt. I check my screen for a text from Xavier when my foot connects with something hard, and I topple over, landing on my hands and knees.

"*Shit!*" I hiss, feeling along the dark ground for my phone.

A twig snaps behind me. I hold my breath. Something scuttles out from under a fallen tree and takes off, a dark shape low to the ground.

"Get it together, Bett," I whisper. I find my phone, flick the flashlight on again, and point it toward where the animal went to make sure it keeps away.

There's nothing there. Only a tree, a shiny pink lump wedged in its roots. Probably more garbage. Some people treat any wooded area as a public landfill. I stand, wipe my hands on my skirt, and start walking toward home.

Three steps later, I stop and turn around.

I've processed what I've seen. Why go back?

The back of my neck grows cold as I slowly, slowly step up to the tree again.

I shine my phone at it, swing it toward the pink shape. It's all wrong. It sprouts appendages—arms and legs, curled in on themselves. My light slowly moves toward what I know I'll find, but hope I don't:

A face.

It's gray and mottled, its eyes open, and I drop the phone again. The light disappears, and I'm plunged into darkness.

I'm almost glad the face has disappeared. But the *smell*. The wind has changed, and the stench invades my nose and mouth, as foul as the time a racoon died under our veranda. It's a smell you can't forget, the smell of death and decay. Of fear. This body must have been out in the heat awhile. Nature has already started to take it back.

I collapse to the ground and run my hands over the leaves until I grasp my phone, hands shaking so badly I can barely lift or point it.

The pink lump isn't trash at all—it's a blood-splattered coat, wrapped around a woman curled up on her side. The light strobes over her frozen face, her blond hair crusted in mud and leaves and blood. But it's not just *any* woman lying there.

It's my mother.

Her blue eyes stare at me, but they don't blink. Her mouth has been carved into a demented smile. For a moment, the woods disappear, and I'm back in that bedroom in our old house, shaking her, begging her to wake up.

The woods deepen around me. Panic claws from inside my chest.

There's something scratched into her forehead. Tilting my head, I steady the light until I can make out two words:

I'M BACK.

I open my mouth to scream, but I can't catch my breath.

That's when I fall.

CHAPTER
Three

Officer Andre Richardson towers over me at the edge of the woods on Dogwood, a flashlight aimed at my face. "Are you all right?"

After I woke from fainting, I stumbled out of the woods and called the police. I've known Andre my whole life; I feel a little better now that he's here.

"There's a woman," is all I can manage to say. I can't say that I think she might be my mom; that maybe she's been alive all these years and died *today*. I don't want him to think I'm crazy. "In the woods, under a fallen tree. About a hundred feet in."

"Is she hurt?" Andre asks.

"More than hurt," I squeak out. I'm in danger of throwing up.

"Wait out here." Andre goes into the trees. "Oh shit," I can hear him say. He's found her. It isn't a dream. He reappears, out of breath. "Did you find her like this?"

I nod.

"You didn't touch her, did you?"

"N-no," I stammer.

He calls it in to the station with his radio. Soon, Chantal Avery, the other officer in town, arrives. It's all a whirl after that; I tell them where I found her, why I was out there so late, and then I wait as they disappear into the green.

"Looks to be a white female, early twenties."

"Stab wounds to the chest and mouth, something scratched or carved into her forehead."

"We better call the medical examiner."

Shaking, I squeeze my eyes shut.

The blood.

Her broken eyes.

Just like Mom.

And those *words*. Even with my eyes closed, they dance on my lids. Hacked into her like she was nothing. Disposable.

I'm back.

Suddenly the food from dinner turns traitor in my stomach, and I vomit into a mulberry bush. The woman looked *so* much like my mom.

Seeing my digestive fireworks, Andre runs to his squad car and returns with a bottle of water. I swish some around my mouth and spit. "Sorry," I mumble.

"Nothing to be sorry for, Bett. Let me get you home."

He drives me to Magnolia House. My grandparents are already waiting on the veranda. Grams pulls me into a crushing hug immediately. "Sweetheart, are you all right?"

Her eyes are red, and her hair, usually perfectly done up, hangs lank. Her bald patches show. For the first time, Grams looks like an old woman to me.

Andre explains the situation briefly.

"You scared me to death!" Grams scolds when he's finished. "You know I like you back by sundown. I saw you come home—why did you go out again?"

"I'm not hurt, Grams. It wasn't me laying in the woods."

"No, but it could have been. It's too much like…" She stops and covers her mouth with her hands.

She doesn't have to say it. We both know what she means.

Her blue eyes meet mine, wide and moist, and then she swallows. "I'll run you a bubble bath to help calm your nerves."

Granddad kisses the top of my head. "We're just happy you're safe, Bettina. We can discuss what you were doing out so late tomorrow." He turns to Andre. "Any idea of who this woman might be?"

"Not yet, sir. But we'll keep you updated. And I'd like to question you, Bett, if I could. Formally."

Granddad shakes his head. "Absolutely not! She's in no shape for that. You can speak with her tomorrow morning."

Andre looks at me. "It really would be best if we could speak tonight, while the memory is fresh…."

"*Tomorrow*, Andre," Granddad warns. "I'll bring her to the station myself."

Andre hesitates, but Granddad has influence in this town. So he nods, tips his hat, and walks back to the squad car. That man has patience.

After I assure Grams for the tenth time that I'm okay, I head upstairs and slip into the bubble bath. She wanted to sit in the bathroom with me; I almost had to shove her out the door.

The first thing I see when I close my eyes is that woman's face. My mother's face. Already turning gray...her mouth, hacked wider on either end...

I touch my own face, half convinced I'll find torn flesh instead of smooth skin.

How long would she have been out there if I hadn't found her? Days? Weeks? I shudder, even though the water is scalding. I try to wash away what I saw in the woods. No matter how hard I scrub, I don't feel clean.

The words on her forehead taunt me, picking at the wound of my story—of my family's story. My father was convicted of murdering my mother, in no small part based on my testimony. But the truth is...I never actually saw his *face* when he went to the bedroom where my mother died. Only his back.

What if it *was* some other man?

And now *he's* back?

The tiny seed of doubt I've pushed down my whole life threatens to bloom. I barely have time to lean over the side of the tub before I'm sick again.

———

The next day, I wake up tucked into my bed, my eyes so dry it's hard to open them. When I sit up, the room spins, and I flop back down.

Everything that happened last night comes flooding back—the woman's body, her dead eyes searching mine, the fear that maybe my father isn't as guilty as I always thought. Shaking my head, I force myself out of bed.

No. Trapper's guilty. The forensic evidence proved that, didn't it? Someone else killed this woman, and it has nothing to do with my mom.

It can't.

As I peel off my pajamas and turn on the shower in the adjoining bathroom, it hits me that the novelty of losing my virginity is gone—I actually forgot I even had sex. It's like something that happened to somebody else. I let the warm water beat against my back.

After toweling off, I throw on my uniform, a pleated green skirt and white polo, and hurry downstairs. My phone dings: it's an email from some loser who's starting a podcast on famous murders and wants to interview me about my mom.

Delete.

Lucky for me, I get fewer and fewer requests these days. I hate them. Loathe. Them. Never, ever, *ever* would I give an interview about—

My scalp prickles with a realization: there's been a fresh murder in Wolf Ridge, and my mom's case will be a hot commodity again.

Downstairs, the clanking of silverware drifts from the dining room. No one's talking, which never bodes well. My grandfather is a notorious talker. After what happened last night, will he be waiting to pump me for every detail?

I hurry down and enter. Grams sits at her usual spot, her green-tea facial mask smeared heavily under both eyes, a bright yellow scarf tied around her head to hide her curlers. (She got very sick when she was a kid and lost a lot of her hair, so she goes to the salon almost every day and wears hairpieces.) She smears jelly on a piece of toast and bites into it, holding her hand beneath her chin to catch any crumbs. Our cook, Ardis, has set up the typical Friday breakfast spread on the buffet, and I make a beeline for the biscuits and gravy. She always makes an extra batch of meatless gravy just for me.

"Not too much, now." Grams sniffs. "Leave room for your beet juice. You need your antioxidants."

Granddad looks up from his newspaper and gives me a terse smile. "Good morning, Bettina Jane."

He's the only person who calls me by my full name. "Morning, Granddad."

His silver hair is freshly cut, parted, and combed to one side. His mustache grazes his top lip, and he dabs at it with his cloth napkin. "Did you get any sleep?"

Did I sleep? Hell no. But it's easier to pretend. "I slept okay."

"Good, good." He slurps his coffee; it's always black. He says cream and sugar are for weaker men. Women, I guess, are free to be as weak as they like. "We've got something to discuss with you."

Grams clears her throat. "Wells," she warns.

Here it comes, I think, bracing myself.

He folds up the newspaper and tucks it under his plate. He's already dressed for the day: a three-piece suit, watch, cuff links. He owns a law practice, and no matter how much Grams begs him to cut back his hours, he works like a dog. "She's going to find out, Vivian. Let's get ahead of this now while we still can."

"Is this about the dead woman?" I ask, feeling faint. For a moment, I can *smell* her, and I set my fork down.

He stands and pours himself a fresh cup of coffee at the buffet, ignoring my question. "Would you like one?" he asks me, looking over the top of his rounded glasses.

Coffee this early makes my heart race. But I need something to do with my hands. "Yes, please."

"You shouldn't drink coffee," Grams scolds. "You're too young for that much caffeine. Bad for your heart!"

Granddad places a steaming cup in front of me and winks. Then he resumes his spot at the head of the table while Grams rubs her forehead. The coffee burns my tongue, but I drink anyway. Granddad takes off his glasses, sets them on the table, and looks me square in the eyes. "Do you remember Jack Ledbetter?"

"Jack Ledbetter," I echo, blankly.

"He was the prosecutor on your mother's case." Granddad never says my mother's name aloud—Prudence. But at least he still talks about her. Grams never talks about her at all.

I finish off the coffee and set the cup down with a thunk.

"Jack died last night," Granddad says. Grams wrings her hands.

"Was he sick or something?" I ask, knowing there's got to be more to this story.

He nods. "Yes…I suppose he was, in a way. Chief Bigsby gave me a call early this morning, said he hanged himself. With his belt. Terrible way to go." He pauses. "I'm sorry, I shouldn't have said how."

We've never really discussed the trial. I have a vague memory of riding in the car to the courthouse with Grams. We sat in the back seat while Hank drove, and she held me so tight I could hardly breathe. I thought the building was a castle. I don't remember what happened inside, just that it made Grams cry. I only went once. When I actually testified against my father, the judge let me do it via a live feed, so I didn't have to see his face. We've avoided talking about it for so long that it feels impossible to start now.

"Why would the chief call you? Were you friends?"

"No, no, nothing like that," Granddad says quickly, wiping his mouth. "We barely knew each other apart from the trial. It was just a . . . courtesy, is all."

"What does his death have to do with me?"

"It doesn't—at least not directly. Bettina Jane, listen to me. The ten-year anniversary of your father's conviction is next month, and the suicide of the man who put him in prison won't have the best optics, I'm afraid. And now that another woman's been killed in Wolf Ridge, in a manner that—I'm to understand—was similar to Trapper's victims . . . well, I have no doubt he will use it to bolster his claims of innocence. I want you to be prepared, so you're not blindsided by the attention that's bound to rain down on us. I may hire a security guard for the house, just for the time being. To keep reporters away. Do you have any questions?"

He asks this as if he's just explained how to change the oil in my car or fill out my Harvard application. Calmly. A mundanity.

I'm well-versed in my father's woe-is-me tale. He's convinced a lot of people he was set up for my mother's murder, even though *his* fingerprints were found on the knife. Her blood ended up on *his* clothes. And *he* wrote her a threatening note the night before she died. Unlike me, *he* is always willing to do interviews, and he has maintained the same simple story: Sometimes they argued, which was why he wrote that note. My mom often had nosebleeds, which explained the blood. And his prints on the murder weapon? He'd used it to cut his steak the night before she died.

Granddad doesn't wait for me to answer. "And it's not just the media that concerns me. Wolf Ridge is a small town, and people around here love their gossip. They're like hens, pecking the dirt for a morsel. Just keep your guard up, is all. Damn vultures!"

"Wells!" Grams hits the table with her fist, sending a jolt through her silverware. "That's enough."

Granddad puts his glasses back on and picks up the newspaper. "Yes."

Ardis comes into the dining room with a fresh carafe of coffee and refills our cups.

"Are you *really* all right, honey?" Grams asks me. "Maybe you should stay home from school today."

I shake my head. "Don't worry, Grams. Some talk isn't going to break me."

"Break you?" Ardis asks. "What's this about?" She wears her grayish-blond hair in a beehive and has what Grams calls *a full bosom*.

"Just Trapper things," I say, my stomach twisting. Sometimes I think I should wear a scarlet *MD* across my chest for Murderer's Daughter. That's all anyone sees when they look at me.

"You got nothing to feel bad about, Bett," Ardis says firmly. "You ain't your daddy's sins, understand me?" I'm left wishing I could believe her as she retreats to the kitchen.

"You don't look quite yourself," Grams pushes. "Are you coming down with anything?"

I hold my breath for a moment. Try to banish the memory of Xavier on top of me juxtaposed with the woman's unblinking eyes. "Please just stop, Grams," I mumble. "I can't breathe when you get like this."

Grams looks off toward the front parlor and its picture window overlooking the street. The purple blooms of our redbud trees pop against the gray sky. Her hands shake so badly when she raises her teacup to her lips that some sloshes over the side.

———

Chief Bigsby waits for us on the steps of the police station. He has a big, fleshy nose, a wad of chew tucked into his bottom lip, close-set blue eyes, and dark gray hair that's severely lacking on top. It's weird to see him without his aviator sunglasses on; he never goes anywhere in Wolf Ridge without them.

"Wells," he says, shaking Granddad's hand. "Wish you were here under better circumstances."

Granddad nods. "Shall we get this out of the way, then? Bettina Jane has school."

Bigsby finally looks at me, as if he forgot I was there. "Bettina. Looks like you got dragged into it last night. What were you doin' out in those woods so late?" He doesn't give me a chance to reply, just turns and opens the door, motioning for us to follow.

Bernadette Myers works the front desk during the week; on the weekends, she runs the farmers' market. Her hair is white as cotton and kept in a tiny bun on top of her head. She beams at Granddad; most people in town do. "Hello there, Mr. Holland," she purrs. She has a voice like Betty Boop, if Betty Boop had smoked Winstons her whole life. (Which Bernadette still does behind the Baptist church, though she professes she quit years ago.)

Bigsby leads us into the back room. There are only two desks set up; one belongs to Andre and the other to Chantal. They look up when we enter. We pass through to Bigsby's office and he shuts the door. "Grab a seat," he says, spitting tobacco-stained spit into an empty soda bottle. "This won't take long."

"Do you know who she is?" I ask.

"Who?" he asks, leaning back in his wooden desk chair. It creaks and groans.

"The woman in the woods."

"Ah, her." He opens a folder on his desk. "This'll be in the paper tomorrow morning. Her name is Melissa Atkins. Worked as a waitress over at Lydia's. Just moved to town a couple months back."

"That poor girl," Granddad says. He reaches over and pats my shoulder.

"Why would someone…do that?" I ask. "To her?"

Bigsby snorts. "That's what we're tryin' to find out. Now, what were you doin' in the woods so late?"

"Going home," I say. I can feel Granddad's eyes on me, but I won't look at him.

"From where? No place is open that late. And we got a curfew around here for you teenagers."

I shift in my seat. The clock on the wall behind him ticks loudly. "The cemetery." Granddad inhales quickly. "I was visiting my mother's grave."

Bigsby scratches the back of his head. "Why the middle of the night?"

I shrug. It's none of his damn business.

The chief spits into his chew bottle again. "You see anyone strange around the woods the last few days? Or last night?"

"I didn't see anyone." *Except you on your front porch, about to hit your wife.*

"And you didn't touch nothin', did you? On the body, I mean."

The back of my throat aches. "I didn't touch her," I say, my voice thin. At least I don't think I did? I try to remember, but my heart races and my breath grows shallow, and I have to blink those thoughts away. "What about the words?"

"What words?"

"On her forehead."

He shakes his head, barely containing a smirk. "Her forehead was a little scratched up, probably by some animals. But there weren't no words."

"But I thought—"

"Anything else you can remember?" he interrupts. "Anything at all that we should know about?"

The blood.

Her broken eyes.

30

Those words.

A tear escapes down my cheek, and I try to discreetly wipe it away.

"I think that's enough. That's all she knows." Granddad rises and shakes the chief's hand. "You better find the animal who did this. It's not good for our town, this happening."

Bigsby hikes up his pants. "We will, don't worry. Probably just some drifter come in off the highway, long since left town. There's that new gas station just off I-40. I'll check there first, talk with the long-haul truckers."

My ears feel stuffed with cotton. "A *drifter*?" I repeat, unable to stop myself. "Why would a *drifter* stuff her body in those woods—how would he know no one ever goes there? And why would he carve up her face like...like *that*?"

Like my mother.

The chief scratches his jaw, as if he's considering it. "Stay out of trouble now, you hear? And leave the police work to us."

Bigsby's already moving around the desk and opening the door, done with me, and I slip out without uttering another word. He can't honestly believe some random trucker cut a smile onto Melissa's face...can he?

CHAPTER
Four

"Settle down, everyone." Our teacher, Mr. Fisher, stands next to his desk, hands on his hips. As if an awkward pose and slightly raised voice can bring us under control. It's almost summer break, and nobody can concentrate.

I sit at my assigned desk, smack-dab in the middle of the room, and stare out the windows. Wolf Ridge is just a jumble of buildings on the horizon. Granddad says when they built Smoky Mountain Academy, the town was booming. But then the mining companies sold out to foreign conglomerates in the nineties for obscene amounts of money, and everything went downhill. There's still some money left here—my family included—but today the school is surrounded by quiet fields of cotton and tobacco. There's no boom here anymore.

The woods where I found Melissa are a dark mass of trees. I try not to look at them, but no matter where my eyes drift, her face follows. Trapper's words come back to me, the same ones he says at every visit—*I've been locked up for a crime I didn't commit. Someone else did. That someone else is still out there.*

Squeezing my eyes closed, I shake my head, trying to make his gravelly voice go away. I wish I could remember my mother's voice. But he took that from me.

I'm back.

Brady Adams sits behind me breathing down my neck, way too close. I pretend to flick away an imaginary fly on the back of my head. My fingers connect with his nose, and I spin around as he jerks away.

"Can I help you?" I ask sweetly.

One of his dreads hangs over his face; it must've come out of his ponytail. "Nothing," he says. "I was just wondering…"

"Wondering what?" I bristle, afraid news of the body in the woods has already gotten out. It wouldn't surprise me; no one in this town can keep a secret.

I really don't want anyone to know it was me who found her.

"Nothing," he says after a while.

I lean back into my chair and roll my head on my neck, take a deep breath. I catch Natalie Baker watching me, and she smiles.

I don't return it. She sits by Madison Tran and Holly Walters. The four of us used to be a group, but they took Nat's side after our friendship fell apart. I shouldn't be surprised: they were always closer to her than to me. Holly and I, especially, never gelled. She really blew my ass up during a confrontation last year, telling me I'd been cruel to Nat, I was a shitty friend, I clearly didn't understand what it was like to have a single mother doing her best… which, obviously, I don't, since my mother is fucking dead. Whatever. Ever since then, we've been enemies.

But it still hurts sometimes, seeing the three of them together.

"Looks like *someone* fell off her diet again," Holly whispers. I can feel her eyes stabbing into the back of my skull.

I turn slowly. "And what? I look good, and you know it."

She smooths her hair. The black stone ring she always wears glints on her middle finger, which is raised slightly. Subtle. "As long as you're happy, honey." Her boyfriend, Hunter Jackson, is playing on his phone in the seat behind her. He doesn't look up, but he's frowning.

She's always doing this. Little jabs. "I'd keep my mouth shut if I were you."

"Or what?" she asks, cocking her head slightly to one side.

Madison touches Holly's arm. "Stop," she whispers. Madison, always the peacemaker. Except when I needed her.

Part of me wants to leap out of this chair and slap Holly across her pointy little nose. Instead, I just glare at her. Hunter shifts in his seat, and I almost hope he'll say something. But of course, he doesn't.

Mr. Fisher begins tapping his foot loudly, and a hush finally falls over the room. I face forward again, sweating with anger. "There, that got your attention. Okay, we're reading our final poems today." Someone groans, and a few people snicker. "Yes, we're *all* reading our poems. Out loud. You've known this day was coming. Does anyone want to go first?"

No one volunteers, so he goes in alphabetical order. Brady's up first. He drags his too-big feet up to the front of the class and reads his poem. It's about video games and how he likes playing them with his mom on the weekends. His voice shakes a little as he reads. I look down at my desk. My mom had an old Nintendo, and we played *Super Mario Bros.* a lot that spring before she died. The memory of her laughter, of the endless bowls of popcorn she set on the couch between us, makes it hard to breathe. I hate when a memory comes from nowhere and chokes me like this. Good memories aren't supposed to make you feel shitty.

"Well done, Brady," Mr. Fisher says as Brady hands him the paper and hurries back to his desk. I catch our teacher sneak a look at the clock. He's probably as ready to get away from us as we are to get away from him.

"Eugenia?" he says. "You're up next."

Eugenia Cline sits in the far back corner. It's easy to forget she's there. When she scoots back her chair, it makes a scraping sound, sharp and unsure. Her long, dark hair hangs down in stringy pieces, like she hasn't washed it in a while. I shudder as she shuffles to the front of the room, head hanging down. Even though it's well over eighty degrees outside, she wears an oversized gray cardigan. She must be roasting.

"Whenever you're ready," Mr. Fisher encourages.

Eugenia stands pigeon-toed in front of us, many pairs of judgmental eyes trained on her, and I suddenly want to scoop her into my hands and protect her, as if she's a butterfly that got trapped inside. Or, perhaps, to crush her underneath my size-eight boot. I can't decide which.

She clears her throat and lifts the notebook page close to her face. Unlike Brady, her voice doesn't shake. As she begins to read, my body breaks out in a cold sweat.

Death follows me around the house,
as I brush my teeth, when I close my eyes at night.
Its cold fingers graze my skin, marking me.
Death has shown me too many things
to Unsee.
Too much violence. Too much grief.
I keep myself in a coffin, too.
Invisible. I can't reach anyone outside of it.
I want to join the living.
But I stay inside, reaching out only after they walk by.
My fingers find only the air they leave behind.

Eugenia peers out over the top of her paper, her eyes meeting mine. And it's like she *knows*. Like she wrote that poem just for me. Like I'm part of her morbid fixation.

Poor little Bettina, her daddy killed her mommy. And now she found another dead body. An angel of death.

"*That* was uplifting," I snort, sitting up straighter in my seat.

A couple of boys behind me snigger, and my ears burn. Why did I say that? "Yeah, nice poem, *Eugene*," they tease.

"That's enough, everyone." Mr. Fisher frowns. "Great work, Eugenia. That kind of honesty is exactly what I'm looking for in this assignment." Eugenia practically tosses her paper at Mr. Fisher and dashes back to her desk.

"Real nice, Bett," Natalie whispers at me, but I'm Teflon. Nothing she says can stick anymore.

After class, though, Natalie follows me to my locker. I spin the dial, pretend she's not there, check my hair in the mirror.

"What the hell, Bett?" she asks. "Eugenia Cline is harmless—and obviously lonely. That was a shitty thing you did."

My eyes flash with rage. "Fuck off, Natalie." Xavier saunters down the hallway, talking to some girl who weighs at least twenty pounds less than I do and stands at least a foot shorter. He smiles at me, but keeps walking.

"I know why you did it," she says. "You're stressed because of your dad."

My ears ring. "What did you say?"

She shifts her books onto her other hip. "My mom reminded me the anniversary is coming up. That's a lot to deal with."

I slam my locker door shut. "Don't pretend that you care. It may have worked back when we were friends, but it doesn't work now."

Natalie's mom, Lydia, owns a bar in town and started a walking tour based on my mother's murder last year. (Okay, it's touted as a ghost tour, but everyone knows what it's *really* about. The town is *only* famous for that murder.) When I found out, Nat made excuses for her—said they were drowning in debt, needed the extra money. I tried to accept those reasons for as long as I could. I didn't want to lose my best friend.

But…after a while, I just couldn't pretend that it didn't hurt me. That it wasn't a betrayal.

Madison and Holly told me I was being unfair and overreacting, that Natalie had no control over her mother's business decisions. Maybe they were even right. A little. But I can't forgive it. And Natalie would never just apologize.

"I do care," Natalie insists.

"Yes, I can tell by the way you stood up for me in class when Holly was talking shit about me. You're a *real* good friend."

Natalie looks down. She opens her mouth, like she's going to say something. But then she spins on her heel and takes off down the hallway.

Once upon a time I would have called Natalie to tell her I lost my virginity. I would have showed her the letter I wrote my dad. I would even have told her about finding that poor woman in the woods; that I'm afraid my whole life is unraveling; that I'm terrified of what this murder *means*. She would have come over and watched old Adam Sandler movies with me all night, just so I wouldn't have to be alone.

Once upon a time is over.

CHAPTER
Five

My mom's sister, Ada, is determined to make my quest for ano-nymity impossible.

I'm sitting on my bedroom floor after school watching one of Bette Davis's earliest movies, *Of Human Bondage,* and running lines for my drama final (a monologue) when I get an alert on my phone.

Ada's just dropped a new podcast episode.

She started a show called *Sister of Doubt* last year, and it's huge. She delves into cases that aren't what they seem, almost always murders. It's so big now that she's beyond selling merch or running a subreddit—she's on tour. People fill auditoriums to listen to her pick apart homicides and to gawk at bloody photos. It's fucked up.

What's even more fucked up is that Ada has deluded herself into believing in Trapper's innocence. She's so into conspiracies that she even sees one here. Or maybe she's just pretending to, so she can stoke the public's interest.

The success of the podcast didn't come from nowhere. Ada was the one who found my mom and me the morning she died. She wrote a book about it, appeared in documentaries about true-crime victims and their families…basically, she hocked the story everywhere she possibly could. My mom's murder didn't even go national until Ada wrote her shitty book calling Trapper's conviction into question. The media drooled over every word she said—after all, *a murder victim's sister who took the killer's side?* Who does that?

She's no better than Natalie's mom with her tour; actually, she's worse. Ada's *family*, and she's profiting off her sister's brutal murder.

Obviously, we don't talk. But I like to know what she's up to, just in case she tries to drag me into it again.

Today she has. When I quickly scan the newest episode's summary, I see that it's about Jack Ledbetter's death. That means it's an episode on our family too.

"Bitch," I whisper. It's no wonder my grandparents disowned her. She has no shame.

And I will never listen to this.

When I finally go downstairs, Magnolia House is alive with dinner preparations. Grams takes her dinners very seriously, even when it's only us. When she was growing up here, her family always dressed for dinner—gowns and suits—but I refuse to wear uncomfortable clothes to eat. That hasn't stopped her from going all-out every night.

"Bett!" she says when she finds me in the kitchen, drooling over a plate of jumbo shrimp. "There you are. I need you to go light the candles in the dining room." She puts a lighter in my hand and practically shoves me through the kitchen's swinging door, away from the cream puffs and coconut layer cake and fried green tomato sliders. I try telling her it's too hot for candles, but Grams won't hear of it. *"Ambiance,"* she trills.

This is the first time I've seen her since breakfast, and she doesn't ask me about being questioned at the police station. She doesn't ask about Melissa, either.

It's easier to pretend.

A spray of tulips, magnolias, and baby's breath spreads out across the dining room table. I light the white candles in each of the three glass hurricane lanterns in the table's center, and they cast the room in a calming glow. Light flickers on the antique cross hanging from my necklace. It dangles just below my breasts, its size borderline obnoxious. Grams raised an eyebrow the first time I wore it (she knows I'm not a churchgoer anymore), but she didn't say anything. Raised eyebrows are the closest she ever comes to criticizing my outfits, or anything else about me.

After I light the rest of the candles, Grams stands with her hands on her hips and surveys the room, her hair perfect, dressed in a pastel pink skirt and matching cardigan. She is the picture of Southern perfection: demure and regal and nonthreatening. I spot a glint of silver in her hair. It's the clip from one of her hair pieces, and I adjust it, making sure it's hidden beneath her honey-tinged locks.

Grams takes my hands and gives them both a squeeze. "What would I ever do without you?"

For a moment, her eyes and smile look exactly like the portrait of my mom that hangs behind her, and it knocks me back. I'm five again, and Mom and I are watching television on the couch, slurping cereal out of bowls.

I shrug and swallow away the lump in my throat, afraid I'm going to spill open, staining the carpet, the walls, everything.

Making my escape onto the veranda, I collapse onto the swing that hangs from the ceiling. The sun stains the sky as it dips below the trees, and I pull out my phone. Texts from unknown numbers fill the screen (a common problem—it's *always* about Mom), but nothing from Xavier. We haven't spoken since last night, and my chest constricts whenever I think of him. Does he know I found Melissa, I wonder?

I'm due to get my period next week, and I fight the urge to run to the drug store and buy a dozen pregnancy tests. I was a fool for not asking him to wear a condom. He was an idiot for not offering.

A flash at the end of the drive brings me out of my pity. At first I'm afraid it's reporters, but then a cluster of people on the sidewalk comes into focus. It's Lydia Baker—Natalie's mother—and her "ghost" tour.

She makes a sweeping gesture toward our house, as if she's a museum docent. Our driveway is fairly long, and it's getting dark, so I can't be sure they've spotted me. Someone takes a picture of our house on their phone, and I scan the veranda for a deterrent. A projectile, perhaps. Something I can chase these people away with. I creep down the steps and spot a paint can nestled next to a rosebush. Hank must've done some touch-ups on the risers and forgotten the can.

Lucky me.

I peel off the lid and march down the driveway, no longer caring if anyone sees me coming. The group is small tonight—only four of them, plus Lydia, her brown hair pulled into a limp ponytail. It gives me a thrill that hardly anyone is on her pathetic tour. They loiter on the other side of our boxwood hedges, stupid smiles pasted on their faces.

"And her father, Wells Holland, put up a huge reward for information," Lydia is saying. When she spots me, she stiffens.

I stop just on the other side of the hedge, paint can hidden. "What are you doing here?"

She manages a smile. "Taking my tour on a walk of our haunted hamlet. How have you been? I haven't seen you in a while."

One of the women has the audacity to snap a photo of me.

"Actually, I was just thinking of you, Lydia," I say, "which reminded me I needed to take out the trash."

Lydia sniffs. "There's no need to get nasty."

"Nasty? You're the one who comes to my house and gossips about my family." I grip the can's handle tighter.

"I'm not gossiping," she assures me, as if I would believe a word she says. "What happened to your mother is a part of our town's history, and I'm only interested in preserving her memory. I mean no harm or disrespect. I adored your mom."

"What happened is *no one's business*." I try to sound tough, but my voice wobbles. She's so different from the woman who used to make homemade pizza for Nat and me whenever I slept over. The woman who would listen when my grandparents were being impossible. The woman who always made me feel welcome at her home. Why did she ever start this tour?

"Prudie was one of my dearest friends," Lydia says quietly. "It's my mission to keep her name alive." Her justifications echo Ada's a little too closely. She turns back to her group. "Let's move on to the next stop, ladies. The house is only a few blocks from here; the ghost of a Civil War veteran allegedly haunts the attic...."

The tour group stares at me one last time before following behind

Lydia like lemmings. My mom is just a character in a story to her, a way to earn a few extra dollars. *Adored her* my ass. When one of the women stops to take another photo of me, I leave the safety of my yard.

"Hey, Lydia?" I call.

She stops and turns back. As she opens her mouth to speak, I place one hand under the bucket and thrust it upward. White, gloppy paint hits her full in the face. It spills down her chin and chest, some getting into her mouth.

She spits it on the sidewalk and wipes furiously at her eyes. "*What did you do?*" she screams.

Some of the paint splashed onto the others, and they look down at themselves as if they're bleeding. I back away and run up the driveway, shame and exhilaration licking at my heels.

CHAPTER
Six

Grams paces in my bedroom as I dab perfume behind my ears. "I think you should stay home tonight. I'd feel better having you close."

They say good news travels fast; bad news, apparently, travels at hyperspeed. I've already gotten texts from a few people at school, asking if I've heard about the dead body the cops found in the woods. I didn't respond. I'm just glad my name is out of it...for now.

"I need a distraction, Grams. I'll be fine, I promise." Xavier texted about a party at the abandoned cemetery tonight, the one where Mom *isn't* buried. I should probably lay low, but I can't stand to be stuck inside this house another minute longer. Not with Grams hovering.

She wrings her hands. "I don't know, sweetheart. I think a quiet night at home is what you need."

Sighing, I rise from my vanity table and hug her. She feels so small in my arms, every bone in her back sharp.

"I wish you'd *stay* with me," she repeats, her voice needy, and I let go.

"I love you," I say tersely, "but I wish you wouldn't try to suffocate me. Please. All my friends are going. I'll text you when I get there and when I'm leaving. I won't stop anywhere, I won't talk to anyone I don't know, and I'll keep my phone on. It's just a party at Sam's house. I need to do something *normal*."

Grams looks hurt. "If you don't text me, I'm going to send someone after you."

She leaves, and I sprawl out on my bed. I shouldn't push her away like that, but she is *so certain* that I'm going to end up just like Mom.

I'm not.

I change into a tight black tank top, a flowy black skirt, and a pair of black suede thigh-high boots. I leave my hair down, my curls pouring in every direction, and add some brow gel and light cream blush. Then I grab my mom's old black shawl with the fringe and wrap it around my shoulders. She wears it in a photograph Grams keeps on her nightstand; it was the night of her senior prom, and she and Grams stand cheek to cheek in the photo, smiling brightly. Grams gave it to me the first time I asked to see it.

Quietly closing the front door behind me, I walk around the side of the house to our garage. It fits four vehicles, but we only have two. I drive a 1971 black Rolls-Royce Corniche my grandfather bought for me at a car auction last year. We have to service it a lot, and it doesn't have air, but it's the best car I've ever driven. I slide into the cushy driver's seat and turn the key. Driving is freedom, and as I back down the drive, I try to leave my troubles behind in Magnolia House.

This boat absorbs every bump in the road like I'm driving in a waterbed. The fountain on Market Street bubbles as I cruise past, and the downtown shops are buzzing with customers—as well as with rumors about the dead woman, presumably. The Rolls glides to a stop at the red light next to the bus depot.

A girl sits on the bus bench reading, head down, greasy hair hanging. She glances up and back down quickly.

It's Eugenia.

The car behind me honks, and I realize I'm idling. I pull over to the curb and get out.

"Hey," I say as I approach. She looks up but doesn't say anything. "Why are you reading on a bus bench at night?"

She places a bookmark in the book and closes it. I tilt my head to read the title: *A Confederacy of Dunces*. Never heard of it. "I was going to ride around for a while," she says quietly, "and read my book."

"Do you do that a lot?"

She shrugs. "It beats spending Friday night at a funeral home. Or driving around in the hearse."

"Fair enough." My phone vibrates with a text from Xavier asking where I am. "Listen…I'm going to a party at the old graveyard if you want to tag along."

She tucks her hair behind her ears. "No thanks."

"You'd rather ride around on a city bus with a bunch of weirdos?"

"Those *weirdos*, as you call them, don't make fun of me."

I sit next to her. "Listen…I was a bitch in class today."

"That's something we can agree on."

She has pale skin and freckles, and a long, graceful neck. I don't think I've ever really looked at Eugenia Cline. She's kind of like a locker in the hallway—something you knew was there but never felt the need to acknowledge. The weird mortician's kid.

I've reduced her, the same way so many have reduced me to Trapper's kid.

A breeze whips into us, and I wrap my shawl tighter around my shoulders. "If I promise not to be a horrible person, will you come along?"

She looks at me, distrust in her dark eyes. "Why would you want me to? We're not friends."

I fumble for a reason. "There's this guy I like, and—I'd rather not show up alone. You'd be doing me a favor."

"Is it Xavier Hart?"

"Yeah, do you know him?"

"I know *of* him." She doesn't elaborate, and I don't ask her to. Everyone knows Xavier, the Brooding Hottie who's at our school on scholarship (like Nat, incidentally). His dad works in one of the quartz mines and does yard work on the side.

Wolf Ridge's only bus pulls up to the stop. Eugenia gets on without another word and takes a seat at the very back.

Her loss, I decide as I walk back to the Rolls. Who cares that Eugenia Cline doesn't want to hang out with me? I mean…*Eugenia Cline*. What was I thinking? There will be plenty of other people at the party—and beer. I can make my own fun.

At least when you're by yourself, no one can let you down.

A few miles outside town along an empty highway is the run-down parking lot of Blue River State Park at the base of the Smoky Mountains. The lot is over half full, so any passing cops will know exactly what's going on…but lucky for us, Andre and Chantal don't bother much with drunk teens at cemeteries. They're busy busting meth dealers inside city limits. And now they've got a murder to solve (if the chief can be convinced to give a damn).

I set out on the well-worn path that leads to the cemetery. The other path goes down by the river. I guess there used to be an old mining village around here, which explains the random cemetery in the middle of the woods. My great-great-grandfather built Magnolia House and owned one of the quartz mines, and it stayed in our family until Grams's dad sold out a few years before he passed. There's still a dichotomy in our town—you're either blue collar (the majority) or obnoxious rich (the minority). Old money, as Granddad likes to say. A hundred years ago, Xavier's family would've probably worked for mine. In a way, they still do.

Actually, I'm pretty sure his dad laid some new sod for us last summer, and sometimes Xavier is our cashier at the Food Lion.

The noises from the party filter through the trees, and then the cemetery's first stone appears out of the murky blue-gray light. The words have mostly worn away, but the name says ELIZABETH. I always wonder about her when I come here: who she was, where she lived, what she liked to do, how she died. If my parents partied at this same place. If they read her name. If Melissa Atkins died in the woods or if the killer moved her body there.

No, I tell myself, shaking my head.

But then I see that pink coat in the woods, Melissa wrapped up in it, her face a wreck, discarded, forgotten…and I think maybe I *should* have stayed home, not voluntarily come to a party with dead people under the grass.

I see a keg, so I make my way there, weaving around headstones half sunk into the dirt. The stones are thin and rounded on top, some covered with moss, many busted in half by rowdy drunks. A lot of my classmates are here, and I suddenly feel naked, like everyone's watching me.

"Can I get a beer?" I ask one of the basketball players near the keg. They always run in a pack, and tonight's no different.

"Sure thing," Liam Cunningham says. He has curly hair and dimples. He hands me a full red plastic cup (too much foam), but now that I have something in my hands, I can blend in. "How's it going?" he asks, his eyes traveling to my breasts.

I stand up a little straighter and smile. "Better now that I'm here," I say, scanning the faces for Xavier's. He's tall enough to be on the team, and I easily spot his mop of black hair. He's wearing his black hoodie, sipping from a cup, talking to some guys I've never seen before.

"You ready for the final?"

I look back at Liam, with his straight teeth and Tar Heels sweatshirt. Grams would love it if I brought him home. He's the polar opposite of Xavier. His dad's on city council, and I wonder if Chief Bigsby has told him about Melissa's body…or me. Mr. Cunningham *does* seem to know all the business in this town, and he's close with his son. Is that why

Liam's being so chatty with me? I study his face for signs he knows my secret, but Liam is hard to read.

"Which final?" I ask.

"For Sipe's class."

"Oh, right." Xavier glances my way but must not see me. I take a big gulp of beer. "The Civil War unit. Yeah, I'm pretty ready. It'll be a short essay—'The South was a bunch of racist, murdering assholes. The end.'"

Liam laughs. "Right?" A couple guys are trying to start a fire inside a ring of rocks behind us, but they're not having much luck. "You hear about the body in the woods?"

I take a long drink of my beer.

His dad must have told him. Why else would he ask? Carefully, I look at my nails, pretending not to be interested, but my heart hammers and my hands shake.

"It's crazy, right? Nothing like that's happened since..." His eyes grow wide when he realizes who he's talking to and what he was about to say. His cheeks turn pink. "You going to prom?" he blurts out instead.

"I stopped going to school dances." Closing my eyes, I take a deep breath.

"I might have people over after the dance. My parents are out of town. You should stop by. If you want."

"Who's gonna be there?" I ask, watching as Xavier and the guys he's talking to move toward the other side of the cemetery.

"The guys from the team, Hunter, Holly and Madison, Natalie, the normal crew. You should come," he repeats.

"I don't know what my plans are yet for that weekend."

In truth, no one asked me to prom, and I doubt anyone will. Last year I went with Hunter to the sophomore spring dance. We'd been dating a little while, sort of—mostly just friends. I'd had an awful visit with Trapper the day before the dance; he basically accused me of being brainwashed by my grandparents and called me a "stupid brat." At the afterparty, I drank too much and projectile vomited all over Hunter. We never officially broke up, but I never reached out and neither did he.

"Cool, cool," he says and slurps his beer. I imagine his tongue in my mouth, sloppy and wet, and I shudder. No. Liam is definitely not a possibility. Too nice, too bland.

Maybe I *am* a bit like my mother when it comes to boys. I don't think Trapper was exactly a choir boy. I look at Liam again. Maybe I should choose him. Go to all his games, get drunk after with the other players' girlfriends....

"Man make fire!" One of the boys pounds his chest as flames rise from the stone circle. Xavier still stands at the edge of the cemetery, smoking. The moon is rising, and that's when Natalie, Holly, and Madison saunter up the path.

"Fuck," I mutter under my breath. I don't want to deal with this right now. I tell Liam I'll see him later and disappear deeper into the crowd.

Everyone's talking about Melissa Atkins now—I hear whispers from every direction about a *dead body*—and eyes dart toward me and back again. My scalp tightens.

It seemed like I was finally starting to shed that *girl-whose-dad-killed-her-mom* identity. That *true-crime* identity. That *death-aura* identity.

But maybe death does follow me.

Xavier notices me and waves me over. I take my time, stopping once to send a text to Grams, letting her know I'm still alive.

"Hey," Xavier says when I reach him. He's with two white guys, one with a shaved head, the other with long, tangled hair. I've never seen them before; they look older. The messy-hair one wears work boots and greasy jeans splattered with paint. He passes a joint to the bald one, whose cut-off T-shirt reveals a dragon tattooed on the side of his chest.

"This is Bett," Xavier says, wrapping an arm around my waist. Electricity slithers through my stomach.

Messy nods at me. "Jax."

Shaved Head exhales and smiles at me. "I'm Dave. Smoke?"

His eyes are hollow, like he hasn't eaten in a while. I pull my shawl tighter. "I'm already drinking," I say and hold up my beer.

"And?"

"*And* I don't want to barf all over myself later."

Dave snorts and rocks back on his heels, as if I'm no longer worth talking to. I'd rather be alone with Xavier, but his hooded eyelids tell me he's already stoned and probably not going anywhere for a while.

Something pale blurs behind him, like a smudge on a photograph. When my eyes focus, it's the woman from the woods lying at the base of a tree.

My mouth turns dry.

Same hair, same gray skin.

I blink and shake my head. When I look again, she's gone. I drink what's left of my beer in one swallow.

Messy shakes a clear plastic bottle at me, snapping me back to reality. Remnants of the label remain stuck in a few places. "How about my special mix? You want a pull?"

"What's in it?" I ask, trying to buy time. Guys like this are always trying to push girls into drinking or getting high, obviously in the hope they'll be too wasted to resist.

"It's good, trust me," he insists.

"Why should I trust you? We just met." Bigsby insisted the guy who did this is probably long gone. But he could be anyone, it occurs to me.

He could be here.

He could be this guy.

"Are you a *prude*?" Shaved Head asks.

The way he emphasizes *prude* makes me wonder if he's referring to my mom, Prudence. Suddenly everyone here feels suspect, like they're all in on something. I narrow my eyes at him. "No, I just don't feel like getting date-raped tonight. But thanks."

Xavier laughs nervously and moves a little closer to me. I lean into him, and Messy and Shaved Head turn to each other. "How do you know these guys?" I ask.

"They were friends with my brother, Joaquin," he says, his lips brushing my ear.

This is the first time he's ever mentioned his brother. I want to ask him if the rumors his brother died in a car accident are true. But I don't want him to ask about my mom, which would be fair turnabout, so I let those questions die on my tongue.

"Are you okay?" he asks, quietly so no one else can hear. "I heard about the body in the woods."

My ears begin to ring. "What?"

"My dad mows the lawn at the police station, overheard Bigsby talking. Your name got tossed around, I guess."

I close my eyes. "That asshole," I mutter as the dam breaks completely, cold water rushing over me. I'm sinking again. It's like the sick feeling I get each time I visit the prison, each time a reporter shows up on our veranda.

"Are you really all right?" he asks again. "That had to have been pretty awful, finding her." Before I can say anything, his phone rings. "I gotta get this. It's my mom." He walks about twenty feet into the trees. Why can't he talk to her in front of me?

Without Xavier, the older guys close in on me. They don't touch me, but I can feel them on my skin anyway.

Shaved Head says loudly, "You're that girl who found the dead body."

"I don't know what you're talking about," I say.

"Nah, I think you're lying." The way he smiles at me makes my skin crawl. "From what I hear, you called it in."

"Are you Xavier's girlfriend?" Messy asks abruptly.

I don't know *what* we are to each other, and there's no way I'm going to try to figure it out with these two morons. "We're friends."

"Friends with benefits?" Shaved Head raises an eyebrow. "You wanna be *my* friend?"

"I've got enough friends, thanks."

"Oh, so you're a tease?" Shaved Head reaches toward me and flicks a piece of fringe on my shawl. "What are you wearing, anyway? I think my grandma has one of those."

"Your grandma sounds like a cool lady," I say, keeping my voice cold.

Messy drinks from his bottle. "You kinda look like a witch, only it ain't Halloween."

Shaved Head runs a hand over his stubbled jaw. "I read in a book once that you can't drown a witch. They float."

"*You* read a book?" I say, immediately regretting it.

He clenches his jaw. "The river's close by. Maybe we should toss you in, see what happens."

"Funny. I'm gonna go." I take a step toward the other partiers—I didn't realize we were so far away from them—but Shaved Head grabs my wrist, the bones flexing in his grip. "Hey," I say, trying to twist out of his grasp, but he pulls me closer, all humor drained from his eyes.

"I know you. You're that girl whose daddy killed her mommy. The Smiley Face Killer's flesh and blood." His breath smells like weed and beer, and my stomach roils.

"Please, just stop." I try to back away.

"Oh, come on, princess. Jax and I are into that true-crime shit. Maybe you can tell us more about it. I heard your daddy didn't do it and that your testimony was coerced. Is that true?" The harder I try to wrench away from him, the stronger his grip becomes.

"You're hurting me!"

Shaved Head smiles. "I'm just talkin', sweetheart. Wouldn't kill you to talk back, would it? Unless you think you're too good for us."

"Let her go," someone says behind me.

It's Eugenia, her book tucked under one arm.

Shaved Head lets go, and I stumble toward her, the heel of my boot catching on a broken headstone. "We were just talkin'," he says, smiling. "No worries."

She steps toward him, no fear. "It didn't look like talking to me. It looked like you were scaring her."

"Bitch, who even asked you?"

Eugenia looks at him for another moment, sizing him up. "We're leaving. But I'd watch what you call women. One of these days you might meet a real witch."

"We'll see *you* later, daddy's girl," Messy slurs as we hurry back toward the keg.

"What are you doing here?" I ask. As we cross the clearing, Eugenia guiding me, everyone looks at us. Eugenia *never* comes to parties. Part of me, and I'm not proud to admit this, wants to get away from her. But the set of her jaw tells me she means business.

"I just had a bad feeling," she says. "I caught a ride with some girls from school."

I follow Eugenia past Elizabeth's grave and back up the path to the parking lot. "I could've handled myself," I tell her when we get to the Rolls, a little embarrassed. "I'm not helpless."

"I never said you were." She tucks her hair behind her ears. "Anyway, I'm going to need a ride home."

Footsteps pound down the path behind us, and my body tenses, afraid it's one of those guys returning to finish what he started. I'm relieved when Xavier touches my arm instead. "Where'd you go?" he asks, like I'm the one who's done something wrong.

"I'm out," I say, fishing my keys from my bag.

"Why? Did something happen?"

Eugenia steps out from behind me, startling him. "Those *friends* of yours were threatening her."

He looks at me, and his normally aloof expression morphs into one of panic. "Did they hurt you? Dave and Jax?"

I shrug. "It's fine. I don't need you to save me."

"What did they do?"

I look at my wrist, at the red marks revealing what happened. "The bald one grabbed me."

He gently touches the bruise. His eyes search mine, and then he turns and stomps back up the path.

"What an asshole," I mutter. I wipe my eyes discreetly as I put my key into the lock. *He didn't even say anything.*

"How about that ride?" Eugenia asks.

"Yeah, right." I unlock her door, then mine. After I slide into the driver's seat, I readjust my mom's shawl on my shoulders, only to discover it's been torn.

CHAPTER Seven

When I was a kid, the Cline house was my favorite place to go trick-or-treating. Mr. Cline would answer the door, somberly give each kid one piece of candy, never two, and then shut the door without a word. Eugenia's family didn't have to decorate to have the creepiest house in town.

Pulling up front, I try to imagine living inside those walls. It reminds me a bit of my house, actually, with its wraparound porch and curtained windows…but without all the dead bodies inside.

I put the Rolls into park and say, "Here we are." As if she doesn't already know that.

She picks up her book and grabs the door handle. "You gonna be okay?"

I swallow. "Yeah, why wouldn't I be?"

"Thanks for the ride." She climbs out and shuts the door, the sound echoing inside the car's roomy interior. I watch as she walks up her sidewalk and onto the lighted porch. Before I can stop myself, I honk. Startled, Eugenia turns around. I'm already out of the car, playing with my fringe.

"Did I forget something?" she asks.

"Well," I say, meeting her in the yard, "I have kind of a strange request."

"I live in a funeral home," she says, gesturing at the house. "You'll need to be much more specific than that."

"Right. I was wondering if I could crash here tonight."

Her eyebrows shoot up her forehead. "You want to sleep *here*? At *my* house?"

"Unless you don't want me to. I can go home, it's fine. I just…"

Eugenia taps her book against her thigh.

"Yes. You can stay over." Then she turns back toward the house, and I follow.

The heavy oak front door opens onto a wide hall, a set of stairs running up the right-hand wall. A large red rug covers the wooden floor. Closed pocket doors line the left-hand wall. A desk next to the front door has a computer and a phone and a wooden placard that says RECEPTION.

"You can leave if this creeps you out," she says. She starts to take off her sweater before putting it back on. "Most people can't handle it."

"I spend two afternoons a year at a maximum-security men's prison. I'll be fine." I never talk to anyone about Trapper, but I know that Eugenia isn't going to spread the news all over school. She just wouldn't.

"Are you hungry?" she asks. "My mom made short ribs for supper. There's leftovers."

"I don't eat anything that bleeds."

"Suit yourself." She heads for the staircase, but I linger by the first set of pocket doors. They're open a touch. The room's dark but I can just make out shiny, rectangular boxes.

"That's the coffin showroom," she says over her shoulder.

"Oh shit." I hurry to the bottom of the stairs where she's waiting.

"You can look at them, if you want."

"Thanks. I'm good."

Eugenia stares toward the room for an oddly long amount of time. I turn back, wondering if she sees something. But it's just a door. No ghosts—or parents—lurking about.

"Did they let you see your mother's body when she passed?" she finally asks. "In her coffin, I mean?"

In the third grade someone asked me about my mom's coffin—what color it was, what it looked like. I punched that kid in the nose and got sent home. But Eugenia isn't asking to be rude. There's no judgment in her face.

"Can we just go to bed?" I ask, and she drops it.

The stairs groan—loud enough to wake the dead, as Grams would say. Speaking of Grams, I send a quick text that I'm staying over at a friend's house, and a selfie for good measure. She responds immediately, telling me to be safe.

Eugenia turns the glass knob on the first door at the top of the stairs and flicks on the light. Her walls are a buttercream yellow, cluttered with framed prints of various species of ferns and moths and beetles. Her bed is under the window. It's a daybed, with a black wrought iron frame. A gray quilt has been meticulously folded over the mattress. She pulls out a trundle bed. "Will this work?" she asks.

"Perfect," I answer. "Where's the bathroom?"

She shows me to the door across the hall, and I close and lock it behind me.

The bathroom is tiny. The toilet is crammed so close to the wall my thigh hits the toilet paper roll when I sit to pee. I try to avoid my reflection as I wash my hands with a bar of lavender soap, but I can't resist. My hair is limp, my eyes hollow. I soap up my entire face, try to wash it all away. Finding the body in the woods. Mom. Dad. Xavier and his asshole friends. But it's all still there, whether my eyes are open or closed.

Eugenia's changed into a huge Panthers football jersey when I get back. It hangs to her knees, its colors faded away. The sleeves are so long I can't see her arms, and it falls off one shoulder. "Football fan?" I ask.

She looks down and shrugs. "It was my uncle's. I have a couple nightgowns I never wear if you want one."

I play with my fringe. "I'm fine sleeping in my clothes."

She just stands there, white socks falling down around her ankles, staring at me. "What do girls usually do at these things?"

"What do you mean?"

"At a sleepover. That's what this is, right?"

"You've never been to a sleepover before?" I shouldn't be surprised. I can't remember Eugenia arriving at any of our houses with her pillow and overnight bag in elementary school.

"No."

"Well," I say, sitting on the trundle bed. "It's been a while, but usually we just watch movies, eat junk food, and talk about boys. Sometimes we steal our parents' liquor. The usual stuff."

"How about we just sleep instead?"

"Sounds good to me."

After Eugenia gets back from the bathroom, she turns out the light and moves past me like a shadow. Her bed squeaks as she climbs in, and I slip off my boots and lie down. It's too humid for covers, so I fold my hands over my stomach and stare at the ceiling. A clunk from downstairs sets my heart racing. I picture her parents embalming someone.

Embalming. Death.

My thoughts drift to my mother, and I roll onto my side, trying to make them go away. I *don't* remember much from her funeral—only that it was closed casket. Afterward, everyone gathered at Magnolia House and gave me lots of sad, worried glances while they ate their finger sandwiches and sipped glasses of wine. Grams and Granddad fed me cake and candies, probably to keep me quiet. It may have been their daughter's funeral, but they were still entertaining people in their home. Expectations had to be met.

Hank was the only one who talked to me about it. I had gone out to the veranda with my second piece of chocolate cake. Hank was crying, and when he saw me, he didn't try to pretend he wasn't. "Come sit with me, baby girl," he said, and we sat together on the swing. His blond hair hadn't turned gray then. I asked him when my mom was coming home, and he told me she wasn't. "Your mama's in heaven now, Bettina. She's an angel watching over you. A perfect, beautiful angel who will never get old or sick."

He was only trying to make me feel better, but I'd take an old sick mother over a young dead one any day of the week.

"I can't sleep," Eugenia whispers.

"Me neither."

She flips on a lamp with a black shade and sits cross-legged on her bed. I sit up, too. "She's in the basement, you know."

"Who?" I ask.

"Melissa, the woman who was murdered. The one you found."

My heart races. "Does everyone in Wolf Ridge know it was me?"

"You know Carl Bigsby can't keep his mouth shut," she says. "They brought her here after the medical examiner finished."

"What did he find?"

Eugenia leans closer. "This stays between us."

"Obviously."

"She'd been dead about six to eight hours based on her body temperature and amount of rigor. Mouth slashed, three stab wounds to the chest. One cut straight through her aorta, and she bled out. Theory is she was killed somewhere else and then dumped in the woods. What time did you find her?"

"I think it was around eleven." My hands were shaking so bad it had been hard to read my phone, but I'm pretty sure the screen read 11:11 when I called the cops.

"Then that would mean she was killed between three and five in the afternoon on Thursday," Eugenia says.

"What about the words on her forehead?"

"*I'm back*," she says, shuddering.

My stomach twists. When the room starts to spin, I lie on my side and close my eyes. I *knew* Bigsby was lying when he said they were animal scratches. This wasn't some random crime. This wasn't some drifter.

"Should I not have told you?"

"No, I'm glad you did." I swallow a few times to keep the beer from coming up. "That's exactly how my mom died, minus the word-carving part."

"I know."

My eyes snap open, and I look up at her. "How?"

She watches me for a moment. "My parents did her funeral too."

"Oh." I sit up and push the hair out of my face. "I guess I should have remembered that."

"My mom still talks about her case sometimes. How sad it was. Of all the cases we've prepared, I think it made her the saddest."

"You call them *cases*?" I don't know why that pisses me off this much, but it does.

She shrugs. "That's what my parents have always called them."

"That's pretty messed up, don't you think? They're people."

"They call them cases to create a cognitive distance. It's better than breaking down over every dead person who comes through our house." She peels back her covers and sits next to me on my bed. "I've been thinking about Cherry Hobbs."

Sitting this close to Eugenia, I can smell her. Lavender. "Why?"

"She was also stabbed. Three times in the chest."

"Yeah. Everyone thinks my dad killed her."

"Possibly. But he couldn't have killed Melissa, which means someone else did." She sighs. "I don't know about you, Bett, but I'm tired of murdered women being carted into my house like slabs of meat." She gets this faraway look on her face, almost trance-like.

"Jesus, Eugenia," I mutter. "Tact?"

She focuses on me. "Aren't you tired of it? You should be, given your history."

My mind flashes to the woods, to Melissa's face that was also my mom's face. To a woman, cut up and dumped.

"We have an obligation to stop whoever is doing this," she continues when I don't answer. "Women are clearly expendable in this town. No one cared about Cherry. No one really cares about Melissa, either. And I for one am sick of it."

"So what would we do exactly?" I ask, my voice strained. "Start some true-crime podcast and solve it, just like that? This isn't a movie, Eugenia. We have no power. We can't change a damn thing. I tried pushing back against Bigsby this morning, and he completely blew me off."

"We start simple," she says, clearly immune to my dark mood. "Look at the records my parents kept on your mom and Cherry. We look at Melissa's body. See if there are any similarities, any connections. If we find one, we'll share it. Make it public."

"Hold up. You think Melissa's murder is connected with my mom's, even though Trapper didn't do it?"

She shrugs. "Could be. And, I mean, your dad has always maintained his innocence. Your aunt believes him. Add the 'I'm back,' which seems cryptic, taunting...."

I shake my head. "There's no way he's innocent. I saw him that day. I saw him come out of that bedroom." I ball my hands into fists, reminded of the last time I saw Ada. It ended in a similar argument and her storming out of last year's Christmas Eve dinner, the first we'd had in a long time. I haven't seen her since.

"I'm not saying he's innocent."

"So then what are you trying to say?" I seethe, suddenly furious. "I'm about two seconds away from leaving."

"What I'm trying to say is that women need to look after other women," she says calmly. "Like tonight at the party. No one else will. Certainly not anyone in Wolf Ridge. No women on city council. Never had a female mayor. I'm shocked they hired Chantal for the police force. Maybe she has dirt on one of them. Anyway—I'm saying we have to investigate, and we have to consider all the possibilities."

"Chief Bigsby already decided it's some drifter who left town," I say, my heart rate slowing. "He didn't seem concerned. Like, at all."

"See? He won't put much effort into solving her murder. What happens if another woman ends up dead in the woods? Your Grams or my mom? Or one of us? What if you had just missed the killer when you found Melissa? You could be *dead* right now, Bett." She pauses. "How well do you know Xavier? He hasn't been in Wolf Ridge very long."

My ears ring. "What are you insinuating?"

"I'm not insinuating anything. Simply making a statement."

"Fuck this. No. Can we just go to bed?"

"Fine." She turns off the light.

My teeth clatter as I lay back down. Melissa's discarded body flashes before me, wedged under that tree like she wasn't human. Like she was just something to get rid of.

The fact remains that *I'm* the one who found her.

This is going to blow my life up whether I like it or not. And I'm connected to her, whether I like it or not.

I think more about what Eugenia said...about looking closer at the murders, including my mom's. It might not be a terrible idea. Instead of being a victim, maybe I could be the girl who stopped a killer. And I can finally prove to myself, beyond all doubt, that my father is guilty of his crime.

If there's really a killer running loose in Wolf Ridge, then Eugenia is right. None of us is safe.

"When do we start?" I ask suddenly into the gloom, surprising myself.

The light flicks back on. I think this is the first time I've ever seen Eugenia Cline smile. And I'm not sure I like it.

CHAPTER
Eight

I lay awake all night, and when dawn comes, I scribble a note for Eugenia, who snores softly. I slip my boots back on and sneak down the stairs, closing my eyes as I pass the room with all the coffins. I've had enough death for one day.

Only when I get home, I come face-to-face with my mother's ghost.

She stands on the veranda with a green duffel bag thrown over one shoulder and a cigarette hanging out of her mouth. My chest grows cold.

"Quiet," she whispers. "Don't want to wake Wells and Vivian."

It's my aunt Ada. Blue eyes, platinum blond hair with pink streaks, dark brows, the scar on her chin that she's never explained. You'd never know my grandparents have two daughters from visiting their house: they don't keep a single photograph of Ada on display.

"What are you doing here?" I ask. "Shouldn't you be out chasing ambulances?"

"Can't I visit my family?" She sets down her bag. "I seem to have forgotten my key."

"Forgot it or did they change the locks?"

"Could you just let me inside?"

I narrow my eyes. "I'm not doing your dirty work for you. Ring the bell."

She drops her cigarette and stomps it with a black boot. "I *am* their daughter, even if they wish I wasn't."

"Gee, I wonder why that could be?" I ask as I come up onto the veranda. "Saw your latest podcast episode came out, by the way. Real classy."

"If I don't cover Ledbetter's suicide and its implications, someone else will. At least this way, we can get out ahead of it."

"How'd you find out so fast anyway?"

Ada sits on the swing. "So how have you been, Bett?" she asks, ignoring my question. The way she looks at me…I can tell she knows about the woman I found in the woods.

I sit in a wicker chair across from her and yawn, pretending she doesn't bother me. "I'm just peachy," I answer. "You?"

"Peachy." She reaches into the pocket of her jacket and pulls out a pack of cigarettes. "So what does Wells make of Ledbetter's suicide?"

"Ask him yourself," I say as a light turns on inside the house. The front door whips open, and Granddad barrels outside, dressed in his robe and pajamas, glasses askew.

"What in God's name are you doing here?" he asks.

"Nice to see you, too, Dad."

Granddad puts his hands in his robe pockets. "What do you want? To steal some of your sister's things and sell them on eBay?"

"Is that what you think of me?" Ada stands, her calmness turning to anger. I kind of want to give my grandfather a high five.

71

"I don't want to play games, Ada Francis. Just tell me what it is you want."

"I came to visit my family." She glances at me. "I promise I don't have an ulterior motive."

Granddad finally notices I'm there. "Bett? Do you have any *idea* what time it is?"

"Late, I think. Or early?"

"You had no right to leave your grandmother last night. She was so sick with worry, I had to give her a sedative! You should have stayed home."

I look down, shame heating up my neck. "Sorry." I go inside, but I leave the door open a fraction—just enough to hear what they're saying.

"Is it true?" Ada asks.

"Is what true?"

"About Melissa Atkins? Bett found her?"

Dammit. She already knows.

He sighs. "You obviously know it is."

"Jesus."

They're silent for a while. Finally, Granddad says, "I want you gone before your mother wakes up. It isn't good for her or Bettina Jane to have you here."

"I'm here to *help* her. And you and Mom. Shouldn't we stick together? Try to be a real family?"

"Our family died when your sister was murdered and you took her killer's side."

I carefully click the door closed and go upstairs, my stomach in knots.

———

I wake up from the same dream I've had since I was six years old: Mom and I are watching TV in our old house. She goes away. She's gone for a while. Then I find her lying in her bed.

The blood.

Always the blood.

And her eyes that are broken; they don't blink. They only stare up at the ceiling.

I'm about to burrow back under the covers when I get a text from Eugenia.

> Eugenia: Parents gone. Good time to start our investigation.

I dress, then go downstairs to grab breakfast. I won't mention Ada to Grams—it would only make her sad, and I do that enough on my own.

After I eat, I tell my grandparents where I'm headed. As I back my Rolls onto the street, I notice a woman in a tailored blazer and dark jeans approach me. She stands in front of the car so I can't pull ahead. "Are you Bettina Holland?" she asks.

I silently curse my car's lack of air-conditioning, which forces me to keep my windows rolled down.

"If you're a reporter, I'm not interested."

The woman holds her phone toward me, undeterred. "Do you have any comments about the suicide of the man who helped convict your father of murder? And what about reports that another woman has been brutally murdered in Wolf Ridge, ten years after your father's conviction?"

"Move. Now," I say slowly, then rev the engine. The woman startles before quickly backing away.

As I peel down the street, my hands are shaking so bad I can barely grip the wheel. If I see her again, I won't be so *nice*.

Eugenia's waiting on the porch when I arrive. Her hair looks clean today, and she's wearing a black sweater dress and gray scarf patterned with tiny black spiders.

"My parents will be back in an hour," she says, hurrying me up the porch steps. "Getting supplies for tonight."

"Supplies? For what?"

"The prosecutor's wake." She slams the front door behind us. "You know…the one from your dad's case."

"Oh. Here?" I ask, surprised.

"Didn't you read the obituary? He moved away to Wilmington years ago, but he grew up in Wolf Ridge. So, yes, here. This was his hometown."

I don't speak. Finally, she gestures behind her. "The basement door is over here."

The small door has been papered over, making it blend in with the floral wallpaper. It squeaks as she pulls it open and hits a switch.

Fluorescent lights buzz to life. I follow her down a staircase that ends in an open room lined with doors, the cinder block walls painted a sickly sage green. The temperature is at least twenty degrees colder down here, and now I understand the sweater dress.

"Embalming room's through there," she says, pointing to a set of closed double doors. "Your friend the prosecutor is in there right now."

I shudder. "How do you get the bodies down here?"

She points to another set of doors. "Elevator that leads into a small garage my parents had built at the back of the house." She turns and types a code into a metal door's lock pad. "This is the records room. It's fireproof in case the house ever burns down."

"That's a lovely thought," I mutter.

She goes into the room, but I linger just outside. The basement smells strongly of bleach. I wonder if it looked like this when my mom was here? The hairs on my arms rise, and I hurry into the records room. Eugenia's already pulled open one of the filing cabinet drawers and is quickly flipping through it.

She lifts out a file and sets it on a small table. "Your mom's," she says, pushing the drawer shut and opening another.

The file isn't very thick. I reach out and touch it. Her life, reduced to a dusty folder in some funeral home basement. A heaviness settles on me, and I can't decide if I want to cry or rip this folder to pieces. Her life was so much more than this—wasn't it?

Eugenia lifts another file and sets it next to my mother's. "And this one's Cherry's."

"Wait," I say. "Where's the woman from the woods? Melissa?"

"She's in the garage freezer."

I blow out a breath and join Eugenia at the table. We sit on a couple of rusty folding chairs. "Which should we look at first?" she asks.

"Cherry's," I answer quickly, pushing the file toward Eugenia. I'm not sure I even want to see my mom's.

Eugenia places her hands on the folder and briefly closes her eyes like she's about to start a séance or something. Then she flips it open. I expect it to look like a police file, with photos and blood and gore, but it's just…paperwork.

She pulls a sheet with an illustration of a woman's body, front and back. "My parents are meticulous notetakers," she explains. "They've marked here where the stab wounds were." Three black marks have been drawn on the chest. "And two superficial wounds at each side of her mouth, made by a knife or other sharp object, inflicted postmortem."

"Like my mom's…," I say, trailing off.

She closes Cherry's folder and opens my mom's without asking me. I push back from the table and move as far from it as I can.

"Don't you want to look at her file?"

"You do it," I say. "I'm good over here."

If I didn't know what she was reading, I'd guess Eugenia was studying for a test at school. Her face is so impassive. She finds another illustrated page and runs her fingers over it. "Here it is. Three stab wounds, again to the chest. Almost in the same location as Cherry's. And slashes to the mouth, both sides, inflicted postmortem. You want to see?"

My hearing wanes. "I'm good with your summary." I glance at the table, then away. "Did you know Cherry's face had been slashed, too?"

As far as I'm concerned, that proves she's another of my father's victims. But Melissa...?

"No, I didn't." Eugenia puts the papers back into their folders and replaces them in the cabinets. "Come on. We don't have much time."

"Time for what?"

"To look at Melissa's body."

She states this as if she just suggested we go see a movie at the cheap theater.

"Wait, wait, *wait*," I say, straightening. "You never said anything about gawking at dead bodies!"

"It's not gawking. It's fact-finding. And you've already seen her."

Melissa's grayish face flashes in front of me, almost like someone's projecting it onto the wall. I turn away, squeeze my eyes shut, and dig the heels of my palms into my eye sockets. "Eugenia, I appreciate the help on this, but seriously? Have I not been traumatized enough this week for you?"

She considers what I've said. "I'll go look. You stay here."

"Um, no thank you! I'll wait upstairs with the living."

Eugenia turns without another word and goes up the elevator. Once I'm upstairs, I sit in a chair at the reception desk and take deep breaths. My lungs ache, and I wonder if I inadvertently breathed in some formaldehyde that's now turning my tissues cancerous. I don't know how Eugenia can stand to live here.

The front door handle turns, and the door creaks as it opens. I assume it's Eugenia, back from her trip to the crypt. Instead, her parents walk in—and freeze when they see me.

"Hey there, Mr. and Mrs. Cline," I say as cheerfully as I can, rising to greet them. "I'm Bett, a friend of Eugenia's."

Eugenia's dad has pale skin, his dark hair slicked back off his forehead like a vampire. Her mother stands about half a foot taller than him, dressed in a long, shapeless peach dress, her black hair pulled into a braid that hangs down her back. They look at each other and then back at me. I guess when your only visitors are corpses, a flesh-and-blood one can be startling.

"Hello," her father finally says, a grocery bag tucked under one arm. I'm reminded of the cliché that undertakers are creepy and socially awkward. As if he senses what I'm thinking, he smiles. "Sorry, I'm exhausted. Busy few days around here."

I have to stall them. Eugenia's still in the freezer playing a real-life version of Operation. If we get caught, I'm guessing the Clines aren't going to just laugh it off as questionable teenage behavior.

"Eugenia said you're working on a school project?" her mom asks as she closes the front door and slips off her shoes.

We forgot to come up with a shared cover story, so I try to think fast. "Yes, for science class. Human anatomy."

It's not a *total* lie.

Mr. Cline frowns. "So much homework right at the end of the year doesn't seem fair."

A creak comes from behind me, and Eugenia appears at the basement door, blinking rapidly with slightly pink cheeks. She quickly shuts it behind her and acts as if nothing is amiss. "Did you get all your supplies for tonight?" she asks coolly.

"What were you doing in the basement?" Mr. Cline asks, all humor gone from his voice.

Eugenia looks at me, and I say, "Getting that textbook for our anatomy project?"

"Textbook?" he asks.

"Yes," Eugenia answers. "I thought maybe you and Mom had some old medical textbooks downstairs."

"You know those are in the library," Mrs. Cline scolds. She rests the back of her hand against Eugenia's forehead. "You're flushed. Are you coming down with something?"

"Maybe end-of-the-year-itis?" her dad asks, and I force a laugh.

"We better get that project finished before one of us spontaneously combusts." I grab hold of Eugenia's hand and pull her upstairs and into her room before they can ask any more questions. I close the door behind us as she flops down on her bed.

"That was close!" she says. "Way too close. They don't like it when I go down there alone."

"What, ever? I just assumed…"

She shoots me a look. "What? That I help embalm the bodies?"

"Actually, the rumor is you do the dead people's makeup."

She shakes her head. "I'm not *quite* the freak everyone in this town thinks—not that I care."

I sit at her desk, leaving her statement to hang between us. "What'd you find?"

Eugenia sits up and tucks her hair behind her ears. "It was… disconcerting. Usually if I see a body, they've already been taken care of. You know, dressed and stuff. But my parents haven't done anything for her yet."

I pace the room, trying to outmaneuver the images of Melissa's body in the woods. The outlines of her body glimmer anytime I focus on one thing for too long, like when I rub my eyes really hard and still see shapes dancing. "Get to the point, Eugenia."

She gives me a look. "She had three stab wounds to the chest, but her mouth is slashed from the right corner only."

I stop. "So not *exactly* like my mom and Cherry, then. Copycat killer?"

"Perhaps. She looks so much like them. This murder definitely seems linked somehow.…It's just too similar to be a coincidence. Three pretty blond girls, all killed in the same manner. And then of course the taunting 'I'm back.' "

I sit back down. "It makes no sense. Trapper's already in prison. Why would someone stage a murder to look like one of his?"

"That's the question we need to answer. I think it's someone who lives right here in Wolf Ridge or who has connections here. There's something I want to show you."

She motions for me to follow, and we go into the hallway. She opens a tiny door at the end of the hall. Heat and dust roll down the set of stairs beyond. She hurries up them, and I follow behind her into the gloom of the attic.

A circular vent at the top of the stairs lets in a few strands of light.

Eugenia lights some candles, then plugs in twinkle lights wrapped around a large whiteboard. She's already written Melissa's name in the center and circled it. The suspect list is pitifully small:

Who Killed Melissa Atkins?
Suspect List:
Drifter from out of town

"What the hell?" I ask, stepping closer.

"It's our crime board. I googled how to solve a murder, and this was the first piece of advice."

"*Of course* you researched it. But why up here?"

"My parents never come up here. My room? They'd find it in there. They have no boundaries."

There's a photocopy of a handwritten note taped to the board too. As I'm reading it, Eugenia says she found it online in one of the Reddit groups dedicated to my mom's case, but I barely hear her.

PRUDIE,

WHY'D YOU HAVE TO BE SUCH A BITCH ABOUT THE MONEY STUFF LAST NIGHT? YOU MADE ME LOOK LIKE AN ASSHOLE IN FRONT OF EVERYONE. I'M TRYING MY BEST TO FIND WORK, WORK THAT ISN'T BENEATH ME. DON'T YOU WANT ME TO BE HAPPY? I'M SORRY I'M NOT SOME IVY LEAGUE PRICK WHO CAN GIVE

YOU DIAMONDS AND PEARLS. I SWEAR. I DON'T
KNOW WHAT TO DO ABOUT YOU SOMETIMES.

—T

I step back. I need to put distance between me and Trapper's ugliness.

I'd never read the note before. Now I wish I hadn't. I can picture him hunched over the page, angrily scratching out those words. Was I asleep in my bedroom when he wrote it?

I look up, just to look away. Someone must have painted the attic's peaked ceiling white decades ago. The paint peels as if it's wax dripping off a candle. The floor's no better: old dress forms and water-damaged boxes look like they've just been tossed up here and forgotten.

"I tried to make it less gross." Eugenia points to a couple of old lawn chairs set up in front of the board, a wooden crate with two unopened cans of Coke set out between them.

"*Tried* being the operative word."

"Anyway," Eugenia says. She grabs a marker and writes: *three stab wounds to chest, slash at right side of mouth, "I'm back" carved into forehead.* Then she pops the cap back on. "We're going to nail this bastard. I can feel it."

My face burns hot, and I pop the tab on one of the sodas and gulp half of it down. "Next time, bring a fan up here."

"Noted." Eugenia sits on one of the lawn chairs and stares up at the board.

I sit next to her and finish my soda. "Do you have any theories yet?"

82

"More than half of all female murder victims were killed by an intimate partner or a family member. I think that's where we start. Figure out if Melissa was dating anyone, where she came from, if she had any family issues. She has a past, and we need to find out what it is."

"But if it's a copycat murder, doesn't that make *everyone* a suspect?"

"The copycat killing is still just one theory, Bett. We need to find out more about Melissa first. Keep our minds clear of bias."

I stare up at the board, at the black words and circles and arrows. Was my mom a name on a board ten years ago? If she was, my name was probably up there too.

Suddenly this feels too invasive. Too personal.

"I gotta go," I say, jumping up so fast my chair tips over.

"Okay," she says slowly, watching me.

"We'll talk later." I hustle down the narrow staircase before she can say anything else, the words on her murder board burned into my retinas.

CHAPTER
Nine

Granddad is outside pruning the rosebushes when I get back from Eugenia's, making careful cuts with garden shears. "How'd the school project go?" he asks, stepping back to admire his work.

"Oh, just swell." I slip off my sunglasses. "Have you seen Ada today?"

"No, and good riddance. I don't like that she's back in town. Doesn't bode well." He pulls a rag out of his back pocket and wipes his brow. "Anyway, enough about her. You've got your Harvard interview in only a couple weeks. Do you have any questions on how you might prepare? We need to make an excellent first impression."

"I don't know, Granddad. I've been a little preoccupied, what with finding dead people in the woods and all."

"That's over and done, Bett. Your life lies in the future, not in the past." He looks off in the distance. "Those were the days, I tell you. Cambridge is a magical town—you'll see. We'll visit when my schedule is less busy. We can have a picnic in Dudley Garden."

"Can we talk about it tonight? I feel a headache coming on that could wake the dead."

"We'll talk tomorrow. Vivian and I will be at Jack Ledbetter's wake tonight."

"Right, the wake. It's weird, isn't it? Trapper's still alive, but the man who put him in prison is dead."

Granddad clenches his jaw. "Bettina Jane."

"What? Don't you find it unfair? Maybe the bad guys really do win in the end. They tell you in fairy tales that good always prevails, but…"

Granddad raises an eyebrow. "Maybe if you'd ever read a real fairy tale, you'd know that they're dark and filled with sorrow."

"Geez, Granddad, *that's* uplifting. And you act like I'm maudlin." I stoop to smell one of the roses. "Maybe I should go to the wake, pay my respects to his family. It might actually be good for me. Cathartic even."

"Absolutely not!" Granddad practically shouts. "I don't want you anywhere near that wake."

I stare at him, caught completely off guard. "Why not?"

"It has nothing to do with you."

"Actually, it has everything to do with me. He got justice for this family. For us."

He shakes his finger at me. "Just do as I say, understand? Leave the past where it belongs."

"Is this because of Melissa Atkins? Are you afraid of how it looks that I found her? Little too much death in the family?" I ask. I immediately wish I hadn't as Granddad's face gets very red.

He takes a deep breath, then lets it out. "I'm trying to remain calm, but that is very difficult to do when my own granddaughter accuses me of such vanity in my own front yard."

"Sorry I brought it up," I mumble, heading back down the driveway. "I'm going to the library." I pull out my phone and send off a text to Xavier.

Me: Where are you?

Xavier: At home. You?

I get to the other side of the hedges and stop. There's still white paint everywhere.

Me: Wanna hang out?

Xavier: I'm here.

I'm not sure if this is an invitation or not, but I head downtown anyway. I pause in front of the mailbox I put Trapper's letter in, wondering if news of Melissa's death has reached the prison yet.

I look down at my phone again, at Xavier's vague text. I used to think his dark broodiness meant something. That he was deep. That he would understand what it's like to have everyone decide who you are without your input.

I don't know now.

An Instagram notification pops up; it's someone from a true-crime podcast, asking if it's true about me finding a body in Wolf Ridge and if I'd agree to an interview. I delete the message just as my phone rings. The screen says UNKNOWN CALLER, probably someone digging for information about my mom. I shut off my phone, knowing I'll need to change my number.

It's starting all over again, just like I knew it would.

A car drives by slowly, the people inside staring at me. One of them points their phone at me, and I quickly hurry down the block. The door to Sheila's Diner dings as I step into the air-conditioning. Sheila, the owner, says she runs hot, which is why she keeps the air cranked up. I'm glad I wore my mom's jean jacket today.

Everyone stops to look at me, then quickly back at their food.

Sheila's behind the counter, pouring Leo Richardson a coffee. Leo is Andre's dad. He's a mailman who's forever going on and on about all the dog attacks he's escaped. He swears an Akita almost took one of his toes. Sheila waves to me, and then Leo whips around.

"Hey, Bett!" he calls. He really is the cutest old man I've ever seen, always dressed in perfectly ironed button ups. "What's the word?"

Leo thinks I know all the hot gossip and can keep him up-to-date. (He has three grandchildren and says he needs to stay fresh or they might demote him from favorite grandfather.) These days, though, the only "gossip" I know is too depressing to repeat.

"The word is my feet hurt and I could eat a horse." I slide onto the stool next to him. If he's heard about Melissa Atkins, he doesn't let on.

Leo frowns. "That's not exactly going to make me sound cool to the grandkids. Didn't that pop star marry the actor's daughter after only two dates? I think I saw that on the TV."

"They're divorced now," I update him. "Apparently, he has a bunch of pet ferrets, and they ran all over the house, pooping on everything. She couldn't take it and moved out."

He slaps the counter and laughs. "Ferrets will do that to a marriage," he says, and Sheila chuckles.

"What can I get for you?" she asks. Most of the white women her age—my Grams included—dress the same and have similar hair styles, like they pass around a book of appropriate looks and you have no choice but to adhere to them. Not Sheila. First off, she doesn't dye her hair. It's silvery white and long, almost to her butt. She is also under the delusion that we're all living in a Wild West frontier town instead of the middle of nowhere in North Carolina. She wears jeans and cowboy boots and an array of western shirts with pearl buttons. She lives above the diner and keeps her horse, Clint Eastwood, out at the stables, and she rides him in every town parade. She divorced her husband for cheating, and that is something women in Wolf Ridge just don't do. Rumor says she keeps a gun under the counter.

"How about a chocolate malt and a big plate of fries smothered in cheese and jalapeños?"

She winces. "That'd have me on the toilet praying to Jesus in half a minute. God bless your digestive system."

"Shoot," I say when I realize I forgot my money. "I left my purse at home."

"I'll add it to your tab." She leans on the counter and lowers her voice. "Say...I heard you found the girl in the woods."

Here, too? My heart drops. "Why am I not surprised?"

"We're just worried about you, honey. You okay?"

"Honestly? Not really. But there's not much I can do about it."

Leo looks behind him, then at me. "Andre said she bore a striking resemblance to Cherry…and your mama."

"Should Andre be sharing the details of a case like that?"

Leo shakes his head. "He knows his old man can keep a secret or two."

He and Sheila stare at me, waiting, so I give them something. "Yes, she did. Eerily similar. Though I never saw her when she was actually alive, so I can't say for sure." I keep the worst detail—the words hacked into her face—to myself.

"I met Melissa a few times down at Lydia's place, and she ate here a couple times a week, at least. Sweet girl. Beautiful. Such a shame." Sheila wipes down the counter.

"Do you know much about her? Where was she from?" I ask.

Sheila drapes the rag over her shoulder. "I think she was from Raleigh. Single. No kids. Told me she wanted a fresh start."

"Was she running from a bad relationship?"

"It's possible, though she never mentioned that to me. She said her mama had died of cancer, and she didn't have any other family. Being home made her too sad. She was saving up for nursing school."

"That poor girl, may she rest in peace." Leo puts his money on the countertop. "I'll see you later, Bett. Stay safe, you hear?"

"Sure thing, Leo. Don't go breaking any hearts tonight."

"I can't make any promises!" he laughs.

Sheila touches my chin. "You go sit; I'll bring your food. You shouldn't worry a lick. The police will find whoever did this."

"Just like they found whoever killed Cherry Hobbs?"

Sheila's face darkens. Cherry's unsolved murder haunted the town for months. Mothers didn't let their daughters out after dark, and Chantal started giving self-defense classes on the weekends. But eventually Cherry's death just…faded away, became another story, and everyone carried on like normal again.

Until my mom's murder.

I settle in at my favorite table in the back, away from the door, next to a bookshelf filled with old games and decks of cards. Whispers fly all around me, and I do my best to tune them out. Sheila drops off my food, invites me to come to church tomorrow, and then goes back to cooking. It's just Sheila and her son, David, running the diner. He's always in the back making food. He waves when he sees me, and I wave back. He has shaggy dark hair, and if I squint, he looks a little like an unauthorized copy of Keanu Reeves.

The malt goes down smoothly, and the jalapeños have just the right amount of heat. I turn my phone back on, ignoring all the new texts and notifications and voicemails. I'm about to order a cup of coffee with cream and sugar when Natalie comes in.

She doesn't see me, and I sink lower into my chair. Sheila's face lights up when she sees her, which really pisses me off. For some reason I assumed Natalie stopped coming here when our friendship imploded. After all, it was *my* place first. Natalie orders a coffee. She's got a notebook with her, which she opens and starts flipping through.

Sheila comes to my table. "You need anything else?" I look around her at Natalie, and Sheila huffs. "Wish you two could just make up."

"Tell *her* that," I mumble.

"I'll tell her no such thing. You want anything or not?"

"Coffee with cream and sugar, *please*."

"Nice to see you manage to say it every now and then." She smiles and brings me the coffee. I forget to blow before I take my first sip, and it scalds my tongue. Natalie spots me, a pinched look on her face. She turns back around, back stiff as she pulls out her phone.

"I know you saw me," I say. The diner's small, and my voice carries easily. She ignores me, so I go up to the counter. I try peeking at her phone, but she places it screen down on the counter.

"What do you want?" she asks. She won't look at me.

"Can't I say hello?"

"You haven't said hello to me in more than a year, Bett."

"I wonder why that could be?"

"I came here to study for my algebra final, not fight with you. Can you leave me alone?" Her voice quivers, and she clears her throat. Natalie hates crying in public.

I consider her for a minute—the fights, the day I told her I'd rather die than be her friend anymore. She made it clear back then there was nothing left for us. I shrug and say, "Never mind. I have more important things to do."

"No, you win. I can't focus now." Natalie closes her notebook and gives Sheila a few crumpled dollar bills. "By the way, my mom told me what you did to her with the paint."

"Did she?" I try not to smile.

"It's always about you, Bett, isn't it? Even now. I've told you a hundred times that I can't control my mother and that we need the extra money. You're just a spoiled heiress who doesn't know what it's like for the rest of us. I've got things going on in my life too! Big things. At least Holly and Madison care." She brushes a tear off her cheek, says goodbye to Sheila, and rushes from the diner.

"What the hell is her problem?" I say, exasperated.

"Language," Sheila warns. She keeps a big glass jug on the end of the counter, and I know the rule: a dollar for each curse word. It's nearly full. "I'll add that to your tab," she says, and drops in four quarters. David laughs from the kitchen.

I'm disoriented as I leave the diner and wander aimlessly around downtown. If anyone's selfish and self-centered, it's Natalie and her mother. How can she blame *me* for being upset that Lydia turned my family horror story into entertainment?

Eventually, I find myself across the street from Lydia's bar. Natalie and Lydia emerge, dressed in black, and wordlessly head toward the funeral home. They must be going to the wake, I realize. They'll say it's to pay their respects, but it's really because Lydia wants juicy gossip to add to her tour script.

And because they want to be extras in this true-crime story. Be part of the *saga*.

I step off the curb and follow them.

CHAPTER Ten

I'm one of the first to arrive at Eugenia's house. (Natalie and Lydia aren't even here; I outpaced them.) The front entry is mostly empty; only a few people have lined up to pay their respects to the man's wife. I can see her through a set of sliding doors at the back of the house, next to a spray of flowers and a glossy black casket.

There's a fountain attached to the wall, and I go in for a drink. The secret door to the basement looks so innocent tucked behind its wallpaper. But I think of Melissa, frozen in the garage out back, and shudder.

More people arrive, and I press myself up against the wall to let them get into the line. Most are older people, the women holding tissues, the men with mouths pressed into straight lines. Perfumes and colognes mix together, a vomit-inducing potpourri. Even Sheila and Leo step into the line. People murmur about Trapper, my mom, and Melissa Atkins; a few mourners, recognizing me, cast furtive glances.

When Lydia finally arrives, I turn my back to her. Odd. Natalie's not with her.

"You're here." It's Eugenia, dressed all in black, standing before me with her hands folded together. Her hair is curled at the ends, and she actually looks pretty. Almost…normal.

"You're observant."

"I thought you didn't want to come."

"Changed my mind."

"Why?"

I shrug one shoulder. "He fought for my mom. I feel like I owe it to her."

"Just don't do anything stupid."

She goes to the door to greet more people. I finally step into the line myself, and immediately wish I was wearing something more appropriate.

As I shift back and forth, we slowly move forward. Fragments of whispered conversations float past me, either about what a great job Jack Ledbetter did putting my father away or who might *really* have killed Melissa…and Prudie.

Wolf Ridge always has murder on the brain.

When I'm almost to the pocket doors, I finally see the widow clearly. Short hair, honey-butter color, and a black pantsuit. She's hugging someone, wiping her eyes. "It's been very hard," she says, holding a tissue over her mouth. The couple she's talking to nod their heads sadly.

There's only two people ahead of me now, an older woman in a green floral dress and an older man drowning in a brown tweed suit. The woman leans toward the man. "Why do you think he did it?" she whispers. "Was it…*that case*?"

The man glances at the coffin. "You know how much guilt he

carried," he says quietly, and I inch a little closer, pretending to examine a button on my jacket.

"I thought he'd moved past all that," she breathes. "Man was evil as sin, everybody knew it. Jack had nothing to feel remorseful about."

"We only spoke of it a few times over the years. Jack couldn't get past it. Said he'd never be able to see it as clean."

As he and the woman approach the widow, my heart starts to thump and my stomach rolls.

It's possible the man and woman were referring to some other case…but I know they're not. Jack Ledbetter didn't die by suicide ten years to the day by coincidence.

Coming here was a mistake—what could I possibly have to say to his wife?—and I turn to go. But then the floral dress whips by, and it's just me and the widow. She wipes her nose and looks at me.

"I'm so sorry," I say, hating to use the clichéd words that have been used so many times on me.

"Thank you, dear."

My eyes dart to the coffin. Jack Ledbetter rests on a bed of white satin in a black suit and tie. He looks like a wax figure. If the belt left marks on his neck, Eugenia's parents covered them with makeup.

"How did you know Jack?" she asks.

I can't very well tell her the truth: *I didn't, although he put my father in prison for life!* But I have to say something. "He knew my grandparents."

"Oh? Who are your grandparents?"

"Wells and…Vivian Holland…," I say, trailing off. But she heard me clearly.

Her eyes lose their spark, and she swallows. "Oh dear, I don't…" She's either uncomfortable with my answer or confused by it.

"I'm very sorry," I repeat. "For your loss."

"Thank you, Bettina," she says, giving me a taut smile. "And I'm so very sorry about what happened to your mother."

Her directness throws me off, and I stare at her.

"Thank you," I finally croak, tears building behind my eyes. I can't remember the last time I cried in public, and I don't want to do it here. "I should go."

"Wait," she says, grabbing my hand. She searches my face, her lips slightly parted, as if she's trying to find the right words to say. "Thank you for coming." She lets go.

"Sure," I mumble as she looks to the next person in line. Chief Bigsby's wife waits a few spots behind me. She keeps her head down, but the bruise yellowing on her cheek is clear as day.

"Bett?"

Grams's voice snaps me back to reality. She and Granddad are standing at the back of the line, dressed in their Sunday finest. Granddad's eyes flash confusion, followed by recognition, and then anger.

He steps out of line and hurries to me. "What in God's name are you doing here, Bettina Jane?" he asks quietly. "I told you not to come."

I swallow. "I needed to see him."

He takes my arm to lead me outside, but I shake him off. *"Bettina Jane,"* he whispers, keeping a smile on his face for appearances. "It is time for you to go on home. This wake is the last place you should be."

"I'll go when I'm ready," I reply, also keeping a smile plastered on.

"I'm glad you wanted to pay your respects," he says tightly. "A man has died, a good man, a decent man who did the best he could to keep our town safe. To bring justice to your mother. But you need to let the past lie and leave the visiting to us."

"Safe? Safe from people like my father, you mean?"

"Are you defending that man? Has Ada gotten to you, too?"

"I'm not defending him," I say, as sweetly as I can. "But why are you so protective of Jack Ledbetter? Are you trying to hide something from me?"

The conversation I overheard echoes in my mind. *Said he'd never be able to see it as clean.*

"That's absurd." He takes a deep breath. "We're going to have a good long talk when I get home." Granddad straightens his tie, nods at a gentleman passing as if nothing is wrong, and gets back into line. Grams says something to him, and he touches her back and whispers.

As I head for the door, I look back at him. He's watching me, and I swear he looks afraid.

Outside, I stomp down the driveway. I have *every* right to be there, maybe even more than he does. I'm so mad I almost walk right past Nat, who's sitting on a bench in Eugenia's yard.

"How come you're not inside?" I ask, surprised.

"I didn't want to see him. Dead bodies scare me."

"Since when?" I ask. We were ten the first time we saw *Day of the Dead*. I'd stolen a copy of it from Ada's room, and Nat had laughed when the zombie tried to use the phone. I had nightmares for weeks. There's no way that's the reason she's out here.

"Since always," she says, not looking at me.

She's lying, but I let it go. "What do you know about Melissa Atkins?"

Her attention snaps back to me. "Why do you want to know?"

"I'm curious about her," I say, keeping my true reason to myself. "Did she have a boyfriend back home? Family?"

"I didn't know her," she says. "I only met her, like, one time."

"What about your mom? Melissa worked for her."

"We already told the police everything we know." She stands abruptly and heads in the direction of her house. I follow, even though it's clear she doesn't want to talk to me.

"You talked to the police?" I ask.

"Please, Bett, just leave me alone."

"I'm only asking a few questions. Aren't you curious about who may have hurt her? It's so much like what happened to my mom."

She stops, and I wait for her face to soften, for her to realize I've been through all this before, maybe offer a bit of support. Maybe I *am* playing the dead mom card, trying to guilt her a bit, but don't I deserve sympathy right now? Only Nat doesn't say a damn word, just walks away, leaving me standing by myself. She doesn't even give me a second glance before she disappears around the corner.

CHAPTER
Eleven

Returning to an empty house, I leave my boots in the middle of the front hall (which will piss off Granddad) and go upstairs for a shower. As I'm shampooing my hair, I can't help but wonder if someone I *know* killed Melissa. Then I shake my head, loosening the idea until it falls away. The only person I know who would kill a woman and dump her body in the woods is currently sitting in prison.

Except…Melissa's dead. And he couldn't have done it.

Once I'm in my pajamas, I boot up my tablet and settle onto my bed. Since no one seems to know much about Melissa, I'll have to stalk her the old-fashioned way. She doesn't have Insta or TikTok, but she's on Facebook. I hesitate before I open her page; it feels like an invasion of her privacy. And that's something I would know about—every time I open a social media account using my real name, I have to shut it down right away. *So* many messages asking for interviews, for my thoughts on other cases; *so* many threats, so many claims that I put away an innocent man; and some things too ugly to think about. But I remind myself that Melissa is gone, and I can't hurt her by snooping.

When I click on her page, she's smiling in her profile picture. She looks healthy and happy, a whole life ahead of her. Until someone decided to take it all away. Now she's just some pixelated photo online. Soon this page will become a tribute wall, and people who barely knew her will leave sappy comments about how much she'll be missed, how great a person she was. Grief porn.

One of the last photos she posted is of Lydia's bar. She's standing outside, hand on one hip, smiling in her apron. The caption: "My new life in Wolf Ridge." Her page is public, so anyone could have seen what town she was in and where she worked. They could have followed her for days, weeks.... This is why I never post photos of myself online. Too easy for bad people to get bad ideas.

She doesn't have any relationship info posted, but I scroll down her wall and find a photo of her with some white guy named Grayson from three months ago. They're cheek to cheek, all smiles. He has dark hair and an eyebrow piercing. When I click over to his page, it's filled with right-wing memes about gun rights and abortion. I text a pic of his page to Eugenia.

Me: See?! It's always the boyfriend

Eugenia: She really picked a winner...

Me: We should add him to our suspects list.
I don't trust him

Eugenia takes a while to respond. While I wait, I wonder how I can make sure Chief Bigsby gets this guy on his radar. If I suggest it, he'll blow me off. Maybe an anonymous tip?

Eugenia: Not so fast. He was in Mexico for the past week. Scroll down more.

Sure enough, I find a picture of Grayson in Mexico with a bunch of other white dudes (probably also all named Grayson). They're standing on a beach in cutoff jeans, drinking beers.

Me: That's just great. Our only person of interest, gone

Eugenia: Narrowing it down suspect by suspect is how we catch him. Good work on this.

Me: FYI, asked Natalie about Melissa tonight, after the wake

Eugenia: What'd she say?

Me: That she didn't know her and to leave her alone

Eugenia: Don't worry, we'll talk to Lydia instead. Going to sleep now. Funeral in the morning.

Me: Do you have to stay for the whole thing?

Eugenia: No, I just help them get things ready. Why?

Me: Let's meet at Sheila's for breakfast...go over the case

Eugenia: See you then.

I toss my phone on my bed and lay back, shoulders popping. I was so sure it was the boyfriend. But if I'm going to find whoever killed her, I need to keep an open mind.

Something bangs outside, and I bolt upright.

As I creep up to my bedroom window, movement near our pool catches my eye. A hooded figure moves slowly around the pool furniture, stops, and stares up at the second floor. My mouth goes dry. The figure hesitates before lowering their hood, moonlight catching curls of dark hair. I exhale and heave open my window.

"*Xavier?*" I call down. "What are you doing here?"

"Can you come outside? I need to talk to you."

He's staring at the water when I reach him. I turn on the string of white globe lights that zigzag over the brick pool deck. When he shifts toward me, I gasp. One of his eyes is purple and swollen shut. "What happened to you?" I ask. "You look like the guy who loses in a boxing movie." I move to touch his eye, and he jerks away.

"It's really sore," he says.

I wait for him to elaborate on why he showed up in my backyard, but he stares at his shoes. "What happened to your face?"

He finally looks at me. "Dave happened."

"That shaved head guy from the cemetery party?" He nods. "Why?"

"He hurt you, didn't he?"

I swallow. "Yes, he did. But you didn't have to fight the man."

"I did, actually. He's an asshole. I don't know why I ever started hanging out with him."

"I'm not your girlfriend. You don't have to defend me."

He shrugs. "I thought you might come over today, after you texted. Wanted to see if you were okay."

"I don't know what I am, but 'okay' definitely isn't it." I cross my arms, numb. "Text me before you come over. Lurking around my pool when there's a killer at large is a bit much."

He frowns. "What, you think I'm lurking?"

"It was the literal definition of lurking, Xavier."

"Sorry I scared you. Come here." He pulls me close and kisses me—only this time his kiss is soft and tentative, nothing like the times before. It feels like kissing a new version of him. His hands find my waist, and the way he holds me—gently, like I might break—makes my insides dissolve. When he pulls back, he rests his forehead against mine. "You're not like everyone else, Bett. I feel like I can tell you...things."

I swallow. "Things?" I think of Melissa's body stuffed in the woods, and my yard suddenly feels a little too dark.

"*Bettina Jane Holland*, just who in the hell is that attached to your face?"

I turn toward Granddad, still wearing his dress coat from the wake. Grams hurries inside through the patio doors. Xavier and I quickly break apart, as if we can trick my grandfather into not believing what he just saw with his own eyes.

"Answer me!" he shouts, and I'm startled by how angry he is.

"Th-this is Xavier," I stutter. "He was just leaving."

"You're goddamn right he is."

"I'll text you," Xavier says before disappearing around the side of the house.

Granddad strides toward me and grabs my hand, pulling me. "Get inside this instant," he orders, as if being dragged doesn't make his intentions obvious enough. It reminds me of Dave at the party, of Xavier's black eye.

Violence seems to be a language all men speak.

Grams sits at the kitchen island, sipping a glass of water. She won't look at me, and as soon as Granddad releases me, I head toward the kitchen door.

"Wait right there, young lady," he barks. "We're going to have a talk about what's been going on around here."

I freeze. "I'm tired. Can't we talk tomorrow?"

"This can't wait until tomorrow. What were you thinking tonight? Practically the whole town was at that wake!"

"So? Why couldn't I go? I wanted to pay my respects to him, Granddad."

"For what purpose?"

"I don't know. For closure. And I was curious, I guess."

"Curious about what?"

"About the man who put my father in prison for life."

"Your father deserved the death penalty," Granddad says.

"Wells," Grams cautions.

"It's okay, Grams," I say. "Whatever Trapper does or doesn't deserve, I'm alive because of him. I'm *a part* of him, and you hate that. I do too." I stare directly at Granddad when I say that last part.

"That's a completely unfair thing to say," he answers.

"If you hate him so much, why'd you agree to visitation in the custody agreement?"

Granddad sighs. "I had my reasons."

Pain at the back of my throat warns me I'm about to cry. "I'm going to bed."

"Stay away from Jack Ledbetter," Granddad warns.

"That'll be easy now that he's dead."

"I'm serious, Bett. No more digging around where you shouldn't be."

I narrow my eyes. "*Why?*"

"Don't test me, Bettina Jane," he says. "My patience is running thin. And no more boys, either. You've got Harvard to focus on."

"What if I'm not sure about Harvard?"

They both give me worried looks. "What do you mean?" Granddad asks. I can see the tension in his face, see that he's trying not to yell at me. "Please tell me it's not this acting nonsense again."

I look at Grams. "Don't you ever wonder what else you could have done with your life? Another path you could have taken?"

Grams gives me a sad smile. "I took care of my house and my children and my husband. That's one of the most important jobs a woman can do."

Sighing, I leave the kitchen without uttering another word, and they don't try to stop me. As I climb into bed, the idea of going to Harvard—of any kind of future—seems as gray and unreal as the face that haunts me the moment I close my eyes.

Who Killed Melissa Atkins?
Suspect List:
Drifter from out of town
~~Grayson, creepy ex-boyfriend~~

CHAPTER
Twelve

My grandparents have already left for Jack Ledbetter's funeral by the time I come downstairs the next morning. Granddad stuck a note on the dining room table that reads *Stay out of trouble*. I crumple it up.

My skin feels like it's on fire. I've gotten dozens of DMs on Insta overnight, each from the same people as always: wannabe podcasters with zero tact who want me to bare my soul. I delete the app.

Sheila's is packed when I arrive. Holly and Madison are sitting at my usual table, and I stare at them, hoping they'll feel my rage and leave. But they just keep sipping their Cokes and laughing at something on their phones. Natalie isn't with them.

"Missed you at church this morning," Sheila says from behind the counter, handing me a paper menu. Today's outfit is a long jean dress with a sequined cow on the front.

"Sorry, Sheila. You know I don't really go anymore, even with my grandparents."

She shakes her head. "Looks like your table's opened up."

When I turn around, the girls are moving toward me. Holly whispers something, and they flash me fake smiles as they pass.

I sit and scan the breakfast choices. The front door clangs, and when I glance up, I see Eugenia lugging a giant messenger bag between the cramped tables. People scoot their chairs aside, annoyed.

"Hey," she huffs, dropping the bag onto our table. It rattles the salt and pepper shakers.

"What the *hell* is in that?"

"I checked out some crime books from the library." She makes a stack on the table. One of them is literally called *Crime Solving for Dummies*.

"I love the effort, but this is a covert mission. Let's keep those out of sight."

"Good point. The librarian did give me the side-eye.... We can read them later." She quickly shuffles them back into her bag before sitting. "What's good here?"

"You've eaten at Sheila's before, right?"

She looks at me over the top of the menu. "Not in years. My parents don't care for restaurants."

"Okayyy...but what about with your friends?"

Eugenia doesn't answer; she simply goes back to studying her menu.

I clear my throat. "Can I ask you a question?"

"Yes. But I might not answer it."

"How come I never see you with anyone? Like, at lunch, you're usually by yourself in the corner."

She shrugs and sets the menu down. "People tire me. I hate small talk. Being alone is less draining."

I can't help but smile at her honesty. "We should sit together next week. Also, since you asked, the waffles are delicious."

After we order some, Eugenia takes out a notebook and pen. "All the books say to start your investigation by questioning people who knew the victim. Melissa worked at Lydia's, so we have to talk to her. I also think we should get the transcripts from your dad's trial, to cover the copycat angle."

"Forget Lydia," I say after Sheila delivers our food. "I'm not her favorite person."

"Why not?" Eugenia asks through a mouthful of waffle.

"It's a long story involving a can of paint."

"I'll do it, then."

"You need a reason, though, for asking around. Something that won't rouse anyone's suspicion, especially the chief's. People can't know we're doing this."

We sit in silence, trying to think up a believable excuse, when Lydia and Natalie enter the diner. They go to the counter and order breakfast sandwiches to go. Natalie's hair is stringy today, and when she looks at me, there are deep purple bags under her eyes. I've never seen her like that before. I almost feel bad that she got left out of breakfast with her friends.

Eugenia drizzles more syrup on her waffle. "I could say I'm writing an article for the school paper?"

I shake my head. "Madison's editor-in-chief. She'll never let you join this close to the end of the school year. She's very serious about it."

"Let me handle her." She scribbles something in her notebook as Nat and her mom leave. "I can be pretty persuasive when I want to be."

I laugh, impressed. "Good. So can I."

After breakfast, I convince Eugenia to return to the crime scene with me, hoping being there again might shake something loose in my memory. (I'll be less freaked out with her along, too.) When we get to the yellow police tape on Dogwood, I stop and look behind me. The street is empty. No one is watching, and the cops aren't around, so I duck under.

"Are you sure we should be doing this?" Eugenia asks, hesitating.

"Nope. But we're doing it anyway."

She sighs and steps over the tape, muttering something about felonies, and follows me as I retrace my steps. The area where Melissa's body was lying looks innocuous enough—just some broken plants and dead leaves and a few yellow crime scene markers. There's a small smear of blood on the side of the fallen tree, one I wouldn't have been able to see the night I found her, and part of me wants to reach out and touch it, see if it's real or if I'm just imagining it.

"She was right there," I say, pointing to the tree. "Kind of…jammed underneath it."

"Disposed of," she says, shaking her head. "This isn't all that far from where Cherry was found."

I close my eyes, trying to remember every detail of that night. I'd fallen, tripping over something. A raccoon ran by. Then I was going to leave, but I stopped.…Why did I stop? Why did I go back? I had a feeling I *should*.

My mind flashes to the morning my mom died. I cried out her name as I walked down the hallway to their bedroom. I'd been watching TV, and when I called for her, she didn't come. My mom always came for me. Finding her on the bed, I had a moment of relief, but then I saw the red on her face—saw how she wouldn't look at me, just staring at the ceiling—and I knew something was terribly wrong.

I'm back.

I shake my head.

My eyes sweep over the detritus again, looking for something. Anything.

A strange feeling comes over me, like I've already lived this. I guess I have, in a way. Only this time I'm not in the dark...and I'm not alone.

Suddenly, I spot a book of matches half hidden under some leaves. "A clue?" I ask, bending to pick it up.

Eugenia leans over for a better look. "If it's a clue, you probably shouldn't touch it."

"Too late." The matchbook is wet, probably from the rain we had last week. It has a white cover with SHEILA'S DINER printed in shiny red letters. On the inside, only two matches remain.

"It's probably just a coincidence," I say, disappointed. "This could have been lying in the woods for weeks—months. The cops probably think it's garbage."

"Maybe, or maybe they just didn't see it," Eugenia says. "I don't trust that their detective skills are up to the task at hand."

"You think it's actual evidence?"

"Could be," she says. "Which means whoever killed Melissa could have dined or worked at Sheila's—or known someone who'd been there. Let's go back, see if she has more. I want to see what one looks like dry."

"Why couldn't it have been Melissa's, though?"

"Was she a smoker?" Eugenia asks coolly. "Didn't look like it on Facebook, did it?"

"Okay, fair. But what if one of the cops dropped it? Or the medical examiner?"

"For now, let's assume they didn't."

We leave the woods and retrace our steps. Back at Sheila's, the breakfast crowd has mostly cleared out. I stop short at the sight of Andre Richardson at the counter in his police uniform, drinking a cup of coffee. He's chatting with Sheila. I quickly stuff the matchbook in my pocket.

"Play it cool," I whisper to Eugenia, who blows past me and straight to Sheila.

"Back so soon?" Sheila smiles. "I've got a peach pie about to come out the oven if you wanna wait."

"Do you have any matchbooks?" Eugenia, apparently oblivious to social norms, doesn't even turn down the pie first.

Sheila narrows her eyes. "You're not smoking, are you?"

"No, not me. But my mom does. Stressful job, you know?" Sheila nods. "Anyway, do you have a book of matches? Her old one ran out, one she'd gotten here. She's superstitious about the matches she uses."

I'm impressed—and a touch troubled—by how quickly Eugenia passed this off as the truth without batting an eye.

"No, darlin', we don't hand out matchbooks anymore. It's been, gosh…at least ten years? Ain't that right, David?" she calls toward the kitchen. While David's asking what she's going on about, I feel Andre watching me.

"How are you doing, Bett?" he asks.

I finally meet his gaze, but there's only concern on his face, no suspicion. I breathe out. "Not that great. Any leads on Melissa's case?"

"I can't discuss it, but I promise we're doing all we can. Try not to worry." He leaves some money on the counter. "Thanks, Sheila, I needed that."

She pushes the bills back toward him. "Free of charge when you're on duty, you know my rule!" He laughs, secretly deposits it into her swear jar, and leaves.

"Anyway," Sheila continues, "to answer your question, we stopped orderin' the matchbooks after some kid burned a finger usin' them to mess around with fireworks. David reminded me—memory is impeccable, that man."

"Thanks anyway," Eugenia says. "Come on, Bett." As soon as we get outside, she leans against the building and puts her hand on her chest. "That was scary! I thought Andre had seen us coming out of the woods."

"You didn't look nervous. Didn't even break a sweat."

"My dad says I have a good poker face."

"That's putting it mildly."

"So, ten years," she says thoughtfully. "Kind of blows the chief's theory out of the water. A drifter who only passed through Wolf Ridge to kill wouldn't have had this matchbook. Melissa just moved here; she couldn't have been carrying it either. It'd have to be someone who lives here—or who visited a decade ago."

"If it even belonged to the killer at all," I say, and hand her the soggy matchbook. "You're making a big assumption. I still say it's junk, but you better keep this in your weird attic crime lab. With my luck, our housekeeper would find it and throw away our first possible clue."

CHAPTER Thirteen

Monday morning comes way too early. I slept horribly the night before, dreaming about my mom and a dark figure walking out of her bedroom, and now I'm fumbling through my locker in a fog, trying and failing to locate my only working pen. When something touches my shoulder, I whip around, heart racing.

"Relax," Eugenia says, backing away. "I didn't mean to scare you."

"Sorry. I'm a little tense, I guess."

"Could've fooled me." She leans in. "I talked to Lydia yesterday afternoon."

I glance around, but no one's looking. "You did *what*?"

"It needed to be done, and it couldn't wait. She saw Melissa more than anyone. She was the best place to start."

I slam my locker door closed just as Natalie, Holly, and Madison walk by. Holly and Madison laugh with each other. Nat keeps her eyes straight ahead. She looks thinner than normal. Pale…almost gray.

"Did she buy the lie that you're on the newspaper?" I whisper.

"I didn't need to lie. Madison couldn't say no when I swung by her house." She smiles. "I pulled out my very best Wednesday Addams impression."

"No offense, Eugenia, but it's not an impression. It's who you are."

"That's the nicest thing anyone's ever said about me." She smirks. "Well? Don't you want to know what Lydia had to say?"

"Not really. You know I hate her guts, right?"

"You have to stay objective."

"Objective about the woman profiting off my mother's murder?"

"Yes, if we want to catch this person. Isn't that what you want?"

Sighing, I lean against my locker. "You're right. Tell me."

Eugenia takes out her notebook and flips it open. "Melissa started working at the bar two months ago. She moved here from Raleigh. She hadn't really made any friends yet, but she had gone out a few times with someone." She looks at me. "David Dennison."

"Sheila's son?" I ask, pushing off the wall. I try to look at her notebook, but she presses it against her chest.

"Yes, Sheila's son. Lydia didn't know how serious they were. She said Melissa was a good employee but pretty much kept to herself. That's all I got."

"David is harmless," I say as we head down the hall. "I can't imagine him hurting someone." I've known him for as long as I can remember. He's on the volunteer fire department and does Meals on Wheels. I've never known him to be violent; Sheila wouldn't tolerate it.

Although…seemingly nice men *do* kill.

"Lydia said the same thing. But we still need to talk to him. Maybe he knows who might have wanted to hurt her."

"Sheila wouldn't like us doing that. She'd be pretty offended."

Eugenia shrugs. "Then we'll talk to him somewhere outside the diner."

We split up, and I head into drama class. Today is my monologue final, I remember suddenly. Shit! I'd completely forgotten about it. My lower back breaks out in a sweat, and I lift my T-shirt off my stomach, trying to fan myself. I'm not ready—not even close. Everyone says drama is an easy A, but clearly, it is not.

Holly is staring at me more intensely than usual.

"What's your problem?" I ask as I take my assigned seat next to her. I look up at the clock, wishing I could somehow stop time. Liam sits on my other side. He looks worried too. Probably dreading this as much as I am. Even though I've been in a few plays, standing up in front of a classroom makes me nervous. At least when I'm on stage, the bright lights blind me from really seeing anyone's face.

Holly angles herself toward me. "Oh, nothing."

"Okay, whatever." I dig my phone out of my bag. That's when I notice what Holly's wearing. A black T-shirt with a yellow smiley face and some names printed on it. Names I recognize in big block letters.

TRAPPER. CHERRY. PRUDENCE. MELISSA.

"Do you like it?" Holly asks. "A new docuseries about your family was just announced online. They've already got a bunch of merch for sale on their website—overnight shipping available."

Before I have time to formulate a blistering comeback, my body comes up with an alternative plan.

I drop my phone, spring out of my desk, and shove my closed fist into Holly's nose so hard it bursts red.

She falls backward out of her chair, stunned, then covers her face with her arms like the coward she is. I shake out my hand just as Ms. Jones comes into class. "What's going on in here?" she asks, hurrying to our own unfolding drama.

"Bett knocked her out cold!" Brady says, overexaggerating.

"Is this true?" Ms. Jones asks as she kneels to check on Holly. She's sitting up now, holding Liam's T-shirt to her face.

Suddenly my monologue rushes back to me; I can hear Bette Davis's voice as clear as if she were standing next to me.

I look at Holly. "I never cared for you, not once."

CHAPTER
Fourteen

Holly and I sit outside the principal's office, three empty chairs between us. Principal Thomas hasn't emerged from her office.

As soon as Ms. Jones deposited us outside her office, I looked up the docuseries, hoping Holly was full of shit. But sure enough, some streaming service is rushing to make one about my father, with the angle that our family is somehow cursed. They've titled it *Poisoned Blood*, and from the trailer, I can see that they've included a juicy tidbit: me finding another murdered woman in Wolf Ridge.

If Ada's involved with this production, I'll kill her.

Holly holds an ice pack to her nose. The bleeding's stopped, and her nose really doesn't look that bad.

She notices me watching her. "You can't just go around punching people, *Bett*. My parents are totally going to sue, you know. Just wait."

"Bring it on, Holly. My grandfather is a lawyer, remember?"

She faces forward then, wincing when she moves the ice pack. I almost feel sorry for her, until I look at the blood drying on my mother's name.

Grams's worried voice reaches me before she does. I groan and stand up just as she and Granddad round the corner into the waiting area. Grams immediately hugs me, no questions asked. Granddad gives me a serious look. Then Holly's parents arrive, wearing business suits and pinched looks on their faces. Her dad is about as tall as an NBA player. He glares down at me, and I can tell he wants to say something.

That's when Principal Thomas opens her door. At only five feet, she still commands the room. Twists are piled atop her head, giving her added height. "Come in," she says, waiting as we shuffle past her.

Inside the office, Holly's family sits on one side of the room. We sit on the other. Principal Thomas moves with confidence around the desk and sits. She folds her hands and looks at me and then at Holly.

"Well?" Holly's dad practically shouts. "What are you going to do to her? She assaulted my daughter. I want her expelled!"

"Now hold on, Chip," Granddad says. "Let's not get nasty."

"Nasty?" her dad echoes, looking at Granddad with disgust. "I should call the police and press charges."

Principal Thomas clears her throat. "Please, everyone, stop talking. I want to address these young ladies." The men fall silent. "Girls, I think I have a strong idea of what happened today after speaking with Ms. Jones and your schoolmates. Bettina, you came into class today and saw Holly wearing a T-shirt about your mother's murder."

Holly's parents finally notice their daughter's shirt. Her mom gasps. Holly crosses her arms.

"And Holly," Principal Thomas says. "You told Bettina that she herself could purchase one of these T-shirts. Is that right?"

"Yes, ma'am," Holly says.

"Bettina, did you then strike Holly in the face?"

"I did, ma'am," I say. The thrill of punching Holly Walters has passed. Now I just want to go home. A fan on the desk barely moves the air around, and I can't breathe in this stuffy room.

Principal Thomas looks to Holly again. "Holly, can you understand why Bettina may have been hurt by your T-shirt and your suggestion that she should want one of her own?"

Holly nods. "I can, ma'am. But she's been awful to Nat, so awful, and—"

"And Bettina, do you understand that we have a zero-tolerance policy for violence at our school?" I nod. "Okay. Here's what's going to happen. You're both good students. I'm not going to expel anyone." She shoots a pointed look at Holly's dad. "But there has to be a punishment. First, no prom for either of you."

"What?" Holly cries.

"But she already bought her dress," her mother pleads.

Principal Thomas ignores her. "Second, you are both finished with drama class as of today, and both of you will receive failing grades. You can retake the class next year, and whatever grade you earn then will replace this one. And Bett, if you ever hit another student, you *will* be expelled—immediately. Now go back to class. Holly, you're excused to the doctor."

⌒

After school, Eugenia and I drive downtown and park about a block away from the diner.

We're waiting for David to exit; he usually goes home for an hour before the dinner rush. (I feel slightly creepy for knowing that, but then again, everyone is in everyone's business here. You can't take a dump in this town without someone knowing about it.)

As my grandparents were leaving school today, they told me we would have a "big chat" tonight at dinner. I hope we can skip it—just sweep it under the rug like we do everything else. I flex my hand; my knuckles are sore.

"It's true, then," Eugenia says, watching me. "About Holly."

I nod.

"I won't ask why. I assume she had it coming."

"Damn right she did."

Like clockwork, David exits the diner at three fifteen. He unlocks his bike, slips on his riding gloves, and pedals off down Rose Street. "Come on," I say to Eugenia. We ease out of the Rolls, carefully closing the doors. Eugenia steps off the curb without looking, and I yank on the back of her sweater with my sore hand just before a pink moped takes her out.

She shakes her fist. *"Watch where you're going!"*

"Geez, Eugenia. Maybe look before you cross a street?"

She rolls her eyes, and we cross Market Street and sneak onto Rose. First Baptist Church watches us from the corner, its stained glass windows glowing. I haven't been in years now, no matter how much Grams and Sheila beg. Services just felt…hollow.

Eugenia nudges me. "There he is."

David parks in front of a yellow two-story house, puts down his kickstand, and goes inside.

"You didn't happen to ask Lydia where Melissa was living, did you?" I ask.

"On Storybook Lane."

"So, close by, then," I mutter as I stare at David's presumed home. It has two house numbers, so it must be a duplex. "Should we wait for him to come back outside? What do we say?"

Eugenia gazes at the house. "Let's knock and offer our condolences."

Then, without waiting for me to answer, she marches ahead. Dumbstruck, I follow, my heart slamming in my chest.

David *couldn't* have done anything. Once, when I was a kid, I crashed my bike in front of the diner. He carried me inside, bandaged my knee, and called Grams. Does he have a darker side I'm just refusing to see?

I'm back.

Eugenia knocks on the rusted screen door. David steps onto his porch a few seconds later. He's eating a banana, carefully peeling back a section.

"Hey there, Eugenia. Bett." He takes a bite, looking a bit confused. "Can I help you with something? Did Sheila send you?"

I assume that David Dennison was a heartbreaker in his day. His shaggy black hair and stubble are hot-adjacent. The cargo shorts and sandals with white socks? Not so much.

"We wanted to offer our condolences—about your friend Melissa." Eugenia folds her hands in front of herself and tilts her head sideways. It reminds me of Grams when she's being fake nice to people.

David lowers his eyes before taking another bite of his banana. "Thanks."

"I'm really sorry, David," I say.

He looks up at me, his eyes filling with tears. "I can only hope she didn't suffer. Not like how your mama did."

"You knew my mom?"

He nods. "I thought you knew that, Bett. Sure, we went to school together—even dated for a while. She was the nicest girl in class. I was even at your house the night before it happened. I still can't believe she's gone." A tear slips down his cheek, and he wipes it away roughly.

My mom dated *David*? My grandparents never mentioned it before.

"I wonder who would do something like this?" Eugenia asks, casually glancing back at me. "Would anyone want to hurt Melissa?"

"Gosh, I wouldn't think so. She was a real sweet lady. Went to church, even."

I bristle. Do only certain types of people deserve to be murdered? I know he's not really implying that, so I take a deep breath. "Lydia said you two were sweet on each other?"

"We'd gone out a few times. It wasn't anything serious."

"When's the last time you saw her?" Eugenia asks, no tact left, apparently. She sounds like Mariska on *SVU*. I cringe.

David looks startled. "Why are you asking me this?"

Eugenia doesn't miss a beat. "I'm writing an article about Melissa for the school newspaper. I'm interviewing everyone who knew her."

"Well, let's see…it would've been that Sunday at church. We were supposed to go out to a movie Thursday night, but she never showed. I figured she was standing me up. Now I know better."

"Where were *you* on Thursday?" Eugenia asks pointedly. For such a tiny person, she takes up a lot of space.

"I went to the diner in the morning, stopped home late afternoon to shower, and then I went back to the diner after Melissa didn't show."

"All night?"

He shakes his head. "No, I would have been home around midnight." He gives me a look, and I shrug. There's no stopping Eugenia Cline.

"Anyone who can corroborate this information?"

He sighs, tossing his banana peel off the porch. "Listen, girls, I've got things to do. Good luck with your article." He goes inside without another word.

———

We stay silent as we walk back toward the Rolls. When we reach the car, I turn on her. "Did you have to question him like that? Jesus!"

"Yes. I was reading about this interrogation technique police use. You hit them with some easy questions first, then go straight for the jugular. Catches them off-balance. It makes sense. People feel safe with patterns. Mess up that pattern and they fall to pieces."

"This wasn't *supposed* to be an interrogation," I say. "Just ease up next time, okay?"

"Fine. But did you see how agitated he was? And he wouldn't answer my question about his alibi!"

"For someone who spends a majority of her time around grieving people, you sure can't read them." I unlock the Rolls, slide in, then unlock her door.

She opens the door but doesn't get in. "What do you mean?"

I motion for her to sit. "David was being genuine."

She puts on her seat belt. "You don't know that."

"Call it a hunch."

Eugenia sticks her hand down the front of her shirt, and then she sets David's banana peel on my lap.

"What the hell is this?"

She smiles. "Now we have his DNA."

I start the car before tossing the slimy peel out the window. "You need help."

As we drive away, something David said nags at me. "David said he dated my mom. That means he's connected to both my mom *and* Melissa."

"And he has a chunk of time with no alibi. The same time frame the medical examiner says Melissa was killed in, he was conveniently 'in the shower.' His name is going on the suspect list."

She's right. I can't assume David is innocent just because he seems like a kind person. I hate to think it, but yes. He's on the list.

"We still need the trial transcript," I say. "If David was with my mom the night before she died, maybe he testified. We could just watch it online, but…," I trail off. I've never been able to bring myself to watch the trial on YouTube, uploaded in chunks by true-crime buffs with a hard-on for tragedy. I don't want to hear any of it spoken out loud—or watch my own testimony.

"I understand," she says. "It's less scary in black and white."

Who Killed Melissa Atkins?
Suspect List:
Drifter from out of town
~~Grayson, creepy ex-boyfriend~~
David Dennison

CHAPTER
Fifteen

The next day, Eugenia and I ditch last period to drive to Wilmington. The County Courthouse where the trial took place looks like I remember: a tall redbrick building with a clock tower. Being the granddaughter of a lawyer does have a few advantages: I know exactly how I can get the transcripts here. I've written down the date of Trapper's trial, the case number, and the names of the lawyers and judge on a slip of paper.

The temperature drops once we step inside the doors; it's cold, like a crypt. The floors and walls are marble, and my footsteps ricochet off them. The clerk's office is on the second floor, and we take the stairs. A glass partition blocks me from the clerk, who smiles when she sees us. "How can I help you?" The woman's dark hair is pulled back into a messy ponytail, her glasses sliding off the end of her nose.

I hand her the paper. "We'd like the transcript to this trial, please."

She looks over the paper. "I remember this one," she says, touching her nose. "Lucky for you it's already been transcribed. I can get you a copy. The fee is twenty dollars."

She has me fill out an official form, and then she disappears into another room. We sit on the empty chairs across the hall. I lean my head against the wall.

"You don't look so good," Eugenia comments.

"Thank you for the compliment."

"I didn't mean it like that. Your skin is pale. Are you feeling okay?"

"Honestly, not really."

Eugenia's quiet for a while. "I'm sorry."

"Sorry for what?"

"For pushing you into this investigation. My motivations weren't entirely pure."

I try not to smile. "*Pure*, Eugenia? What does that even mean?"

She's quiet for a while, working something out in that mysterious brain of hers. She finally says, "I meant everything I said. I wanted to make a difference. But I also wanted to matter, for once, in Wolf Ridge. Not be seen as just the creepy undertaker's creepy daughter."

I nudge her with my elbow. "You do matter, weirdo."

"You're just saying that to cheer me up."

"I'm not. I promise. It's been nice having someone to talk to. Someone who isn't obsessed with my mom's murder."

"We're literally here to get the transcript of her murder trial. I'd say I'm at least a little obsessed."

I chuckle darkly. "That's true...but you're still pretty cool, Eugenia. You make me feel like I can shake shit up now and then."

A small smile blooms on her face. "Thanks, Bett."

After more than twenty minutes, the clerk returns with two large bankers boxes. "Here they are," she says, wheeling them out to us. "You know, you're the second person this month who's requested this transcript."

I touch one of the boxes. "Who else came in?"

"I probably shouldn't say," she whispers, "but some woman who said she runs a bar? I can't remember, but it seemed strange."

I should have guessed. Some people are shameless.

We lug the boxes up the stairs into Eugenia's attic. While she lights the candles, I carefully take the lid off the first box. A smudged photocopy looks up at me, and I run my fingertips across the smooth paper. How can something as ordinary as ink and paper feel so dangerous?

Eugenia drags her lawn chair next to mine and places what looks like two tiny metal sawhorses in front of us. She lays a piece of cardboard over them.

"What are those?" I ask.

"Vintage coffin stands." She lifts out a stack of papers and sets them on the makeshift table. "We better get started. We've got a lot of ground to cover."

```
THE PEOPLE OF THE STATE OF NORTH CAROLINA
   —against—
   TRAPPER MCGRATH,
   Defendant.
```

I dig the heels of my hands into my eyes. Trapper's crimes are all right there, printed in black and white. Every question I've ever had about my mom's death is answered in these two boxes. All the silences at Magnolia House, the whispered conversations my grandparents cut off the moment I come into a room. These boxes hold *everything* they've been hiding from me. Everything I've been hiding from myself.

But a woman has been murdered. Melissa's face crowds my dreams, the taunting words the killer left on her face carved deep. Sometimes she's my mother, and she looks up at me and asks me to help her. But no matter how hard I try, I can't stop the blood that floods the forest floor, carrying me away in a surging wave.

Eugenia picks up the prosecution's opening statement. "Mind if I read this out loud?"

"Be my guest," I say, folding my hands in my lap.

She clears her throat and begins, her voice soft and low.

OPENING STATEMENT

ATTORNEY LEDBETTER: Thank you, your Honor. May it please the Court...

THE COURT: Counsel, you may begin.

ATTORNEY LEDBETTER: Ladies and gentlemen of the jury, the morning of June 25, 2009, was sunny and warm in Wolf Ridge, North Carolina. Flowers were blooming. The city was preparing for its annual carnival and Friendship Days celebration. Prudence McGrath was at home with her six-year-old daughter, Bettina Jane. She fixed her Fruity Pebbles, her favorite cereal. She turned on some cartoons for Bettina to watch. They read a book together and played a game of Candy Land.

On that same morning, Trapper McGrath decided to forever sever the bond between mother and child when he murdered Prudence McGrath. He committed this act of unspeakable violence while their child was at home, watching TV on the living room couch.

Trapper McGrath had been drifting from menial job to menial job for years. He never graduated from high school. He tried and failed to earn his GED. He was a known womanizer. Prudence was a senior in high school herself when Trapper impregnated her. They eloped shortly after she turned eighteen, causing strife in her once close-knit family. The house Prudence and Trapper were renting was more than they could afford. The landlord will testify that he was in the process of evicting them and that Trapper had threatened him with physical violence on several occasions. Prudence would not go to her family for money, which went against Trapper's demands. On the morning of June 25, Trapper McGrath stabbed her to death in their bedroom with their daughter in the next room. Trapper stood to benefit financially from his wife's death.

Throughout this trial, the State will prove beyond a reasonable doubt that around 10:00 in the morning, Trapper McGrath arrived home. He grabbed a three-inch long steak knife from the kitchen, where Prudence had been washing the dishes. Trapper followed Prudence into their bedroom and stabbed her three times in the chest, puncturing her right lung. Prudence fell backward onto the bed. Defensive wounds on her arms and hands will show that she tried to fight back. The attack also cut into Prudence's aorta. She bled to death. Trapper slashed her face with the knife after she'd died, his rage uncontrolled. He then left his small daughter alone with her dead mother and went to the local bar for a beer. The minor child, in taped testimony, will tell you that she saw her father leaving the scene of the crime.

The State will show you that fingerprints on the knife were made by the defendant, Trapper McGrath. Prudence's blood was found on his clothing. A threatening note written by Trapper to Prudence shortly before the murder was found by police in the couple's bathroom. Witnesses will testify that Trapper was acting strangely the night before assaulting Prudence at their home.

The Judge has explained to you one of the counts is murder in the first degree. The State will meet the burden of proof. We will make your job very easy for you, ladies and gentlemen. We will present ample evidence to convince you beyond any reasonable doubt that Trapper McGrath is responsible for this heinous crime.

Thank you.

Eugenia tapes the opening statement to the whiteboard. "This gives us a good summary of the time line." She turns around just as I'm wiping my eyes. "You're crying."

"You're perceptive."

She tucks her hair behind her ears. "Should we stop?"

I clear my throat. "No. We keep reading."

"If you're sure…"

"I said I'm sure!" I snap. "Sorry. I'm stressed, I guess."

"I would be too." She's quiet for a minute. "Do you remember much of that morning?"

I knew Eugenia would eventually have to ask me about my mother's death. Still, I prickle with fear. My testimony convinced a jury, but the truth is…when I try to remember that morning, it's all gray and jumbled. I'm pretty sure I saw the dark silhouette of him coming out of my mom's bedroom. But that's all I remember. No screams, no shouts, no struggle.

"Not much," I say, "apart from him leaving their room." I will keep my doubts to myself. Trapper killed her; on the evidence, he would have been convicted even without me. But sometimes I wish that memory was clearer, more focused, more…real.

We flip through page after page of the transcript in silence. The words bleed together. My armpit sweat has soaked through my T-shirt, and I'm about to demand she bring up a second fan when Granddad's name jumps out from one of the pages.

DIRECT EXAMINATION

ATTORNEY LEDBETTER: What is your relationship to the victim?

WELLS HOLLAND: I'm her father, Wells Walker Holland III.

ATTORNEY LEDBETTER: Can you describe what you were doing on the morning of June 25, 2009?

WELLS HOLLAND: I worked at my law office in the morning. I left the house at 8:00 a.m., the same time I usually head in. I returned home early in the afternoon.

ATTORNEY LEDBETTER: Did you see or speak with Trapper McGrath at any time that morning?

WELLS HOLLAND: No, I did not.

ATTORNEY LEDBETTER: Did you see or speak with your daughter, Prudence, any time that morning?

WELLS HOLLAND: No, I did not.

ATTORNEY LEDBETTER: When was the last time you saw Prudence or Trapper?

WELLS HOLLAND: I last saw them briefly on Memorial Day. My wife, Vivian, was throwing her annual potluck at our home.

ATTORNEY LEDBETTER: Did you notice anything out of the ordinary during that visit?

WELLS HOLLAND: (clears throat) Trapper was very quiet that day. That wasn't usual for him.

ATTORNEY LEDBETTER: What else happened?

WELLS HOLLAND: They departed before all the guests arrived. I saw Trapper and Prudence arguing on the other side of the pool, about what I couldn't say. He tried to grab her arm. They left after that.

ATTORNEY LEDBETTER: Was that the last time you saw your daughter alive?

WELLS HOLLAND: Yes, I'm afraid it was.

I lean back in my chair. "I never knew he testified. I mean, I guess it makes sense. But it must have been really hard for him."

"Do you talk about her death often? About what really happened?"

I give her a look. "Never. We literally *never* talk about it."

"How is that even possible?"

I shrug. "It already happened once. Why keep reliving it?" I realize I'm parroting what my grandparents have always told me.

Eugenia goes back to reading, but I cross my arms and look up at the rafters, the cobwebs gently swaying. Our suspect list for Melissa's murder is pathetically short, and I'm starting to doubt that reading about my mom's murder will do us any good.

"Here's the medical examiner's testimony about the slashes on her face," she says, and I lean closer to read.

MARY QUINTERO: Yes, it's a photo of the slashes I examined.

ATTORNEY LEDBETTER: Can you describe the location of the wounds?

MARY QUINTERO: The slashes are on both the left and right cheek, approximately half a centimeter from the corners of the victim's mouth. You'll notice a small amount of blood around the cut.

ATTORNEY LEDBETTER: When were these slashes inflicted?

MARY QUINTERO: Based on the lack of active bleeding, I believe they were made postmortem.

ATTORNEY LEDBETTER: No further questions.

"What about Melissa and Cherry?" I ask. "Were their slashes made postmortem?"

"Yes, but let's read their files again to confirm."

"Not another trip into your basement of horrors," I groan.

"No need! I made copies." Eugenia crosses the attic, opens an old steamer trunk, removes a few ragged looking quilts, and takes out some paper. She flips through the pages, her brow knitted in concentration. Then she goes to the whiteboard and scribbles down a few lines. "They were made postmortem, too."

"Which means this really *could* be a copycat killer," I say. "He's sticking pretty close to what happened to my mom and Cherry."

"I agree. It doesn't seem like a coincidence." Eugenia tucks the papers back into the chest. "Should we stop for today? Or keep going?"

"I have a feeling this killer won't stop. So neither can we." I flip to the next page. "Holy shit, it's Lydia!"

DIRECT EXAMINATION

ATTORNEY GRAHAM: Please state your name.

LYDIA BAKER: Lydia Lynn Baker.

ATTORNEY GRAHAM: How do you know my client, the defendant?

LYDIA BAKER: We went to some of the same parties together. That's how we met. Became good friends after that.

ATTORNEY GRAHAM: And how did you know Prudence McGrath?

LYDIA BAKER: We went to school together, from elementary through high school. We were also good friends.

ATTORNEY GRAHAM: Where were you on the night of June 24, 2009?

LYDIA BAKER: I was at Prudie and Trapper's house on Elm Street. They were having a small get-together.

ATTORNEY GRAHAM: Who else was at the party?

LYDIA BAKER: Besides me, it was Heather Reyes and David Dennison. And Prudie and Trapper, of course. Trapper was late. We all got there first.

ATTORNEY GRAHAM: What happened that night at the party?

LYDIA BAKER: First we had some beers in the backyard. David brought a few T-bones, and when Trapper got there, he grilled them out back. We just sat around, drinking and eating and talking. We played a couple of games of beanbag toss. It was a pretty tame night.

ATTORNEY GRAHAM: Where was the minor child, Bettina McGrath?

LYDIA BAKER: Prudie had put her to bed around eight.

ATTORNEY GRAHAM: How would you describe Trapper's demeanor that night? Did he seem angry? Agitated?

LYDIA BAKER: Not at all. He was in a great mood. He had even picked up ice cream on his way home, mint chocolate chip. It was Prudie's favorite.

ATTORNEY GRAHAM: Did Trapper and Prudence argue?

LYDIA BAKER: If they did, it wasn't in front of me. She was sitting on his lap almost the whole night. They seemed happy. I know a lot of people think Trapper's a bad guy. But he isn't.

ATTORNEY GRAHAM: How so?

LYDIA BAKER: I'm a single mother, and Trapper fixed my car for free last winter when it broke down. He's always there for his friends, no matter what. He just wouldn't have done this. He couldn't have.

"She was *there*," I say, sitting back in my chair. "Lydia was with them the night before, and she never told me." I squeeze my eyes shut. Does she tell the women on her dumb tour this salacious detail?

"That's so messed up," Eugenia says. "Lydia thinks your dad is innocent, but she's running that tour, acting like she believes he really did it!"

"Lydia has convinced herself the tour is to honor my mother's memory.... At least that's what she told me."

"If it was just to honor her, why charge a fee? Why not make the tour free?"

"Well, exactly. Have you ever heard of Heather Reyes?" I ask, looking back at Lydia's testimony. Eugenia shakes her head.

My grandparents never talk about my mom's life: not her friends, not her hobbies, not her dreams for the future. Newspaper reporters covering her trial probably know more about my own mother than I do.

I keep turning pages until I find Heather's testimony. She was a witness for the prosecution.

DIRECT EXAMINATION

ATTORNEY LEDBETTER: And how did you know the victim, Prudence McGrath?

HEATHER REYES: She was my best friend since junior high. I loved her like a sister.

ATTORNEY LEDBETTER: Were you at the party at 313 Elm Street on the night of June 24, 2009?

HEATHER REYES: Yes, I was.

ATTORNEY LEDBETTER: What time did you arrive?

HEATHER REYES: I got there about 6:00. I was the first one there. Trapper wasn't home yet.

ATTORNEY LEDBETTER: And how did Prudence seem when you arrived? Was she in a happy mood?

HEATHER REYES: No. She'd come home from work to an eviction notice taped to their front door. She was really upset.

ATTORNEY LEDBETTER: Was Prudence aware that she and Trapper were behind on rent payments?

HEATHER REYES: No. Trapper took care of the bills, and she thought he'd been paying them.

ATTORNEY LEDBETTER: Was Trapper employed at the time?

HEATHER REYES: He claimed to have been working at a garage for six months. We found out later he'd been let go only a few weeks into the job. He was showing up late a lot. Sometimes not at all.

ATTORNEY LEDBETTER: What time did the defendant, Trapper McGrath, arrive at the party that night?

HEATHER REYES: Around 8:00. He was the last one to get there. David Dennison was about to start grilling some steaks when Trapper came into the backyard. He grabbed the tongs from David and took over.

ATTORNEY LEDBETTER: What was Mr. McGrath's demeanor?

HEATHER REYES: Trapper was usually a pretty jovial guy. Life of the party. Charismatic. But he was quiet when he got there. He kept his back to us for a while, just fiddling with the grill, not talking. It wasn't like him.

ATTORNEY LEDBETTER: Did you notice anything else unusual that night?

HEATHER REYES: It was later in the night, maybe 10:00. I went inside to use the bathroom. Trapper and Prudie were in their bedroom, arguing quietly. I looked inside, and I saw Trapper grabbing her wrist and he wouldn't let go. Prudie told him to stop, that he was hurting her.

ATTORNEY LEDBETTER: Permission to approach the witness, your Honor.

COURT: Permission granted.

ATTORNEY LEDBETTER: Ms. Reyes, can you demonstrate on me how the defendant grabbed Prudence McGrath's wrist?

HEATHER REYES: Sure. (ATTORNEY LEDBETTER EXTENDS RIGHT ARM. WITNESS QUICKLY GRABS ON TO ATTORNEY LEDBETTER'S WRIST AND TWISTS SLIGHTLY.)

ATTORNEY LEDBETTER: No further questions.

The papers fall out of my hands and drop into my lap. It's not that I'm surprised Trapper laid his hands on her that night. It wasn't the first time, and if he hadn't killed her, it wouldn't have been the last. It's just so ugly.

I consider stopping for the night, almost afraid to search for David's testimony. But then a crow caws loudly outside the attic, and I imagine it pecking at a new victim's decomposing body in the woods. I couldn't save my mom or Melissa. But maybe now I can save someone else.

"It's so hot up here," Eugenia says. "Let me grab us a couple glasses of iced tea."

Once she's gone, I read without her.

DIRECT EXAMINATION

ATTORNEY LEDBETTER: How did you know the victim, Prudence McGrath?

DAVID DENNISON: She was my friend. One of my very best friends. She was always nice to me.

ATTORNEY LEDBETTER: Were you at the party at 313 Elm Street on the night of June 24, 2009?

DAVID DENNISON: I was.

ATTORNEY LEDBETTER: What time did you arrive?

DAVID DENNISON: I don't remember exactly, but it was before Trapper came home. I was grilling some steaks. He didn't like that much.

ATTORNEY LEDBETTER: And why do you say that?

DAVID DENNISON: He walked over and took the tongs right outta my hands, told me he was taking over. He sounded mad.

ATTORNEY LEDBETTER: Did you speak to Prudence that night?

DAVID DENNISON: Yeah, before Trapper came home. When I got there, she was sitting on the front step with Heather Reyes. She'd been crying. Her eyes were all red and puffy.

ATTORNEY LEDBETTER: Did she tell you what was wrong?

DAVID DENNISON: She just wiped her eyes and said it was no big deal. I asked if it was about Trapper, and she nodded.

CROSS EXAMINATION

ATTORNEY GRAHAM: Mr. Dennison, you said you were good friends with Prudence McGrath, is that correct?

DAVID DENNISON: Yes, sir.

ATTORNEY GRAHAM: Were you ever more than just friends?

DAVID DENNISON: We dated when we were in the tenth grade, before I had a bad car accident.

ATTORNEY GRAHAM: What happened after your car accident?

DAVID DENNISON: I got banged up pretty good. Was in a coma for a couple of weeks.

ATTORNEY GRAHAM: When you came home from the hospital, did your relationship with Prudence change?

DAVID DENNISON: She was really nice to me, came by the house all the time while I recuperated.

ATTORNEY GRAHAM: Did you continue your romantic relationship?

DAVID DENNISON: Prudie thought we should just be friends. She said I needed to focus on getting better, and she was right. We were never that serious anyway.

ATTORNEY GRAHAM: So she ended things?

DAVID DENNISON: Yes, sir, I suppose she did.

ATTORNEY GRAHAM: Were you upset by this?

DAVID DENNISON: Honestly, no. I had a long road ahead of me. I wasn't at school for a few months, and I was totally focused on recovery.

ATTORNEY GRAHAM: Are you saying you weren't angry that she broke up with you at such a vulnerable period in your life? So angry you wanted to hurt her?

ATTORNEY LEDBETTER: Objection. This witness isn't on trial.

COURT: Sustained. The jury will disregard that question.

ATTORNEY GRAHAM: No further questions.

"David Dennison," Eugenia says, tapping the page from behind me. I almost scream. "Looking likelier by the minute."

"Don't you know not to sneak up on a person like that?" I grab the glass from her and chug half the tea, wiping my mouth on the back of my hand. "It was just Trapper's shitty attorney trying to seed doubt."

"Yes, but what if David killed Melissa in some bizarro tribute to your mom?"

"Seriously, Eugenia? How much crime reading have you been bingeing?" My head is starting to throb, as if someone is squeezing it from both sides.

She shrugs. "It just makes me wonder." She picks up the page with David's testimony on it. "What if Trapper's lawyer was onto something?"

I narrow my eyes, my heart thumping wildly. "He wasn't."

"I know you don't want to hear it, but what if *David* killed your mom? And now Melissa?"

I stand, my legs shaking. "I'm done."

"Can't we talk about this?" she asks.

"No. We can't. Not now, not ever. My dad is guilty, okay?"

He has to be.

She pauses for a moment. "I think we should go visit Heather Reyes tonight."

"Seriously? Didn't I just say I was done for today?"

"Like you said, whoever's behind this doesn't take nights off. Neither can we."

I give her my empty glass. "*Tomorrow.* Tonight, I need a break." I stop at the top of the attic stairs and look back. Eugenia's standing at the whiteboard, head tilted as she reads. A shot of cold goes through me, and I hurry downstairs and into the sunlight. As soon as I'm outside, I suck in huge breaths of air.

I'm not sure how much more of the past I can revisit, especially now that Eugenia has voiced my biggest fear—that Trapper might be innocent.

CHAPTER Sixteen

'm parked outside a run-down trailer park in Eugenia's parents' hearse.

The Rolls decided not to start, again. My grandparents had driven out for dinner. Eugenia asked to borrow her parents' car, but they said no, she should take the old hearse.

So here we are, two towns over.

"Do you think everyone's watching out their windows, thinking we're here to collect a body?" I ask, sipping my caramel latte nervously.

Her hands are still on the wheel. "It's happened before."

I focus on Heather's trailer. It's blue and leans slightly to one side. Wind chimes hang by the door, clanging in the breeze. The sound is somehow off-key, a warning.

"We may as well get this over with." Eugenia takes the key out of the ignition.

I tip back my cup to suck out the last drops of caffeine. "Let's do this."

I stare at the trailer's windows as we walk up a gravel pathway. They look soaped over. I climb a set of wobbly wooden stairs to the door.

There's no room for Eugenia, so she waits on the dead grass. I hesitate before I knock. Someone moves around inside, something slams, and then the inner door creaks open. A woman with short-cropped black hair and a nose ring opens the screen door so fast it almost hits me. "Yes?"

"Are you Heather Reyes?"

She frowns. "Depends on who's asking."

"I'm Bett Holland?" I say this almost like it's a question. "You were friends with my mom, Prudence."

"Oh my God." She opens the door wider. "You want to come in?"

I look back at Eugenia. "Yeah, if I could. And my friend, too?"

"Absolutely, come in. Please."

The trailer is small but tidy. Not much furniture. All the shades are drawn. "You girls drink coffee?" she asks as she pours three cups of it. She gestures for us to sit on a pink velvet couch. It looks antique.

Heather sits across from us in a worn-out leather recliner. "Gosh, I haven't seen you in years. Probably not since the trial. But grown-up, I'd recognize you as Prudie's daughter anywhere. You're as gorgeous as she was."

I try to imagine her and my mother going to high school together: talking about boys, dreaming about the future. Part of me wants to reach out and touch her, as if that will connect me to Mom.

"You and my mom were best friends?" I ask instead. "I read about you in the trial transcript."

Her bright red lips turn up into a smile. "Since the eighth grade.

147

We had choir together. I was a new student, and she just turned to me one day and introduced herself. She was so loyal. We were friends ever since."

"You were at a party with her and Trapper, right? The night before her murder?"

She grips the mug in her hands. They shake, and coffee dribbles over the edge. "I was, yes."

Suddenly, she looks small, like every word causes her pain. I look over at Eugenia.

"We're trying to figure out exactly what happened to Prudence, including at that party," Eugenia says. "There's been another murder in Wolf Ridge, and we think it may be connected somehow. We're hoping some small detail from Prudence's last days will help us find the killer. The police aren't trying very hard, you see."

Heather stands and removes a framed photo from a shelf. "We were so young," she comments, handing it to me. "But it feels like we were just at that party."

A group of people stand together in a backyard, smiling, holding bottles of beer. My mom. Trapper. Heather with longer hair. And David Dennison. They all look so happy, not like one of them is hours away from killing the other. Lydia's not in the photo, so I assume she's the one behind the camera.

"We read in your testimony that Trapper grabbed my mom's wrist pretty hard that night," I say, finding my voice again.

She nods. "I'd never seen him get physical with her before. I'd seen bruises, but Prudie always explained those away. I got scared and went outside. That's just what people did back then. They stayed out of it. Maybe if I'd said something…"

"So why didn't you?" Eugenia asks.

"I thought they were just arguing about Lydia."

"Lydia?" I ask.

Heather sips her coffee. "Lydia always had a little crush on Trapper. Lots of women did."

Eugenia leans forward, a bloodhound on the trail. "Did something happen with Lydia that night at the party?"

"Sort of. Prudie went into the house for something, I can't remember what, and Lydia was hanging all over him in the kitchen. She was a little drunk—we all were."

"Was Trapper cheating on my mom with Lydia?" I ask, sweat breaking out on my lip.

Heather shrugs. "I have no idea. But honestly? I don't think so. Trapper was controlling, but I never saw him with anyone, and I never heard talk of him stepping out—and in Wolf Ridge, that kind of stuff never stays hidden."

"But Jack Ledbetter told the jury that Trapper had been with other women," I say.

"What about Cherry Hobbs?" Eugenia interjects, setting her cup on a coffee table with photos of Marilyn Monroe decoupaged on its top. "Do you think Trapper killed her?"

Heather shrugs. "He could have. I wouldn't put it past him."

"Was he cheating on my mom with her?" I press.

"Like I said, I don't think so. But Cherry didn't run in our circle."

"Whose circle did she run in?"

"She worked at the gas station, lived over on Rose. Everyone knew she was an addict, that sort of thing. She was in with a rough crowd. I only ran into her a handful of times before she died. Seemed nice enough, if slightly out of it." Heather shifts. "Bettina, I should have done more to protect your mother. It's my fault she married Trapper at all.... I practically pushed her toward him at the prom."

"What happened at the prom?" I ask.

"She was David's prom date that night. She and Trapper had been dating on and off, as I'm sure you know, and they had gotten into a huge fight over it. Trapper was jealous! He showed up outside the school, heartbroken, desperate to talk to her, so I convinced her to go and hear him out. They got back together. At the time, it seemed like they were meant to be—like Romeo and Juliet."

"Romeo and Juliet kill themselves," Eugenia says coolly.

"I know." Heather finishes her coffee. "It was so nice to see you, Bett, but I have to get going. My shift starts in ten. You have any other questions, call me, okay? Anytime, day or night."

She recites her number, and I put it in my phone. Then she stands, grabs her bag, and ushers us outside before climbing into a rusted-out Toyota Tercel and squealing down the road.

"She was sure in a hurry to get away from us," Eugenia observes. "Almost like she has something to hide."

I watch Heather's brake lights blink on and off before she turns the corner. "You think *everyone* has something to hide."

"That's because they do." She unlocks the hearse. "Like Lydia Baker, for example. In love with Trapper! We should take her ghost tour."

"Her *what*?" I practically spit.

"You heard what Heather said. Lydia wanted Trapper back then. She was at the party the night before your mother died, and she was at the center of an argument between them. I bet she fills her tour with all *sorts* of personal stories about them—and David, too. Who knows, maybe she'll even share something about Melissa that she forgot to tell me. I'm sure she's worked that murder into the tour by now."

"I highly doubt Lydia's tour is factual. It's theater. We're not going to get anything useful out of it."

"Maybe, maybe not. But we won't know that until we take it." As the hearse pulls away from the trailer park, she adds, "Cherry lived on Rose Street, same as David Dennison. Don't you find that strange?"

"Very," I say, a knot building in my stomach.

My phone buzzes. Unbelievably, it's a text from Ada. I'm tempted to delete it unread. But since she rarely communicates, I open it anyway.

> Ada: An arrest has been made in Melissa's murder. Chief Bigsby to give a presser in an hour and name the suspect. Thought you'd want to know.

"We need to get to the police station *now*," I say as Eugenia turns onto the highway, the hearse chugging as it gains speed.

"Why? What happened?"

"They arrested Melissa's killer."

"Seriously?" She whips her head toward me, her arms yanking on the wheel and almost taking the hearse off the road. I grip the dashboard, certain we're about to flip over. After she rights the beast of a vehicle, she asks, "Who killed her? David?"

Still holding on to the dash, I try to catch my breath. "Bigsby's releasing a name at the press conference. Can you make this thing go any faster?"

"Any faster and the wheels might come off."

I lean back in my seat, chewing my nails off.

CHAPTER Seventeen

Inside the police station, we elbow our way toward the conference room through the crowd that's packing the lobby. No one asks us if we're with the press as we squeeze inside and hide out at the back; either the chief must want as big of an audience as possible, or the Wolf Ridge PD really is that badly disorganized.

My heart pounds so violently I'm afraid I'll pass out. Chief Bigsby is seated stoically at the table in front of a microphone. He's got his aviators on, flanked by Andre and Chantal. Could this really be the end of it? I take a deep breath and blow it out. On the wall behind them is the Wolf Ridge police logo: a navy blue shield with a protective eagle soaring over the town's name. It appears as if the eagle is about to sink its talons into someone.

Ada stands across the room with her phone out, no doubt preparing to record this and use it for whatever stupid project she's working on next. Xavier leans casually into the far corner, opposite from where we stand by the doors. He doesn't notice me; he's too busy on his phone. I guess this is big news for Wolf Ridge, so I shouldn't be surprised that he's here. Still, something about it bothers me, though it shouldn't.

The chief removes his sunglasses and turns on his microphone. The room goes silent. Bigsby sits up straighter, shoulders pushed back as he looks out across the crowd, his captive audience. "Good evening, ladies and gentlemen. I want to thank y'all for coming down to the police department today. We have an update on a homicide case I'm sure you're all familiar with: the murder of Melissa Atkins. This morning we made an arrest and have taken the suspect into our custody." He lifts a photograph from the table and holds it up for everyone to see. Cameras click away wildly. The man has pale white skin, thinning brown hair, brown eyes. He could be anyone. Nothing about him stands out.

"We arrested a white male, Gregory Hornsby, age thirty-two, at approximately ten forty-five this morning," the chief drones on. "The suspect, a long-haul trucker from Baton Rouge, Louisiana, came into the police station himself and confessed to the killing of Ms. Atkins. It's a terrible tragedy what's happened in our small town. This is still an active case, and we have a ways to go before it can go to trial. But we've executed an exhaustive search of the crime scene and our suspect's home, and we're confident we've got our man. Any questions?"

Dozens of hands shoot up, and the chief calls on Ada first. "Thank you, Chief Bigsby. Did Mr. Hornsby say why he had decided to turn himself in now?"

"Mr. Hornsby said he felt a tremendous amount of guilt for his crime and wanted to give Ms. Atkins's family closure."

Another reporter tries to ask something, but Ada continues speaking anyway. "Do you have any physical evidence tying him to this crime?

Travel logs from his company that can confirm he was in Wolf Ridge at the time of the murder? Anything besides his spontaneous confession?"

"She's good at this," Eugenia whispers, leaning in. "Maybe we should team up with her."

I ignore her.

Bigsby narrows his eyes. I can see them harden for a moment. He's probably regretting letting my aunt speak. "Yes, but I'm afraid I can't share that with you. Not with the investigation still ongoing."

"At the chief's presser after your dad's arrest, he listed out a bunch of physical evidence they had against him," Eugenia says.

"You watched that? When?"

"A few days ago. Fell down a rabbit hole one night when I couldn't sleep. Anyway, it's odd the chief won't list even one piece of physical evidence they have on Gregory Hornsby."

As the chief answers questions from other reporters in the room, the temperature rises. This many people in a small space with no air-conditioning drives the heat up quickly, and soon I'm sweating through my bra. A reporter turns to speak to her camera guy, and her eyes latch on to me. "Bettina Holland?" she asks. Several others turn around, and I've suddenly hijacked Bigsby's press conference. "Do you have any comments on this case?"

Others move toward me, hands outstretched with microphones and smartphones, shouting questions at me. I look down, try to shield my face, but it's no use. Bigsby's at the table, shouting for order, and I know he's going to rat me out to Granddad for this. Eugenia tries to push them away, but she's too small. No match for them.

Suddenly Xavier's in front of me, pushing back at the reporters until they slowly give me a bit more breathing room. "Come on," he says. "Let's get out of here." He takes my hand and we run out of the station and into the lot. It's stuffed with news vans. "I've got my dad's truck," he says, nodding at a weathered old Ford. "Wanna go for a swim?"

"Absolutely," I say, climbing in as fast as I can, my hands so sweaty I can barely get the door closed. We pull out of the lot just as the first reporter stumbles outside, tracking us like we're her prey.

I text Eugenia, telling her I'm with Xavier and not to worry. She texts back that Bigsby can't regain control of his press conference and is fit to be tied. I want to believe the chief solved the case, that this Gregory Hornsby guy turned himself in out of the kindness of his heart. But something about it doesn't feel right. It fits way too neatly with Bigsby's theory of a drifter passing through Wolf Ridge.

———

"Where are we going?" I ask Xavier as he takes us deep into the foot-hills. We're outside Wolf Ridge now.

"It's a surprise," he says, smiling as he dodges a pothole the size of Texas.

"I hate surprises," I mutter, bracing myself against the dash and door handle.

"This is a *good* surprise, trust me."

The sun is just starting to drag all the color down with it when he finally parks in a small clearing of weeds. The trees slowly turn black as day bleeds into night.

Since Xavier's truck has no air, I've drenched my T-shirt. I pull my hair off my neck and tie it on top of my head, then follow him out of the truck. "Please don't tell me you're secretly into hiking?"

He grabs my hand and pulls me close. "Would that be a deal-breaker?" I smile, and then he kisses me. "Come on, we better get going. I have something really, really special to show you."

Xavier leads the way, climbing through patches of wildflowers and weeds and over tree roots that stick out of the ground like arms. "How is this not hiking?" I ask as I wipe the sweat off my forehead.

He looks back, smirking. "We're almost there. It'll be worth it, trust me."

"You keep asking me to trust you," I tease.

He's quiet for a minute. "That's because I mean it, Bett. I want you to trust me." When his eyes meet mine, electricity slithers through my belly. He's so different from the aloof Xavier at school, or even the fearless Xavier at the train tracks.

I want to know which one is the real Xavier.

The faint sound of trickling water intensifies as we pass through a grouping of pine trees. Up ahead, behind more fallen trees and brush, runs a shallow creek. The water is so clear, I can count each tiny stone at the bottom of it, even as the sunlight fades—the surface is as smooth as gemstones. Xavier takes my hand and leads me to the edge.

"My brother used to bring me up here a lot to fish and stuff. It makes me feel better, just being here." A fish darts through the water in front of us.

This is the second time he's brought up his brother. I swallow. "What happened to him?"

"He died of an overdose. Fent. Not a car crash, like everyone thinks."

"I'm sorry, Xavier."

"He wasn't just some junkie." He cracks his knuckles. "He was so much more than that."

I wait for him to tell me more, but he doesn't. "It's very peaceful here," I admit.

He scales a boulder and sits on top. "It's cool though, right? I've never seen water so clear." He pats the spot next to him, and I slip off my sandals and climb up after him, only slipping once. I settle in next to him, and he pulls a joint out of his front jeans pocket. "Smoke?" he asks.

"I better not."

He flicks his lighter and takes a drag, blowing the smoke away from me.

"Can I ask you something?"

"Sure," he says.

"You smoke a lot of weed."

He gives me a lopsided grin. "That's not a question."

I nudge him with my shoulder. "I know. And it's fine. I smoke some-times too. I just wondered."

Xavier looks out across the water. "I don't know. When everything gets all twisted and crazy, weed slows things down. Does that make sense?" He looks at me, brows knitted.

"Total sense."

"I like how I can talk to you about stuff."

"Me too," I say, but I look away. I'm not sure what his angle is, but I suddenly feel like I can't quite catch my breath.

He stubs the joint out on the rock, then leans over and brushes his lips against mine. "Want to cool down?"

"Absolutely."

After we climb down the rock, Xavier peels his shirt off, then his shorts. He looks at me, waiting, and I hesitate. We've had *sex*, yet I suddenly feel too shy to strip down in front of him. "You get in first," I say.

He shakes his head and steps into the water. "It's deeper out that way," he says, still facing me.

"Don't look, okay?"

He frowns. "Why?"

"I don't want you to see, that's why."

"But you're perfect."

My face floods with heat. I hope it's too shadowy in the trees for him to notice. "Shut up," I say, and he laughs and finally turns around. I take off my top and shorts, leaving on my bra and underwear, and step into the water. It's chilly, but it feels good after another hot day.

"Are you in?" he asks, turning his head to the side.

"Yes, and don't look yet!"

Xavier wades farther into the creek, and I follow. The water chills my legs, my thighs, my stomach. He turns around once I catch up, grabs my waist, and kisses me. As my eyes close, I can't believe I'm here, with him. He's so *different*. Not moody, quiet, aloof. I smile through our kiss, and I can feel him smiling, too.

"Thank you for bringing me here," I say quietly.

"Thank you for letting me."

He floats on his back, and I float next to him. As the sky turns deep blue, a single star tries to break through the haze. Xavier's hand brushes mine, and he twines our fingers together. I glance at him, but his eyes are closed. It reminds me of how peaceful he looked at the tracks, the night we were together. But this seems more intimate somehow. And scarier.

"I can feel you looking at me," he says without opening his eyes.

"No, you can't," I say and splash water at him.

He quickly stands up in the water and splashes me back. We push small waves at each other, laughing and darting around the cool water. When our laughter dies down, we come together again. He kisses me until my whole body warms up. I wrap my legs around him, and he grips my hips, lifting me halfway out of the water.

Our kisses slow, and then Xavier rests his forehead against mine. "Are you okay?" he asks.

"I am now."

"I mean, with everything that's going on. Melissa Atkins and stuff."

I slide back into the water, keeping my arms wrapped around his neck. "I'm as good as can be, I guess."

He licks his lips. "I just mean, it's probably really weird. All this happening again."

"What do you mean?"

"You know…with your mom. Does it bring it all back?"

I take a step away from him. "What does my mom have to do with anything?"

I watch as he runs his hands through his wet hair, his face flustered. "Nothing? I'm just saying, it might remind you of what happened back then. Sometimes with my brother…I don't know. It's like I go back to that time."

I cross my arms. "I do *not* want to talk about her murder."

"Okay, you don't have to. That's fine. I'm just worried, that's all. Melissa and your mom were both, you know, killed in the same…" He cuts himself off and looks at me, and my skin grows cold. Goose bumps pepper my skin.

"It's getting late," I say. "We should go back."

"Because I talked about her?" He reaches for me, but I move away.

"I want to leave. I don't need a reason."

"Listen, we don't have to discuss it. Or anything else. Stay." He touches my waist, his hands slippery on my skin, but I pull away again. All I can think about are his loser friends from the cemetery party, digging for dirt on my mom's murder. I'm suddenly exhausted, the weight of this day, this life, pushing down on me too hard.

I hurry back to the edge of the creek and climb out, pull my clothes on over my wet skin. I don't care if he sees me now; I just want to go home.

"Bett, come on," he protests, but I ignore him. I haven't pressed *him* to reveal all his darkest fears to *me*. He has no right to demand mine.

He's quiet as he gets dressed next to me. I head back toward the truck, trying to remember the way we came. As I walk, my anger starts to fade. Maybe he didn't mean anything.

At the truck, I open the passenger door and slide in, trying to come up with an apology of sorts. But a sneeze tickles my nose, and I bury my face in the crook of my elbow, opening the glove box hoping to find a tissue.

Instead, I find a deep-purple wallet sitting all by itself. Small, square. Plain. Curiosity gets the better of me, and I flip it open, thinking I can give him shit for having a purple wallet. But when I see who it belongs to, my body breaks out into chills.

Tucked behind a square of plastic is Melissa Atkins's driver's license.

CHAPTER
Eighteen

Xavier climbs into the truck, and his eyes immediately land on the wallet in my hands before I can hide it. His face twists in fear. "I can explain—" he starts, but I cut him off.

"What are you doing with Melissa Atkins's wallet in your truck?" There's got to be a reasonable explanation, one that doesn't make him a murderer.

"I gave her a ride a week or so ago from Lydia's bar. It was dark, and I was driving home from work. Lydia flagged me down, said Melissa drank a little too much on her shift that night and asked me to take her home."

"And the wallet?" I say, holding it up.

He runs his hands through his hair. "She must've dropped it during the ride to her house, but I didn't find it until after she died. I swear."

"Why didn't you turn it into the police?"

He looks out the windshield. We're miles beyond town. I slowly slide my phone from my pocket. I bring up Eugenia's last text, but I only have one bar.

"I was scared."

"You could have turned it in anonymously."

He shakes his head. "I didn't think of that, okay?"

We're both quiet for a while. "Can you take me home now?"

He turns to me. "What about the wallet? What are you going to do?"

"I'll take it to Andre," I say.

"*Please* don't tell them where you got it, Bett."

"I can't promise that."

He stares at me, jaws clenching, before he starts the truck and drives back down the mountain. I shoot Eugenia a text, keeping the screen dimmed so low I can barely see it.

> Me: Found M's wallet in X's truck! If I don't make it back alive, I'm in the foothills by some creek

> Eugenia: If he tries anything, jab his eyes with your fingers. Saw it on Oprah. Or attack his balls.

Xavier pulls into my driveway, and I'm out the door before the truck is fully stopped. I take a few steps down the driveway and turn back. He's just sitting in the driver's seat, watching me, the truck's engine idling loudly.

"Where were you last Thursday afternoon?" I ask.

The medical examiner said Melissa died six to eight hours before I found her; I have no idea where Xavier was before we met up at the tracks.

"At work," he says cautiously. "Why?"

"No reason," I say, hurrying onto the veranda.

Xavier peels off down the road.

"That doesn't make him seem guilty at all, does it?" comes a voice from the far end of the porch. Eugenia stands up from the swing, and my heart feels like it's being twisted in my chest.

"You've really got to stop scaring me!" I say shakily. "But I'm so, *so* glad you're here."

"Can I see it?"

I pull Melissa's wallet from my back pocket, hanging on to it by the corner. "Probably useless. It's been touched by who knows how many people."

Eugenia holds up a plastic baggie. "I came prepared," she says as I drop the wallet inside. "What was his explanation?"

"He said he gave Melissa a ride home last week, and she must have left it behind."

"Convenient excuse. We better take this in," she says, stepping down off the veranda.

"Right now? It's almost ten," I say, beginning to sweat. I don't want to fuck up Xavier's life if I don't have to. Maybe he really *did* only give her a ride.

But then my mind takes me back to our night at the tracks. Is that why Xavier asked me to meet him there? So I could give him an alibi?

Is that why he was at the press conference tonight—because he's worried?

"This is evidence. *Major* evidence. We shouldn't sit on it any longer." She stops and turns around, her face half hidden in shadows. "I'm happy you're okay, Bett. Just so that's clear. Now let's ride."

The police station is a stark contrast from earlier tonight. No news trucks. No lingering reporters. Just the sound of crickets as we push open the doors and step into the quiet lobby. Bernadette is gone for the night, and Chantal sits in her place. As soon as she sees us, she stands.

"Are you all right?" she asks, her voice tight. She looks behind us into the parking lot. Clearly this whole murder thing has gotten to her.

"We're fine," Eugenia says. "But we have something related to Melissa's murder." She hands Chantal the plastic bag.

"It's Melissa's wallet," I add for clarification.

Chantal's eyes widen. "Where did you find this?"

Now is my chance to lie, to say I found it in the woods or out on the street. I don't even have to say Xavier's name. But if he had anything at all to do with her death, he's left me no choice.

"Xavier Hart's truck," I answer, my skin breaking out in goose bumps. "I found it in his *glove box*. He said she dropped it when he gave her a ride home last week."

"Thank you for bringing this in. We'll question him. We really should question you, too, but…" But Chantal knows who my grandfather is. She checks her watch. "It's past curfew, but I'll let it slide. Do you need a ride home?"

Before I can answer, Bigsby comes sauntering into the lobby from the back of the station. "What's this all about?" he barks. "You girls are out past curfew. I ought to call your folks." His bottom lip bulges, likely from a dip of chew.

"They brought in some new evidence," Chantal says, coming to our defense. "Melissa Atkins's wallet. Found it in Xavier Hart's truck."

166

"Is that so." The chief takes the bag from her and glances at the wallet inside.

"So?" Eugenia asks. "You're going to question Xavier, right?"

"What for?" Bigsby asks. His eyes are bloodshot, hair a mess. He reeks of stale cigarette smoke. He's probably fielded calls left and right today, and I'm sure I'm not his favorite person after I hijacked his press conference. But he has to be kidding.

"We also found this." Eugenia holds up a second baggie, the one that contains the matchbook. I give her a look, and she shrugs. "Figured I better bring it along."

Chantal steps forward, frowning. "And where'd you find this?"

I take a deep breath. "In the woods."

"At the crime scene," Eugenia adds, and I flinch.

Bigsby's face turns red. "You better *not* have been at the crime scene."

"We stumbled upon it by accident," I lie before Eugenia gets the chance to tell the truth. "But the weird thing is, Sheila stopped handing out matchbooks ten years ago."

"Right," Eugenia says. "We asked her. Which means it's doubtful a young long-haul stranger like Gregory Hornsby left it there...which also means he might not be the killer."

The chief takes a deep breath and lets it out. He pinches the fleshy skin between his eyebrows leaving behind an angry red mark. "So let me get this straight," he says. "You went back to an active crime scene, found a piece of trash, questioned a citizen about it, and now you've decided Gregory Hornsby is innocent."

Sensing she's about to put her foot in it, I grab Eugenia's hand and squeeze it. Hard. "No, just that there's some new information to look into. That's all."

"*That's all,*" he repeats, starting to laugh. He looks to Chantal, who's still frowning. "Call their parents," he says, his voice a rumble, "and get Xavier Hart in here right now."

"You don't need to call our parents," I interject. "We'll go straight home, we promise."

The chief shakes his head and steps closer to me. "You're not going anywhere until your parents and grandparents collect you. Now, sit and do as you're told for once."

He stomps into the back of the station. A door slams. "You heard the chief," Chantal says. "Take a seat."

We sit next to each other in plastic chairs across from the reception desk. "We're in deep shit, you know," I say, chewing my thumbnail. "My grandfather is going to stroke out over this."

"We're concerned citizens doing the right thing. They should be thanking us," she says matter-of-factly.

It doesn't take long for a car to pull up out front—my grandparents' Lincoln. Groaning, I sink deeper into my chair as Granddad gets out and marches toward the building. He yanks open the door, spotting me right away.

"Bettina Jane Holland," he says slowly and quietly, yet with force. "Do you have any idea of what it is like to receive a call from the police this late at night?" I know better than to say anything, so I shrug. "That's right, you don't. For a second, I thought…" He stops himself. "I'm glad you're safe. Let's just go."

"Good luck," I whisper to Eugenia.

When I stand, the door swings open again. A short woman with dark hair enters first, clutching her purse. Xavier walks behind her, head bowed, still in the same clothes he wore at the creek. When he looks up, his eyes catch mine, transforming from shocked to something else…something darker.

I stand there mute, unable to speak. What would I even say? Xavier is silent too. But his face says it all. He narrows his eyes at me, mouth tight, and my insides turn cold. Then he shakes his head and looks away, as if the sight of me sickens him.

Who Killed Melissa Atkins?
Suspect List:
Drifter from out of town (Gregory Hornsby, confessed & arrested)
~~Grayson, creepy ex-boyfriend~~
David Dennison
Xavier Hart

CHAPTER
Nineteen

Someone has drawn a smiley face on my locker in permanent marker. When I open it, pieces of paper fall to the floor. They weren't there yesterday, and I'm afraid to look at them, but the words written on them shout up at me: *lying slut*; *murderer's daughter*. I kick them away, my vision blurred with tears, and grab my books.

Xavier's popular, and clearly, the news he was brought in for questioning because of me is making the rounds. I should have expected this. Maybe someday, after I've figured out who killed Melissa, people will thank me for making our town safe again. (Probably not, but it's a nice thought.)

"Don't look at her, Mad," Holly says loudly behind me. "She might accuse you of murder."

Every whisper, every mention of my name is a hot ember pushed into my skin.

Slamming my locker shut, I step into the stream of students and right into Xavier. He looks at me like he's seen a ghost. He quickly rearranges his features into his usual laid-back affect.

"Do me a favor and stay the fuck away from me," he says coldly. Then he stalks off, clipping me with his shoulder.

Fuck him. I remember being alone with him yesterday. I was *afraid*. Deep in the woods with no signal. Homicide evidence in my hand. Him staring. Him and me, alone…

He chose not to turn in Melissa's wallet. He can't blame me for doing the right thing by her.

A small crowd has gathered around me, watching, enjoying the scene, and my resolve begins to crumble. I've always survived by being tough, by not caring what anyone thinks. But maybe I do care.

Just as tears threaten to spill over, Eugenia comes barreling down the hallway.

"Show's over, mouth breathers," she says grimly, glaring at anyone dumb enough not to scatter. A couple of freshman girls linger, and Eugenia literally barks at them. They scream and run.

I laugh, my mood a little lighter. "Did you really just do that?"

She shrugs. "It's effective."

We fall into step, and with Eugenia by my side, the looks and whispers don't feel quite as potent.

"Thanks," I say. "Xavier obviously told the entire school about what happened. Think he left out the fact he hid murder evidence?" It seems impossible that just last week we slept together. Now my skin crawls at the idea of letting him touch me.

"If Xavier Hart hates you for doing what's right, then he's all kinds of wrong."

"Still sucks, honestly."

"I wonder what he told the cops. Will they even bother checking out his alibi?"

Last night was a line in the sand. I chose Melissa over him. I chose seeking justice for a murdered woman, and I won't let anyone make me lose sight of that. I won't regret it.

Even if he's innocent. And it suddenly occurs to me that—with a little sleuthing—I can deduce that for myself.

"Let's ditch last period," I whisper. "There's someone we really need to talk to."

We meet out front just as last period starts, scurrying low across the lot to the Rolls. Minutes later we park outside the new Food Lion, a beige brick building on the outskirts of town, near the highway. We hurry inside, swallowed up by air-conditioning and bad music. A couple of older women push carts, but otherwise the store is empty.

A middle-aged man wearing khaki pants, a white button-down shirt, and a tie is inspecting some oranges in the produce section, clipboard in hand. We approach him, and I smile. "Excuse me. Can I speak to a manager?"

He sets down an orange and pushes his glasses up his nose. I've seen him at Sheila's, but I can't remember his name. Hopefully he won't recognize me. "I'm Thomas, the manager. How can I help you ladies today?"

"My grandmother was shopping here last week, and she said the nicest young man helped her. She's super old and frail and has trouble reaching stuff." Grams would *kill me* if she heard me describing her this way. "Anyway, she wanted his manager to know what excellent service she received, but she can't remember his name."

Thomas smiles. "Does she remember what day she was in, or what the young man looked like?"

"Yes, she was in last Thursday afternoon. She said the man was tall with kind of shaggy black hair?"

"Ah, that sounds like Xavier Hart. Started about a month back. Very nice young man. Let me go check the schedule, but I'm almost positive it was him." Thomas disappears into a back room.

"Good story," Eugenia says. "I was just going to ask if Xavier was working that day or not."

"You know that people get suspicious if you ask point-blank, right?" I ask, eyeing the door. "You've got to get some finesse."

She shakes her head. "I don't do finesse."

"Guess that's why you have me."

Thomas emerges from the office. "Just as I suspected," he says. "Xavier had a shift that afternoon. Clocked in at one, clocked out at seven. Does that match up with when your grandmother was here?"

I nod. "It does, thank you so much." I quickly run the math in my head: if Melissa had been dead for six to eight hours when I found her, she would have been killed between three and five in the afternoon. If Xavier was working here, he couldn't have done it.

"Thank you for coming in! I'll share this with Xavier." As we turn to leave, Thomas asks, "You didn't mention your grandmother's name?"

"Just keep walking," I whisper to Eugenia, pretending I didn't hear his question.

Who Killed Melissa Atkins?

Suspect List:

Drifter from out of town (Gregory Hornsby, confessed & arrested)

~~Grayson, creepy ex-boyfriend~~

David Dennison

~~Xavier Hart~~

CHAPTER
Twenty

"Do you feel better knowing Xavier's innocent? Terrible judgment about the wallet, obviously." Eugenia stands in my room holding a floral bag like the one from *Mary Poppins*. If she pulls out a floor lamp, I'm going to lose my shit.

"No. Let's just say that I'm grateful for the weekend. TGIF and all that."

"Bettina, Xavier made a *choice* to hold on to evidence in a femicide," she says. "You have nothing to feel bad about. I know the cops here don't seem to care much about murdered women, but they *are* the ones with the power of arrest. You had to give them the wallet."

"If you say so." I go into my closet and return with a handful of items. Eugenia looks them over, carefully lifting each one, sizing them up.

"I'll wear it," she finally says, "but *not* the push-up bra."

"Fair enough," I say, dropping the red lace contraption onto my bed.

After we get dressed, we stand at the end of my driveway and wait for our Uber. We can't take my car; it's too recognizable. And the hearse is out of the question. She's dressed in my black leather pants (which are two sizes too big for her, but she pulls them off anyway) and a white puff-sleeve top. I curled her hair and added some red extensions. Her eyes are so heavily lined with black she doesn't look like Eugenia Cline anymore.

And we need to look like totally different people on Lydia's tour tonight.

"What's my backstory?" she asks, studying the brand-new ID I snagged for her. Half the junior class has fakes, and Liam delivered two that are pretty convincing. The women in the photos look a lot like us, and I'm hoping the darkness will help convince the bouncer.

"Does it matter?" I'm wearing vintage jean shorts with patches sewn all over them, neon-green fishnets, a baggy white T-shirt, and a black wig cut into a bob. I've also got on a pair of Grams's cat-eye glasses that she didn't want anymore. They're reading glasses, so they make everything a touch blurry, and the brown-colored contacts aren't helping, either—but I look like someone else.

"Yes, my backstory matters," she says. "If I'm going to become"— she reads from the ID—"*Regina Johnson*, then I need to know a few things about her."

Our Uber pulls up, and I ask the driver to take us out of town first and then to the bar. I don't want anyone to think we live in Wolf Ridge; we *need* to be out-of-towners. As we cruise along the highway, we come up with our backstories. She's Regina Johnson, a university student studying English and journalism, and she's in town visiting her cousin, Ruby, an aspiring actress who dropped out of her Catholic high school.

"Isn't that what you want to be?" she asks. "An actress?"

I shake my head. "I'm going to law school."

"So you want to be a lawyer?"

The driver hits a bump, and I almost smack my head against the window. "My grandfather wants me to be a lawyer. Do you really want an English degree?"

She nods. "I want to be a novelist. Create worlds and people with my words. Play God."

"Wow, Eugenia." I look at her. "That's kind of dark, isn't it?"

She gets quiet for a moment. "Not to me," she says, so soft I can barely hear her.

I nudge her with my elbow. "Forget what I said. You'll be a great novelist. I can't wait to read whatever that singular brain of yours comes up with."

"I've written loads of stuff already," she says, her mood lifting. "Shorts stories, some Poe-inspired stuff, *Wednesday* fan fiction. And the beginning of a novel, but I'm not ready to talk about that yet."

"Could I read some?"

She raises one brow. "You want to read my stuff? Won't it be too gloomy for you?"

"We're friends, Eugenia. Obviously I want to read it."

She smiles. It's the brightest smile she's ever given me.

A neon sign that reads LYDIA'S PLACE hangs over a one-story brick building with a gravel parking lot across from the post office. The tour starts at nine, so we've got about a half hour to kill. The lot is usually only half full, but tonight it's overflowing onto the street.

"Act natural," I whisper to her as we approach the door.

"That's not helpful," she whispers back.

A man in jeans and a black T-shirt sits just outside the door on a stool. "IDs, please," he says, and Eugenia hands hers over. He looks at the card, then at her before handing it back.

"Here's mine," I say, sounding too eager. He reads the card and looks at me for what feels like minutes. My throat grows dry, and I swallow. He flips it over, then back again. Finally, he hands it to me.

Inside, the bar is packed with people, wall to wall. Most of them are women, giggling and drinking fruity-looking cocktails. I spot the only open table by the bathrooms and quickly drag Eugenia to it. "This place is about to bust open. Do you think they're all here for the tour?"

She crosses her arms over her chest. "Relax, would you? You're starting to make me nervous."

"Should we get drinks?"

"Alcohol?" Eugenia's voice shoots up an octave.

"It'll calm us down."

She shakes her head. "Uh, *no*, it will not. We've already committed one crime tonight. I don't need to commit a second."

"Fine. How about two Cokes instead? Sans alcohol." She nods, and I head up to the bar. Lydia's not there. Some guy in a rainbow plaid shirt and pierced ears asks me what I want. "Do I pay here for the ghost tour?" I ask as he pours our sodas.

"Lydia collects that at the door, honey. It's so much fun!" I hate the way he says that, like ghosts and murder are no big deal.

I smile, but even without seeing my face I know it's more of a grimace. "So sad about the lady who worked here," I venture. "What was her name? Melinda?"

He puts two glasses of Coke down in front of me. "Melissa," he says, his voice tender. "We're all devastated about what happened. We had just worked together the night before, too. Gives me the willies just thinkin' about it."

"Did anything seem odd that night you worked together? Like maybe a boyfriend bothering her?" I want to ask him about David, but then he'll know I'm a local. "I heard they made an arrest already."

"Yeah, I saw that on the news, thank the Lord."

"Gregory Hornsby, I think. Was he in the bar at all last week?"

The man squints up at the ceiling, trying to recall. "Honestly, I don't think so. Plain skinny white boys may be a dime a dozen around here, but Wolf Ridge don't get a ton of visitors. If he had been here, I would've remembered."

"Was Melissa acting strangely? Preoccupied, or even scared?"

"Nah, she seemed bored. We all were; the bar hadn't exactly been packed then. Not like tonight."

"Who else was working that night?"

"Just me, Melissa, Harvey out front, and Sasha."

"Is Sasha here?" I ask, watching the woman at the other end of the bar mixing a drink.

He narrows his eyes at me. "You sure ask a lot of questions. Do you run a channel or something? Relax, honey. It's Friday night."

"Sorry! I've just got murder on the brain, what with this tour and all," I say, laughing. I take our drinks as he makes an order for someone else.

When I get back to the table, Eugenia's literally crawling on the ground. "What are you doing?" I ask.

She pops back up with one of the extensions. "This damn thing fell out," she whines.

I roll my eyes. "Come on, let me help." We go into a tiny bathroom with two stalls and a rusted-out sink. As I clip the hair piece back in, the women in the stalls are speaking to each other over the sound of urine splashing into toilet water.

"I saw David out the other night," one says.

"David Dennison?"

"Bingo." She giggles.

Eugenia and I exchange a glance. Drunk people make eaves-dropping way too easy.

"Is he still as hot as he was in high school?"

"Even more so, if that's possible."

"She never should have even *looked* at Trapper, let alone married the guy."

"Oh, come on! Trapper was way sexier back then."

"And look where that got her—six feet under!"

The women cackle. I ball my hands into fists, and Eugenia pushes me toward the door. "Not worth it," she says as she swings open the door. Back at the table, I fill her in on the scant information the bartender told me about Melissa, trying to forget the petty gossip.

"Gregory Hornsby never came into the bar," she repeats. "So how else would he have met Melissa? From what we've learned, Melissa was quiet and pretty much kept to herself. Except for here and church, and a few dates with David, where else would Hornsby have seen her?"

"I guess he could've watched her leaving the bar after it closed? Maybe he followed her home."

"Maybe," she says. "But that feels like a stretch." We fall silent as we sip our Cokes, lost in thought. This Gregory Hornsby angle didn't sit right with me before, and it doesn't now, either. But maybe the chief has some hard evidence that ties him to her murder?

There's a crowd up by the door now, and a platinum-blond woman stands at the head of it. Her mannerisms seem familiar, and it takes me a minute to recognize her—Lydia, with dyed hair. "Would you *look* at her?" I ask as we pick our way through the bar. "How tacky can she be?"

Lydia's talking with some guy, touching his arm and laughing at everything he says. The walls near the door are covered in memorabilia from the case—Trapper's mug shot, court renderings, newspaper articles in cheap gold frames. A woman takes a selfie next to his photo, pouting her lips.

"Is Trapper some kind of sex symbol?" Eugenia mumbles.

A woman behind us starts talking. "Oh yes. He's yummy." I turn around to face a short woman in ripped jeans and a black T-shirt that falls off one shoulder. It's another one of those T-shirts from the upcoming docuseries.

"He's a *murderer*," I say, and she gives me a confused look. "Doesn't that bother you?"

She smiles. "Oh, honey, a girl could do a lot worse. Besides, he just loves too hard. With the right woman, he could change. I'm sure of it."

My muscles start to twitch, and I force myself to look away. I'm supposed to *want* to be here, and I'm pretty sure smacking this woman upside the head would draw negative attention.

"You okay?" Eugenia whispers to me. I nod, but I can't speak.

"All right, everyone!" Lydia trills. "Who's ready for the Wolf Ridge Ghost Tour?" The women hoot and clap. The woman behind us whistles so loudly in my ear, it rings. "Let's head outside, y'all." We pay our twenty bucks to the bouncer as we file outside.

We hang out at the back of the crowd, at least fifty in total. Quite the change from the night they stopped outside my house. Melissa's death is really packing them in. One of the customers is Mr. Fisher, our English teacher. "Look at that shit!" I hiss in Eugenia's ear, pointing.

"That is incredibly unethical," Eugenia murmurs. "You're his *student*. I should report him to the board of trustees."

They've all got their phones out. A few snap photos of Lydia, who claps and brings us all to attention. "Welcome, everyone, to the Wolf Ridge Ghost Tour!" More clapping and hooting, and my face grows hot. "My name is Lydia Baker. I'm a lifelong resident of Wolf Ridge, and I grew up hearing local ghost stories from my granddaddy. This town is full of them—some more recent than others. I went to high school with one of Trapper McGrath's victims, Prudence McGrath. I didn't know Cherry Hobbs, his other presumed victim, personally; she moved to Wolf Ridge a couple years after graduation. She worked at the gas station and lived in an apartment downtown.

"I couldn't believe it when Prudence was murdered," Lydia continues. She puts on a serious face, as if she's delivering my mother's eulogy. "She was the sweetest, most beautiful girl in our class. Everyone liked her. I wondered who could have done something so evil to my friend? And then my mind went to Trapper, her husband. She was underage when they got together. It was quite the scandal. A dangerous older guy, a pretty young girl…"

She shakes her head. "Tonight, we'll travel to some of the last steps Prudence took before her life was snuffed out. We'll also retrace Cherry Hobbs's final days leading up to her still-unsolved murder. It's never been proven in a court of law that Trapper killed Cherry, but it was well known he was having an affair with her. Rumor has it he got her pregnant to boot!

"And, ladies and gentlemen, as I'm sure you've heard by now, *another body* was found in the woods just last week, near where they found Cherry's body. Melissa Atkins, who worked in this very bar and was just the sweetest gal. The police aren't admitting it's a copycat murder, but believe me, it was—the famous Trapper McGrath inspired a long-haul trucker to attempt to claim his *own* notoriety. So be careful tonight, is all I'm saying. Always watch your back in Wolf Ridge!"

The group grows silent as Lydia lifts a backpack from the sidewalk, reaches inside, and holds out a handful of large glow sticks. "Everyone, grab a glow stick." She moves through the crowd, and when she gets to me and Eugenia, we quickly take one each. Her eyes don't meet mine, and then she's gone. Little popping sounds spread around the group, and hot pinks and greens bloom in the bluish tint of dusk.

Lydia slips on the backpack and leads everyone down the street. We lag at the back of the pack. Someone whispers, "Maybe Trapper really is innocent? Could this be a serial killer situation?"

"Serial killer," I repeat softly.

The words turn bitter on my tongue. Everything around me turns gray. My body breaks out in a sweat, and I want to rip this wig off. Lydia and her swarm are at the corner, waiting to cross.

"Let's leave," Eugenia urges. "You look like you're about to pass out."

"No, we need to finish what we started. See if we can get any new information."

Lydia points up ahead. "Here's our first stop: Sheila's Diner. Back in the twenties, a bride jumped out the second-floor window on her wedding day. Some say she was pushed by her betrothed! Sometimes you can see her ghost in the upstairs window."

The woman who spoke to us in the bar snaps some photos at our side. "I'm Regina," Eugenia says to her, holding out her hand.

She takes it. "Sarah Beth. Nice to meet you."

"Have you taken this tour before?" Eugenia asks, giving me a look. I keep my head down. Lydia is talking in the background about how my mom and Trapper used to eat at Sheila's all the time. About the epic fights they used to have. How Sheila had to call the police once—a fact Sheila has neglected to share with *me*, unless Lydia's making it up.

"A few times. I live in Wilmington, but I watched the whole trial on TV. It was amazing, wasn't it? Trapper looks so much like Matthew McConaughey."

I ball my hands into fists, and Eugenia clears her throat. "Do you think he did it?" she asks, which surprises me.

Sarah Beth takes a deep breath and looks past us for a moment.

"That's a really hard question to answer, right? I mean, they had all that evidence. But Trapper has always maintained he didn't do it. Wouldn't he have admitted it to someone in the last ten years? Most criminals confess eventually. And how many people can sustain a lie for a decade without changing their story?"

"Pathological liars are pretty damn good at lying," I mutter without thinking.

Sarah Beth gives me a funny look. "You think he's guilty, then?"

I look away, and Eugenia answers for me. "They found her blood on him, the note he left for her that morning, his prints on the murder weapon. There was no forced entry."

"Yeah. The slash marks on her face seem pretty personal, too, like something a jealous husband might do if he didn't want anyone else to look at her, you know? Maybe she was running around on him. Not that it justifies murder." Sarah Beth puts her phone back in her purse. "But then I read about this new woman who got killed in town? Stabbed and slashed, just like the others. Maybe the real killer is still out there. Maybe Hornsby killed Prudence, too?" She leans in closer. "I heard Trapper's own *daughter* found the new body. Can you imagine? It's like she's cursed."

I meet her eyes, and I swear she knows exactly who I am.

Lydia motions for everyone to follow, and we head off again. She takes us to an alley across the street from Sheila's and stops in front of a dumpster behind our town's only Chinese restaurant. "This," she says, pointing to the ground, "is where the police found Cherry Hobbs's pink satin stiletto, covered in her blood. When they found her body in the woods, she had three stab wounds to the chest, face cut up. Trapper's MO. They never found her other shoe, by the way."

I wish I could show these women Lydia's trial testimony. *She doesn't think Trapper is guilty at all.* But she sure does a good job pretending to make her tour more entertaining.

A man shoves past me to get a closer look. Lydia takes off her backpack and removes two long metal bars that are bent at ninety-degree angles at one end.

"What are those?" someone asks.

"These are divining rods," Lydia explains. "I'll use them to try to make contact with Cherry's spirit. Let her tell us what she wants or needs us to know."

"Is she for real?" I whisper to Eugenia.

Eugenia crosses her arms and shudders. "This is bullshit," she whispers.

"Do you believe in all this? Ghosts and stuff?"

"I live in a house with dead people, so paranormal stuff is bound to happen, right? Wrong. Humans die, their bodies rot. It's science. End of story."

"That's lovely," I mutter.

"I'm not sorry," Eugenia says. "I just don't think it's right to trick people like this."

As Lydia holds the rods in her hands, I crane my neck for a better look. The rods are parallel with each other. She asks everyone to take a step back, and then she walks over to the spot where Cherry's bloody shoe was found. Lydia closes her eyes, and everyone leans forward. "I'm searching for the spirit of Cherry Hobbs," Lydia intones, a terrible imitation of a medium she probably saw on TV. "If you are here with us now, Cherry, please cross the rods. We wish you no harm, only to speak with you."

The rods slowly begin to cross over each other, making an X. "She totally moved those," I whisper to Eugenia.

"Totally," she whispers back.

"Quiet!" Sarah Beth snaps, and we shut our mouths.

"Please uncross the rods, Cherry. Use my energy if you need to." The rods uncross. I look around the crowd, at eyes practically bugging out of heads. "Cherry, if Trapper McGrath killed you, please cross the rods."

The rods cross again, and Sarah Beth snaps a photo. Her camera's flash blasts the alley with light, and then it falls into shadow again. Our glow sticks are already beginning to fade.

"How did Trapper kill you, Cherry?" Lydia asks. "If he strangulated you, please cross the rods." Now Lydia's really got them eating out of her palm. Even I find myself leaning closer. Waiting to see if the rods move. "If Trapper stabbed you, Cherry, please cross the rods."

The rods cross, and some of the tourgoers put their hands over their mouths in surprise. I loathe them. They're all secretly getting off on it, the perverse thrill, knowing whatever evil thing happened to Cherry can't touch them here.

"Did Trapper kill you in this alley, Cherry? If so, please cross the rods." The rods don't move. "If he killed you someplace else and moved your body to the woods, please cross the rods." Again, the rods remain motionless. Lydia takes a deep breath. "Are you still with us, Cherry?" The rods don't cross; instead, they angle away from Lydia. She twitches and takes a small step forward. "Excuse me," she says. "The rods are pointing me this way. I have to follow where they lead."

The group slowly parts like a zipper as Lydia drifts toward me and Eugenia. She stops in front of me, the rods pointing at my chest like knives. I keep my head down, hoping she'll leave. "You there, miss," she says, her voice throaty.

When I look up, Lydia's staring at me. The recognition grows in her eyes.

"Bett?" she gasps. "You shouldn't be here."

Sarah Beth looks harder at me, a flash of realization on her face. Voices begin speaking over one another, rippling through the crowd.

"Is she really his daughter?"

"Does she remember her mama's murder?"

"Did she really find that body in the woods?"

Their questions swirl around me, and I push my way forward until I'm at the dumpster. Frantically, I duck behind it, as if it'll somehow keep them away from me. My foot skids on something wet, and I fall backward, landing hard on the pavement. I lie there for a minute, dazed, half covered in shadow, tailbone aching.

Someone else has fallen with me, their arm by my feet, their body... under the dumpster?

I lean forward to look, to help, but my hand touches something wet and sticky. There's dark liquid on the ground; the person is lying in it.

Wait. I know their face. Pale skin, yellow hair. Eyes wide open. Face slashed into a deranged smile.

It's Holly Walters. Dead.

Something's been written on her forehead. The crowd regathers about me. Someone snaps a photo, lighting up her body in horrific, unnatural blue.

Still here.

"Oh fuck," I say, scrambling backward just as a police car slowly rolls down the alley. Chantal and Andre get out of the car and come straight for me.

"Help," I say, my voice shaking. I point to the dumpster, blood on my hand, and then some of the women in the crowd start screaming.

"You're under arrest for possession of a fraudulent ID," Chantal says, walking quickly toward me. Lydia stands off to the side, a concerned look on her face. She must have called the fuzz—that was fast.

Phones flash behind me. Eugenia has vanished. "Are you seriously *arresting* me right now? Look under the damn dumpster! *It's Holly!*"

"You have the right to remain silent."

My hearing goes sideways as she reads me the rest of my rights and puts me in handcuffs. I let her lead me to the car. She gently touches the top of my head as I slide into the back seat, my mouth dry, my heart pounding. She shuts the door, trapping me inside, and I look out the window. The group is still gawking and taking photos, everyone vibrating with excitement. Andre is pushing the crowd away from the dumpster; some people cry, others gawk. They must have seen her.

I look down at my boots; there's blood on them. "I think I'm gonna be sick," I say as soon as Chantal gets in the car. My breathing is growing shallow as my mouth fills with saliva.

"About what? You'll be fine."

As we drive slowly down the alley, I puke all over her back seat.

CHAPTER
Twenty-One

The police release me to my grandparents, no bail required. I was questioned backward and forward about discovering the body, but frankly, there wasn't much to say.

The ride home is excruciatingly quiet. No one says a word about Holly.

As we make the familiar drive through the darkened neighborhood, I stare at the wig sitting on my lap. It looks like a dead animal. Granddad took my phone, so I can't check with Eugenia and see if she made it home unscathed.

Even though I washed my hands at the station, I can still feel blood on my skin.

Still here.

Holly and I were never close—we were barely even amiable—but we had our moments. For my thirteenth birthday, she threw me a *Golden Girls*-themed party in the park. It had been my favorite show for a while, one I watched with Grams daily. Holly brought along old dresses and wigs and cheesecake, and it was actually the perfect day. I'd almost forgotten it, how she made me feel special…and now we'll never be able to work through any of our shit.

Closing my eyes, I let the tears fall.

I *knew* the chief had the wrong guy when he arrested Hornsby. Clearly, the killer doesn't want Hornsby to get credit for *his* kills. Which means he's still out there, still targeting young blond women, still taunting all of us.

When we pull up the drive, there's a tow truck parked in front of the garage. "What's going on?" I ask, but they don't answer. I get out of the car and walk to the back of the tow truck. A man is hooking a chain onto my Rolls. "What are you doing?" I cry. The man keeps working. I turn to my grandparents; Grams is already walking to the front door. Granddad stands there, watching. "Why is he taking my car!"

"I'm having it sold."

"You're *what*?"

He takes off his glasses and pinches the bridge of his nose. Then he puts them back on. "I told you to leave all this alone, Bett. But you refused to listen."

"So you're selling my *car*?"

He shoves his hands in the pockets of his coat. "I don't know how else to get through to you. Your grandmother may be a soft touch, but I'm not. There are rules, and you broke them."

"But how am I supposed to go places?"

"You can borrow our car—after you're done being grounded."

"I'm grounded now, too? What am I, twelve?"

"When you act like a twelve-year-old, you get treated like one."

"Can I at least have my phone back? I don't really feel safe without one—you know, given there's a *serial killer* on the loose."

He sighs and hands it back to me. "Don't make me regret this, Bettina Jane. I'll cancel your phone plan if I need to. Now come inside, have some tea. You've had one helluva night."

"In a minute," I say, and he leaves me to watch the tow's chains slowly pull my car onto the back of the truck. "Goodbye, loyal friend." I hope Granddad was exaggerating when he said he was going to sell it. Hopefully he'll store it someplace and give it back when all this dies down.

Whatever "all this" is.

The exhaustion hits me suddenly, like I've had too much to drink and it's finally catching up with me. I drop my wig on the veranda and collapse into a chair, weighed down by a thousand regrets, a thousand new worries. Holly Walters is dead. Stuffed under that dumpster, words cut into her face.

What the actual fuck is going on in Wolf Ridge? I quickly text Eugenia.

Me: You make it home okay?

Eugenia: Snuck away before the cops saw me. Poor Holly. Are you in jail?

Me: Nah. Released to family and ticketed. Now . . . Suspect for Holly?

Eugenia: We need to question Hunter. Remember, it's usually the boyfriend, statistically speaking.

Me: God, I hope not. Are you sleepy?

Eugenia: I've got snacks. Come over.

When I go inside, Grams has made tea and heated up some peach pie. We eat together silently at the dining room table, though I don't take more than a couple of bites. Grams looks at me like I'm made of glass.

"You're not hungry," she states, and I shake my head. "I wish I could protect you from this."

"I know you do, Grams."

Neither of us says what we're really thinking: Why do *I* keep finding the bodies? Am I just bad luck…or is there some other reason?

After I let Grams tuck me in, I wait fifteen minutes before sneaking out.

The house is silent, my grandparents locked away in their bedroom suite, and no one comes to investigate as I quietly leave out the back door and run all the way to Eugenia's. It's a bad idea to travel alone in the dark, I know, but I'd rather it was me out here going to her than the reverse. She's so tiny.

Eugenia's already waiting for me on her porch, and we slip inside silently, not speaking until we've made it into the attic. There are two whiteboards now. "Did you buy this tonight?" I ask. "Or do you have ESP?"

"Amazon had a two-for-one deal. Didn't think I'd need it."

On the second board, I write Holly's name in the middle. Under her name I write the words her killer carved into her face. "He's laughing at us now," I say, capping the marker.

"It certainly seems that way. We won't know for sure until we find out how she died, but I'm almost positive it will be exactly the same as Melissa, Cherry, and your mom."

I sink into the lawn chair, my head starting to pound. Eugenia cracks open two cold cans of Coke and hands one to me. Then she goes back to the board. "Suspects?"

"Obviously Hunter," I say.

"What about Madison and Natalie?" Eugenia asks. "Sometimes it's the friends."

"I really doubt it, but we can try to question them." I sigh. "This just got twice as hard. Who connects to both Melissa and Holly?"

I wrack my brain, but my brain won't let me think—it keeps taking me back behind that dumpster. Holly's sticky blood. Her eyes. And those words scraped into her skin. I squeeze my eyes closed, wishing the chief *had* been right about Hornsby. She would still be alive.

I bring up the Friend Finder app on my phone; Natalie and I installed it not long before our friendship ended. I never took her off my list. "Nat's at Madison's right now. Probably sleeping over. We can visit tomorrow—maybe they'll talk to us."

"If they don't slam the door in our faces," Eugenia muses.

She's not wrong. But it's a chance we have to take. Melissa's murder was scary enough, but Holly's feels personal, like something has been circling at a distance but is moving closer.

Who Killed Holly Walters?
Suspect List:
Hunter Jackson
Madison Tran
Natalie Baker

CHAPTER
Twenty-Two

The next morning, I eat a solemn breakfast with my grandparents. Eugenia drove me back a few hours before dawn, and I can barely keep my eyes open.

Granddad clears his throat. "I hope a good night's sleep in your own bedroom has helped your attitude. No more going out alone, Bettina Jane. You are to be with someone else at all times if you leave this house. Not until this animal is caught. It may seem a bit severe, but I won't bend on this."

I take a bite of pancake, which goes down like sandpaper. "I get it, Granddad. I won't." He looks surprised, like he expected a fight. Honestly, I'd rather not go out by myself, either. "Is it okay if I hang out with Eugenia today? You can drop me at her house if you want."

"That's fine, Bett. Fine. I'll take you after breakfast."

Eugenia and I stand on Azalea Terrace, looking up at Madison's house. It's a huge modern two-story with sleek lines and big glass windows, nothing like Magnolia House. A long curving driveway cuts through the sprawling front lawn, which is perfectly manicured with minimalist bushes and carefully placed boulders.

"It looks like an office building," Eugenia says, a box of donuts tucked under one arm. "Not very inviting."

"It's not supposed to feel inviting. It's meant to intimidate."

"It's working."

We walk up the long drive together, my bravery draining out of my body with each step. I haven't been here in over a year. Natalie's phone says she's still inside, and I can't help but feel we're about to intrude on something we shouldn't. They just lost a good friend and should be able to mourn in private. Yet here I am, doing what all those true-crime reporters and fans have done to me since I was six years old—mining someone else's pain for information.

Eugenia rings the bell before I can tell her I've changed my mind. Madison's mom opens the door, her hair swept into a low ponytail. "Bett?" Her eyes are a little red.

"Hi, Mrs. Tran. Is Madison here?" I ask.

"Yes...but she's not really in the mood to see anyone."

"We heard about what happened to Holly and wanted to see how she's feeling. Let her know she's not alone."

Madison's mom smiles a little before pulling me into a hug. "I'm so sorry, Bett. I know you girls had a falling out, but I hope you're feeling all right." I let her hold me for a while. She was always nice.

"Were Madison and Natalie here all night?" Eugenia asks.

Her mom pulls back, nodding. "They were asleep when we got the news. I had to wake them. Let me go see if she's up to visitors. Wait here."

She leaves the door halfway open, and soon Madison and Natalie step outside. They're still in pajamas—sleep shorts and matching tops, their hair in messy buns. Madison's face is blotchy red, and she dabs her nose with a tissue. "Did you hear?" she asks, her voice catching.

Eugenia holds up the box. "We brought condolence donuts."

"Like I could eat at a time like this," she says, taking the box anyway. "But thank you."

"I'm really sorry about Holly," I say, feeling awkward.

Madison wipes her eyes. "I just can't believe it," she sniffs. "It makes no sense. Who would do something like that?"

"I can't believe it, either," I offer. "It's so bizarre."

"Was Holly with you guys last night?" Eugenia asks.

Madison nods. "Holly got a text from Hunter at like, what, six? Do you remember?" She aims her question at Natalie.

Nat wraps her arms around herself. "I think so," she mumbles.

"Did she go to meet him?" Eugenia asks.

"Yeah, and when she didn't come back, I assumed she was staying with him. Her parents are kind of strict—you remember, Bett—so she usually sneaks out of our sleepovers to see him." Madison's voice wavers. "I never even texted her. I should have."

"Do you think Hunter could have done this?" Eugenia prods.

"No way," Madison says, shaking her head. "They were, like, the perfect couple. Never fought. There's no way he would have hurt her. Right, Nat?"

Natalie nods, keeping her head down. She seems so small and afraid—nothing like the Natalie I knew. She must be heartbroken.

"But you can't know that for sure," Eugenia says. "He could have texted her to lure her out on purpose, knowing neither of you would ever suspect him."

I wince, knowing Madison's going to shut us down. Sure enough, she shoves the donuts back at Eugenia. "That's a cruel thing to say, Eugenia."

"Madison—" I start, but she holds up a hand.

"Our friend just got killed, and you're here grilling us for spicy details? What is *wrong* with you?" She glares at me, something hard taking shape in her eyes. "Especially you, Bett. She was your friend, too, once."

"We're sorry about Holly," Eugenia says. "We're trying to help catch whoever did this."

Madison wipes her eyes. "You can help by leaving us alone." She turns and goes back inside with Nat, slamming the door in our faces.

"That went well, don't you think?" I say, walking back to the road.

"She's just upset. Don't take it too hard. Anyway, no joy—they're each other's alibis." Eugenia opens the box and takes out a fresh donut. "Want one?"

I grab a glazed, barely tasting the sugar.

Who Killed Holly Walters?
Suspect List:
Hunter Jackson
~~Madison Tran~~
~~Natalie Baker~~

CHAPTER
Twenty-Three

I always thought that riding the school bus was for losers. Today, I am the loser queen.

I sit at the back Monday morning, head down, earbuds in. The underclassmen stare at me. Everyone's heard about Holly by now, and that it was me who found her. I thought about calling Eugenia for a ride, but I worried she might show up in the hearse.

I skipped breakfast with my grandparents this morning, grabbing a Pop-Tart on my way out the door. I pretended I had overslept, but in reality I didn't sleep at all.

I don't know what to do with all this death.

Blocky white news vans are parked in the grass, with skinny women and handsome men holding microphones and gesturing toward the school. Other random people congregate, filming with their phones. Some are interviewing classmates, and I can only guess what they're talking about. Our bus driver curses when she almost clips one of the vans.

The other students exit the bus, but I hang back, watching. A few students are holding signs that say JUSTICE FOR HOLLY in bright block letters. I sink down in my seat, but then the driver tells me to get off, and I'm forced to step into the middle of the circus.

At first, I go unnoticed...and then a strong breeze blows my hair out of my face.

A few students point and murmur, and then the anchors see me. Leeches. I start booking it toward the main doors, head down, but one reporter shoves her microphone in my face and says, "Bettina Holland, care to comment on the murders of Holly Walters and Melissa Atkins? Have you spoken to your father lately? Do you think there is any connection between these killings and your mother's?"

I stop and face her, and she looks surprised. Even a little relieved. If I speak to her, it'll be on all the major news sites. She pulls her shoulders back and flashes me a megawatt smile as some slobby guy in saggy jeans rushes over with a camera balanced on his shoulder.

"The community of Wolf Ridge has been rocked by two gruesome murders in as many weeks," she says, speaking to the camera now. "I'm speaking with local resident Bettina Holland, daughter of convicted killer Trapper McGrath, who discovered both bodies. Would you care to comment on this shocking wave of violence, Ms. Holland? This must be a terribly difficult time for you."

She holds the microphone toward me, and I stare at it for a moment, weighing my options. I could be polite—play the shy, innocent girl, heartbroken over the recent tragedies.

Or...

I snatch the mic out of her hand and hurl it at her. "You're shameless!" I spit, and then I head up the stairs to the main doors.

Madison and Natalie are sitting on a bench to my right. Madison's face is puffy from crying; she's holding one of the signs. Her normally perfect hair is knotted in the back, like she didn't brush it. Natalie keeps her head down; her clothes are wrinkled. I pretend not to see them and keep going, even as my name is shouted out behind me.

Inside, I open my locker, and a piece of paper tumbles out and lands at my feet. It's been torn from a newspaper. I open it up, and it's the report of my arrest Friday night, with the word *murderer* written in red ink.

"Fuck," I mutter and crumple it up. I know how it looks. Me, finding both women.

"Oh, look, Lizzie Borden's here," someone whispers.

I whip around, but can't tell who said it. Everyone looks away, like they'll catch something if they make direct eye contact with me. I take a deep breath, try to calm myself, and grab my things.

As I head to first period, I bump smack into Natalie. Her books fall to the floor with a loud thud. She looks even worse up close—chapped lips, dry skin.

"How are you doing?" I ask, picking up her stuff. It's a stupid question.

Natalie shrugs. "I'm...okay." She takes her books and tries to move around me, but I step into her path.

"I'm sorry if we overstepped at Madison's." She says nothing. Won't even look at me. "What's going on with you lately, Nat? You don't look like yourself at all. It's like you're dead or something."

Natalie's eyes rage. "Thanks, Bett. That's *real* classy of you to say, considering."

"I didn't mean it like that, okay? You just seem…"

"I wonder why!" she snarls. "My best friend just died!"

Best friend? "Sorry," I say softly.

I've told Natalie Baker to go to hell in a million different ways this past year.

Yet now a small part of me wants to forgive her. We both know things about each other that no one else does. She knows about my secret nighttime visits to my mom's grave. She knows how my grandparents tiptoe around things to pretend we're a normal family. I know how Natalie has to wear her shoes until they crumble off her feet. How her dad stopped sending even a birthday card a couple of years ago.

But every time I see her, I think of my mom's death. Of blood and pain. Of the exploitation of my family. And now that I've gotten an up close and personal look at Lydia's bar and the macabre death parade she leads through town, I can't unsee it.

I hurry away from her, leaving her standing alone. I pass Hunter in the hall, and our eyes meet. He quickly looks away.

Like he doesn't want to see me. Or like he has something to hide.

I turn back and approach him slowly, glad Eugenia's not with me. His shoulders tense up. "Hey, Hunter," I say, keeping my voice soft. "How are you holding up?"

His eyes are red around the rims. "I'm okay," he mumbles. Hunter's never been real big on words, or stringing them together into super-long sentences. But he was always nice to me (up until I barfed on him and he vanished).

"Have you seen the news people outside?" I ask. "It's sick."

He shrugs. "What's sick is I spent my entire Saturday being questioned by the cops."

The hairs on my neck prick up. "You did?"

He clenches his jaw. "Said they had to rule me out as a suspect. As if I'd ever..." His voice catches and he swallows, looking down.

I touch his arm. "I know you wouldn't have hurt her, Hunter. No one thinks that." I don't say that Eugenia thinks that.

"Thanks, Bett." He exhales a ragged breath and leans against the lockers. "God, I can't believe she's really gone. Why would someone do that to her?"

I try to think of a delicate way to phrase my next question. "Madison told me about you guys meeting that night. Can I ask... when you texted Holly to meet up, what was her response?"

"She sent three hearts, same as always. Why?"

I lean against the locker next to him, face casual, not totally sure myself why I asked. "That's sweet," I say. "So it happened when she was on her way to your house. You can't blame yourself."

"Actually, she asked to meet up at the church's playground, not my place."

"First Baptist?" I ask, and he nods. "Why there?" That church is a couple of blocks from Hunter's house, and also a couple of blocks from Nat's. More, it's the same church David Dennison attends.

A connection.

"My parents caught us together in my room last week," he

admits. "We were trying to lay low for a while. And when she never showed up…"

"Is that where Holly goes to church?" I ask, my face growing warm. "I mean—went."

He wipes his nose on the back of his hand. "Yeah. She was supposed to help run vacation Bible school soon. She was so excited."

"Listen, Hunter, if you ever need to talk, or think of anything else about that night, I'm here. Okay?"

Hunter nods. "I need to get to class," he says, pushing past me before I can say anything else. But I've already gotten what I need. Holly attended the same church as David. When I get to English, I skip my assigned seat and sit in the back next to Eugenia.

"I just talked to Hunter," I whisper, and she turns her full attention on me, eyes unblinking, totally focused. Sometimes her intensity catches me by surprise. "Holly asked him to meet her at First Baptist. She and David both went to church there."

Eugenia's eyes widen. "Our first suspect connected to both victims."

"Hunter said the cops questioned him all day on Saturday, but he *didn't* say if they cleared him as a person of interest."

"Did he seem afraid or agitated?"

"He just seemed really sad. I think he actually did love her."

"Still, until we know for certain, we can't officially rule him out. No known alibi."

My phone pings with an alert. Ada's released another podcast episode, and as I read the title, my blood runs cold.

Sister of Doubt *Episode 107:*

Special Announcement—False Arrest in Melissa Atkins Case

I pop in my earbuds and hit play. My aunt's show starts off with some ominous music, almost like chains being dragged through water. And then her voice fills my ears, dropped an octave lower than her regular speaking voice.

> **Ada:** Hello, *Sister of Doubt* listeners. It's Ada Holland, and I have a bonus episode for you today. I'm continuing my deep dive on the Trapper McGrath case. If you're not familiar, circle back to last week's podcast or my debut episode where I cover the murder and trial in detail.
>
> Today, though, there's a new development in the small town of Wolf Ridge, North Carolina. The same town where Trapper McGrath committed his alleged crime more than a decade ago—the grisly murder of his wife. It's a case I am intimately familiar with, the one that spawned this very podcast: my sister was the victim. And I'm not convinced my former brother-in-law is guilty.
>
> In fact, I think the person or persons responsible may have returned to Wolf Ridge. This sleepy mountain town has recently experienced yet another murder of a blond white woman, twenty-three-year-old Melissa Atkins. She was found only a couple of weeks ago, stabbed to death and dumped in some woods near the town's only cemetery,

Mount Olivet. According to my sources, Ms. Atkins was killed in the same way my sister was, including the postmortem cuts to her face.

News recording: We arrested a white male, Gregory Hornsby, age thirty-two, at approximately ten forty-five this morning. The suspect, a long-haul trucker from Baton Rouge, Louisiana, came into the police station himself and confessed to the killing of Ms. Atkins.

Ada: That's the voice of Carl Bigsby, chief of police in Wolf Ridge. He was also lead detective when my sister was killed. I spoke to him at the press conference he held shortly after Hornsby's arrest. Hornsby allegedly turned himself in and confessed to the murder. When I pressed the chief for any physical evidence, he was cagey. So I tracked down the company Mr. Hornsby worked for, Vanselow Trucking, and spoke to his boss, Artie Flowers. I asked Mr. Flowers if Hornsby was on the road anywhere in North Carolina the day Ms. Atkins was killed.

Artie Flowers: Gregory Hornsby was on a route out West the entire week of the killing, delivering diesel fuel. Got receipts for gas and meals, plus I talked to him on his work cell, which has GPS. No way he was anywhere near Wolf Ridge.

Ada: Did Mr. Hornsby make a false confession? Did the Wolf Ridge PD thoroughly vet his confession? Or were they pressured by the district attorney to make an arrest?

Someone killed Melissa Atkins, but it wasn't Gregory Hornsby. The chief got it wrong, folks. Is it really that big a stretch that he got it wrong in my sister's case, too?

Who Killed Holly Walters?
Suspect List:
Hunter Jackson
~~Madison Tran~~
~~Natalie Baker~~
David Dennison
SERIAL KILLER???

Who Killed Melissa Atkins?
Suspect List:
~~Drifter from out of town (Gregory Hornsby, confessed & arrested)~~
~~Grayson, creepy ex-boyfriend~~
David Dennison
~~Xavier Hart~~

CHAPTER
Twenty-Four

Eugenia and I ride the bus to her house after school. She listens to Ada's podcast, her eyes focused on the seat in front of us, shaking her head occasionally. When the bus drops us, we set out on foot toward the inn on Storybook Lane, passing the small apartment building where Melissa lived. A man stands out front, snapping photos with his phone.

I wonder if anyone will come to collect Melissa's things, or if they'll be tossed into storage and forgotten.

The Firelight Inn sits way back at the end of the street, separated from the road by a white picket fence and rosebushes bursting with pinks and purples. The house itself is three stories of ivy-covered red brick with a huge front porch. Planters exploding with color hang from the porch ceiling, and rocking chairs sit empty beside potted plants.

Once we get closer to the steps, cigarette smoke engulfs us. Sure enough, Ada sits in a chair at the far end, smoke curling around her head. She's on her laptop and doesn't look up when we climb onto the porch, its floor painted white and covered in throw rugs. The boards creak a little as we approach, and when I clear my throat, she finally takes her eyes from her screen.

"Bett?" she exclaims, astonished. "Are you all right? Didn't expect to see you here!" She snuffs out her cigarette into a crystal ashtray. Her eyes land on Eugenia, who's wearing an unseasonal black scarf wrapped around her neck. "And who's this?"

Eugenia doesn't wait for an introduction. "I'm Eugenia Cline. You must be Ada Holland."

Ada closes her laptop and sets it aside. "You girls want to sit awhile?" We nod, and she quickly drags a couple of the rocking chairs into a makeshift circle. "Mrs. Jacobs makes great lemonade, if you'd like some."

"That'd be nice, thank you," Eugenia says. As soon as Ada goes inside, Eugenia grabs her laptop and opens it. "Dammit. Password protected."

"Seriously? You're trying to break into her computer?"

She shrugs and places the laptop back exactly where Ada put it. Ada returns with three glasses, and we sit across from her. No one drinks. We hold them awkwardly in our laps, waiting for someone to break the silence.

Finally, I set my sweating glass on a table. "I listened to your newest episode today."

"Really? I didn't think you were a fan."

"I'm not."

She sips her drink. "And? What'd you think?"

"Is it true?" Eugenia asks. "Did you really speak to Gregory Hornsby's boss?"

"I did. He showed me documentation as well. Hornsby's innocent. Clearly, he has some serious mental health issues to deal with, but he didn't kill Melissa Atkins." She takes another sip. "And no one from the Wolf Ridge PD has contacted Hornsby's place of employment."

"Why not?" I ask. "That seems like an obvious first step."

Ada shakes her head. "Bigsby was a lazy detective, and he's a lazy chief. It doesn't surprise me."

Eugenia gives me a pointed look, then nods at Ada. I clear my throat. "We've kind of been looking into Melissa's murder ourselves. And now Holly's."

"Do your grandparents know about this extracurricular activity?"

"Obviously not. Which is why we're here."

"You don't approve of my lifestyle or the way I choose to honor and remember my sister. So why have you come to me now?"

"I still don't approve. But we've…hit a wall, I guess you could say."

Eugenia nods. "We've got two suspect lists going, but only a single name appears on both."

Ada raises an eyebrow. "Oh? Who are you looking at?"

Eugenia and I exchange a look, and then we tell her our theory about David Dennison. "Going to the same church as Holly and a few dates with Melissa isn't a smoking gun or anything," I say. "But it's all we have so far."

"David Dennison," my aunt echoes. "Kind of hard to imagine him murdering anyone, but killers often hide their true selves. I mean, look at Ted Bundy. People thought he was charming."

"When he wasn't off butchering college students," Eugenia mutters.

"I like her," Ada says to me. "So you want to know what I think about David as the killer, and what other suspects are on my list."

"Yes," I say. "Any help you can give us." I keep my motivation for wanting to solve these murders to myself—taking back control of my story from people like her.

She sits back and crosses her arms. "You're not going to like what I have to say."

"We'll be the judge of that," I answer, crossing my arms as well.

"Once we talk, there's no going back," she warns. "There's stuff you don't know that you probably don't want to know."

"I've been dealing with stuff I don't want to know since I was six years old. Don't patronize me, Ada."

"First off, I don't know many details about Holly Walters yet. My source is slow today. But I can say that the boyfriend, Hunter Jackson, has been cleared as a person of interest. His phone shows he was at the park at the time Holly was killed. Eyewitnesses saw him too."

"What else do you know?" I ask.

She sighs. "I hope I'm doing the right thing. Wait here." She goes inside the inn, and I start chewing my nails, my stomach in knots. Her ominous words hang over my head: *no going back*. It's not too late to leave and let the chief handle it from here. But I already started down this path the day I found Melissa. What could Ada possibly tell me that's worse than what I saw that day or the day my mother died?

Ada returns holding a manila envelope. She sits down, setting it on her lap. I don't ask her what's inside, but it must be important. "I agree with your theory that these murders are connected."

"A copycat killer perhaps?" Eugenia asks. "Some twisted fan of Trapper's who's obsessed with him?"

Ada shakes her head. "No. I don't believe there's any copycat killer. Whoever killed Melissa and Holly has come out of dormancy. They're simply continuing what they started, first with Cherry Hobbs and then my sister."

I roll my eyes. "Please don't start with your 'Trapper is innocent' bullshit. It's tired."

"It's not bullshit, Bett, if it's true." She takes a deep breath. "How much of that day do you remember?"

I stand. "I should have known you'd be completely useless."

Ada reaches for me. "Hear me out, please? You said you wanted to know what I know. If you want clarity on these recent murders, hear what I have to say."

"Let's at least listen to her," Eugenia says calmly. "It's not like we have to agree."

"Fine," I say, gritting my teeth as I sit back down.

I'll never forget the night Granddad turned on a cable news show, and there was Ada, giving a sprawling interview about how she didn't think Trapper was guilty. How she thought his conviction was some big conspiracy and his lawyer was incompetent. My grandparents were rapt, giving her their full attention. After, Granddad calmly turned off the television and poured a glass of scotch. Grams slowly went upstairs to bed.

After that, Ada didn't come around much anymore, and I understood without asking that she had betrayed my mother. She had betrayed us all.

"When your dad was convicted, I was relieved at first," Ada says. "We all were. Justice had been served, now we could heal. But then a documentarian contacted me; she was producing a film about the families and friends of murder victims. Being in that was cathartic for me. I got to tell the world about the real Prudie, not the side character she'd become in Trapper's story. Being in that film, though, brought a lot of people out of the woodwork. People who thought Trapper was innocent and I was somehow to blame for wanting justice for my sister. I got a lot of death threats. I had to change my number and move. It was awful."

"I never knew this," I say quietly.

"I didn't realize that by speaking about Prudie, I was opening myself up to a lot of people who thought *they* owned her story." She drinks the rest of her lemonade, setting the glass down with a thud. "A lot of people don't understand why I do this, my parents included. But whether or not I talk about my sister, whether or not I look into wrongful convictions or mishandled cases, Prudie will still be gone. That pain won't ever go away. So I do what I do to make sense of what happened. To retain some kind of control, maybe help a few people along the way. Because what I saw that day when I found you and my sister still haunts me, Bett, and it always will."

As she wipes her eyes, I remain frozen in my chair. I've never seen my aunt cry before or become emotional about my mom. If she truly loved her, I always thought, she wouldn't have turned her death into a career. But listening to her now... She didn't ask for this. Neither did I.

"I know I created a rift with how I choose to live," she goes on. "My parents will probably never forgive me. They come from a different generation, where grief is kept private and boxed away. But I couldn't stay silent in that big house, pretending I wasn't drowning."

"They wanted you to keep quiet," I say, thinking of all we don't say at Magnolia House. All the hurt that goes unspoken.

"They did. Speaking out hasn't been easy, but I've met some good people along the way. Others who have lost family to violent crimes, and some whose loved ones were wrongly convicted." She holds up the envelope. "I didn't only come back to Wolf Ridge to cover Melissa's murder, Bett. I also came back to meet with Marjorie Ledbetter, Jack Ledbetter's widow. I've known for years that Trapper wasn't guilty, and I'll tell you why, but this is the absolute proof."

"What? Why did you want to meet with her?" I ask, my mouth going dry.

"She contacted me shortly after he died, said she had a document I should see. He'd kept it all these years. If you're ready, you can see it too."

"I'm ready." She studies me for a beat before handing it to me, and I open it with shaking hands. The only thing inside is a single sheet of paper. It's a police report dated June 28, 2009, three days after my mother's murder.

POLICE REPORT

<u>DATE</u>: JUNE 28, 2009   CASE NO. 2846

<u>REPORTING OFFICER:</u> CARL BIGSBY

<u>INCIDENT:</u> INTERVIEW WITH BETTINA MCGRATH, VIC-TIM'S DAUGHTER

DETAIL OF EVENT: The minor child, Bettina McGrath, was interviewed with her maternal grandfather, Wells Holland, present. The child was found at the scene by her maternal aunt, Ada Holland. Mr. Holland agreed to the interview.

BIGSBY: Can you tell me what happened to your mommy?

BETTINA: When?

BIGSBY: The day she got hurt real bad. What can you remember, sweetheart?

BETTINA: She was in her room. She got quiet.

BIGSBY: What else do you remember about your mom? How did she look?

BETTINA: Her eyes were open. There was blood. I tried to get her to wake up. (The child cries.)

MR. HOLLAND: Can we finish this another time? She's too upset to go on.

BIGSBY: I'm almost done, Mr. Holland. (To the child.) Did you see your daddy? Did he say anything to you or to your mommy?

BETTINA: Daddy was gone.

BIGSBY: Did he leave after he hurt your mommy?

BETTINA: No, it wasn't my daddy.

BIGSBY: What do you mean, sweetheart?

BETTINA: Daddy wasn't home. It was the monster with the blue hands.

BIGSBY: The monster with the blue hands?

BETTINA: The monster hurt mommy and then he left.

216

And then he left.

I look up at Ada, who's watching me fiercely. "What does this mean?"

"This proves Trapper wasn't the one who killed my sister. You said so yourself—he wasn't there."

I shake my head. "He was there. I *saw* him, leaving their room."

Ada's face is filled with pity. "That's what Bigsby and Ledbetter and Wells wanted you to believe."

"So why wasn't this report in the trial transcript?" Eugenia asks. "It would have been given to his lawyer, wouldn't it?"

"His attorney received a copy of the interview," Ada says. "Just not this one. The interview used at trial was dated the following day." She looks at me. "Do you remember giving either of these interviews?"

"A little…but the memory is fuzzy." I remember talking with someone; it must have been Bigsby. They asked me about my mom. But I can't remember the other details. I don't even remember Granddad.

"I think Ledbetter and Bigsby didn't like your original answer, so they buried this first report and reinterviewed you."

"Planted false memories?" Eugenia asks.

"Exactly," Ada says. "Even before I saw this report, I knew Trapper couldn't have done it. About a year after the verdict, I ran into Leo delivering mail. He seemed…upset. It was coming up on the two-year anniversary of the murder, so I chalked it up to that. But then he told me he had seen Trapper the morning Prudie died."

"*Where?*" I manage to choke out, holding the police report so tightly I'm afraid it's going to rip in two. I fold it up and put it in my pocket.

"Leo said Trapper was standing outside Magnolia House the morning of the murder, arguing loudly with Wells about a loan. Leo swears he delivered the mail at nine thirty. And when Leo passed by the other side of the street an hour later, they were still there. Prudie was murdered around ten. Trapper couldn't have been in two places at one time. After that, he went to a bar. Witnesses corroborated it."

My ears ring. "Why didn't Leo tell anyone? It would have given Trapper an alibi."

Ada shakes her head. "He did, Bett. He went to Bigsby, who told him to keep his mouth shut or Andre would be out of a job. He'd just started on the force, so Leo backed off—he couldn't do that to his son. I checked, and there was no official record of Leo ever speaking to anyone in the Wolf Ridge PD."

My mind flashes back to Granddad's testimony at the trial. He said he didn't see my dad that day. But he had argued with him, and he wouldn't have forgotten that. Granddad never forgets. "He lied," I say, starting to feel lightheaded. "Granddad lied at trial."

Ada picks up my glass of lemonade and puts it in my hands. "Here, drink this."

I drink the whole thing down, which helps some. I no longer feel like fainting, but my stomach still roils. "I don't understand any of this," I mutter, my thoughts tumbling over each other. "They hide a report, Granddad lies about seeing my dad. Why?"

"I can't say for sure, but if I had to guess, they assumed they had their guy. And they weren't going to let a pesky thing like reasonable doubt get in the way of that."

"Bett?" Eugenia asks softly. "Maybe we should go. This is a lot of new information."

I stand. "I need to be alone for a while."

When Eugenia gets up, too, I shake my head. "But I thought your grandparents said you *can't* be out alone."

"Their word is kind of meaningless at this point," I say, stepping off the porch.

Who Killed Holly Walters?
Suspect List:
~~Hunter Jackson~~
~~Madison Tran~~
~~Natalie Baker~~
David Dennison

Who Killed Prudence McGrath?
Suspect List:
~~Trapper McGrath~~

CHAPTER
Twenty-Five

I walk through town, needing to feel my feet hit the pavement, my breath in my chest, no matter how unsafe it may be.

I need to feel something real.

I break into a jog, then a sprint. My lungs are about to explode, and a stitch tears up my side. But I don't stop until I'm on Elm Street in front of our old house. I stand there for a while, just staring at it.

This is where my story began.

There are only a few houses out here. The shittiest, saddest ones. The ones no one wants anymore. All the windows are boarded over. The sidewalk leading to the front steps is heaved up and cracked and exploding with weeds. Gray paint chips off the siding, trying to escape. Ivy grows up over the roof. It's sat empty for years—apparently no one in Wolf Ridge wants to live in a crime scene.

I'm standing in front of the house Trapper killed my mom in. That's my truth. The only story I have.

Only now it's been taken away from me.

I close my eyes and try to remember the three of us inside, happy. No…not happy. All I see is Trapper pacing, his boots thudding the wood floor, ranting about bills and money. My mom shrinking away from him. I see myself, hiding in my closet, playing with my paper dolls, pretending everything is okay, trying not to hear them arguing.

But then I remember the endless games of Uno he used to play with me. The way he used to toss me into the air and catch me, how free I felt. It wasn't all bad, was it? Maybe it could have gotten better?

This house has a tiny front landing, barely enough room for two people. The railing creaks when I grip it. I jiggle the door handle, just to see. It's locked, the rest covered with plywood.

Before I can think it through, I walk around to the backyard. It's mostly dirt with some weeds growing here and there. The shed is still here, but not much else. The back windows have been boarded over, too. But the board on my bedroom window hangs on by a single nail, and when I tug, it comes off. I lean it against the house and look through the dirty glass, the cicadas screaming all around me, but I can't see anything. I push up the sash, but it won't move. I pound along the sides and bottom of the window, and when I try again, it stutters up the frame.

The room beyond the window is diffused in shadows as I climb inside.

Floral wallpaper hangs from the walls in shreds. I hold up a section, put it back against the plaster. I remember this wallpaper, the hundreds of pink roses. I used to pretend my room was a secret garden. White paint bubbles from the window and door trim. The closet door squeals on rusted hinges, and I shine my light inside. It's empty, no old toys or little-girl clothes.

A short hallway leads into the living room at the front of the house. I lift a dirty sheet from a couch under the window; I can't remember if this was our couch or if someone else lived here before it was abandoned. I shove some of the sheet aside and sit. Ledbetter's opening statement said I was sitting on the couch watching television when she was killed.

I settle into the damp fabric and close my eyes, willing myself to travel back in time, to unlock some secret memory I've kept hidden away.

I remember a TV that sat on the floor, cartoons playing. I remember Trapper leaving early that day; he slammed the front door so hard a photo fell off the wall and shattered. I remember my mom sweeping up broken glass, keeping a smile on her face.

She wore that smile hard.

I try to imagine Trapper walking from the kitchen down the hall, knife squeezed in his fist. If I had been afraid, why didn't I go hide in my closet like always? Why did I stay on the couch that morning? My eyes snap open.

I rise from the couch and go into their bedroom.

The blood.

Her broken eyes.

This memory is fragmented; all else has fallen away except me crying out her name, shaking her, begging her to wake up.

I don't remember a monster with blue hands. Why can't I remember?

Something crashes outside, and I freeze. I move deeper into the house, searching for just one window that's not boarded over. But they all are. The panic rises in my chest, and I tiptoe back to my old bedroom. Something moves outside the window, there one second and gone the next. I ease along the wall and peer outside just as a shape disappears around the side of the house, swallowed up by shadows. I wait a couple of minutes until I can no longer stand the stench and the heat and climb outside.

Standing on the half-dead lawn I wait, listening for footsteps or heavy breathing, watching for a glint of sharp metal. My breathing returns to normal, and then all the reasons for Trapper's guilt crowd in around me once more, pushing me, pulling me as I walk around the side of the house to the front yard. The letter. Her blood on his clothing. His fingerprints on the knife.

Motive. Opportunity.

"Fuck!" I scream. My eyes land on a large rock in the yard, and I pick it up and hurl it at the house as hard as I can. It hits a boarded-up window with a thud. No crashing glass. No satisfaction. I look for something else to create damage with, but I'm all I've got.

If I had a match, I'd burn it to the ground.

I charge up the front steps, try to pry the wood off the front door, pulling and straining until my fingernails start to bleed. A yearning pounds through my guts so strongly that it takes my breath away, and I stumble down the stairs, fall onto my knees, and weep.

I want my mom.

I want my beautiful, soft-spoken mother who read to me every night at bedtime. Whose soft hands cupped my face when I was afraid, and whose gentle voice promised me we'd be okay. Everything would be okay.

But nothing is okay. Her body was my safe place, and someone took that away from me.

"Bett?" I wipe my eyes as David comes riding down the street. He flips down his kickstand and gets off his bike. "I was out for a ride and heard screaming. Are you hurt?"

My fingertips are bloody, and I hide my hands behind my back. "It's nothing. Don't worry about it."

"You can take my bike home," he offers.

I hesitate, more than a little creeped out. What is he doing all the way out here? "Thanks, David, but I can walk."

"At least let me ride along next to you. It's not safe to be out alone."

I consider saying no, but I don't want him to know I suspect him. "Yeah…sure."

My heart beats in my ears as I walk home, possibly alongside the man who killed two women, maybe even my mother. Was he in the backyard just moments ago? The spokes on David's bike make incessant clicks, but he doesn't try to make idle chitchat. He keeps his distance, sometimes pulling ahead or falling behind. He seems like the same David I've always known, gentle and kind. Wouldn't hurt a fly. Would he?

I keep my hand fisted around my phone in my pocket.

When we get to my house, he stops at the end of our driveway. "Try to get some rest tonight," he says. "Things will seem better in the morning. They always do." He smiles before riding back down the street.

I turn and face the house, this place I've called home for most of my life.

Why am I suddenly afraid to go inside?

CHAPTER Twenty-Six

A few days with Ardis away and our breakfasts have changed dramatically. Gone are the piles of pancakes and omelets bursting with cheese. Grams sets out a plate of burnt toast, a jug of milk, and a box of Honey Nut Cheerios.

"Sorry about the toast," she apologizes as Granddad and I sit at the table the next morning. "That new toaster is a bit finicky."

"It's okay, Grams," I assure her, spreading some jam on my toast. I take a bite, and it practically crumbles on my tongue. But the jam acts as a kind of glue, holding it together a little. I smile and say, "It's good!"

Satisfied with my answer, she pours herself a bowl of cereal. Granddad stares at the choices laid out before him, and I watch as he gives the toast a critical eye before pouring his own bowl of Cheerios. He's dressed as usual in his suit and tie, perfectly combed hair. But today it seems like a costume he wears to convince the world he's a good man, not a liar.

"I went to see Ada yesterday," I announce, taking a cue out of Eugenia's playbook. No lead-up. Just blunt statements.

Granddad nearly chokes on his cereal. "She's still in town?" A bit of milk dribbles down his chin, and he wipes it with his cloth napkin.

"Yes, at the inn."

"How does she seem?" Grams asks, not quite looking at me, trying to act as if she's not dying to see her daughter. It's obvious now that staying away from her was my grandfather's idea.

"She's doing well, I think. Looking into the murders in town. She found evidence that Gregory Hornsby made a false confession."

Granddad stands and pours himself a cup of coffee. "She should leave police work to the police." I think of the crime boards in Eugenia's attic and almost laugh.

"She spoke with Marjorie Ledbetter, too," I continue, and this time Granddad full-on chokes on his coffee.

"Wells, are you all right?" Grams asks.

"Fine, fine," he manages to say. Once he stops coughing, he asks me to follow him to his office. He tells Grams it's Harvard stuff, that he doesn't want to bore her. "I don't know what you're playing at, Bettina Jane, but I don't want you to spend time with Ada. She's trouble."

"Why? Because you can't control her the way you control everyone else?"

"What's that supposed to mean?"

The idea of being honest with him about the police report terrifies me. I feel like I'm going to come unstitched and float away. But Ada was right when she said there was no going back. Playing happy little family is no longer an option for me.

"Marjorie Ledbetter gave Ada the report of the interview I did with the police."

"And?" he asks. "That's in the public record. I could've gotten it for you if you'd asked."

"The *first* interview, Granddad. The one you and Ledbetter suppressed."

Granddad doesn't move, doesn't even blink. The gears spin behind his eyes, so I pull the copy of the report out of my pocket and unfold it. He takes it from me, eyes scanning quickly. Then he collapses into the leather couch in front of the fireplace. I stand there, unsure of what to say or do.

"I'm not a perfect man," he says after a while. "I've made many mistakes in my life. I never purported to be infallible." He turns toward me. "Vivian tells me I'm stubborn. And I suppose she's right. But when I see something I know is wrong, I try to correct it. Your mother wouldn't listen to reason. I tried to protect her, but all I did was push her closer to *him*. And then I lost her forever."

My heart speeds up, and blood rushes in my ears. "Is that why you had Bigsby interview me again? Did you tell me what to say?"

He runs his hand over his forehead. "That report changes nothing, Bettina Jane. You were a young child who'd been through a trauma. You were confused, that's all. When he spoke to you again, you were much clearer about what happened."

"But you knew about this first report. You were *there*. Why didn't Ledbetter give it to Trapper's lawyer?"

He sighs. "It doesn't matter."

"It does to me," I say, my voice barely more than a whisper. "I said Trapper wasn't there, that it was the 'monster with blue hands' that killed my mom. And you both ignored me. You didn't believe me, Granddad! And then I testified against him and said he *was* there. And now he's in prison for life."

Granddad's lower lip trembles, and my stomach drops into my shoes. "He killed my daughter. My Prudence. We did what we had to do to see him locked away. I won't apologize for that."

"What do you mean, *we*? You and the chief? Jack Ledbetter?"

"Your father is not a good man, Bettina Jane! Any man who puts his hands on a woman the way he did doesn't deserve an ounce of your sympathy. Do you understand me?"

Thoughts slosh around in my brain. "Trapper had an alibi. Did you know that? Leo saw the two of you in our driveway the morning she was killed. He tried to report it, but Bigsby threatened him."

Granddad shakes his head. "Leo must be mistaken. I never saw Trapper the day your mother died."

"Why don't I believe you?"

"Your father," he says, ignoring my question, "isn't worth twisting yourself up about. He's a liar and an abuser. You're not like him. You never were, and you never could be."

"But he's my dad," I say. "I can't just pretend that away. And I can't pretend that first interview doesn't exist. What if he didn't kill her? What if that's why women in Wolf Ridge are dying again?"

"You can't honestly believe that."

"I didn't, until I found Melissa Atkins and Holly Walters. They're connected to Mom's murder somehow. I…I think that might be why Ledbetter died. Maybe he couldn't live with the guilt of putting Trapper behind bars for a crime he didn't commit."

"I'm done with this discussion," he says, standing abruptly. "Let's finish our breakfast, *now*, before we upset your grandmother any further." He leaves me in his office with too many questions. Tears prick the backs of my eyes. There's only one person who can corroborate what Leo saw, who could possibly give me more insight into exactly what happened the day my mom died.

And he's the last person I want to see.

———

Now that the narrative that is my life has been exposed as a total lie, I don't feel the need to keep up pretenses like *going to school* or *telling my grandparents I'm ditching class to see Trapper.*

Eugenia insists on taking me. I'm glad I'm not doing this completely alone.

The drive passes quickly, and soon we pull up outside Bertie Correctional in Windsor. Tall fencing covered by coiled barbed wire surrounds the prison. It's hot outside, but I'm wearing my mom's old jean jacket anyway. I pull it tight as a chill runs through me. As soon as we step out of the hearse, an officer and a leashed German shepherd approach our vehicle.

"Open the doors and trunk, please," the officer says, letting the dog off the leash. When I was little, I thought the search dogs were pets, but when I tried to touch one, the officer gave me a stern warning. I never made that mistake again.

"You're fine to go in," the officer tells us after determining we're not hiding weapons or bricks of cocaine in the back of the hearse. Eugenia and I park and enter through the visitor's section, the warmth of the sunshine shut out behind us. We empty our pockets, and then we get patted down. They touch me like I'm a slab of meat: up one leg, down the other.

"Do you want me to come with you?" Eugenia asks after we get checked in.

"Thanks, but I'll be okay. This shouldn't take too long." I've never visited him without Grams before, and I miss her hugs and positive affirmations. Eugenia's black sweater and maudlin face aren't making me feel quite as empowered.

"Don't let him get under your skin. And don't let him know about the report right away. Feel him out first."

I nod and take off my cross necklace and silver thumb ring and give them to her. You can't wear jewelry in the visiting room or any clothing resembling the prisoners' uniforms. (Of course, my scratchy school uniform is about as far from a jumpsuit as you can get.)

The visitation room reminds me of the lunchroom at my junior high school. The cinder block walls are painted white, and the small metal tables and chairs are bolted to the floor. There's room for four people at each table. The whole place smells like sweat and sadness. Trapper's not here yet, so I pick a table next to a window and sit.

Cameras mounted to the walls point in every direction, and I wonder who's watching me today.

My mouth is dry, but I don't want to go back to the waiting room for a Coke. A woman and a little boy sit at the next table, playing a game of Candy Land with an inmate. Tattoos on his knuckles spell out STAY TRUE, and his eyes sparkle as he watches his son. I turn away as the prisoner door opens.

Trapper stands about a head taller than the guard who lets him into the room. He's not shackled or chained. He spots me, nods, and strides across the linoleum in long, confident steps. He sits across from me and folds his hands on the table, as if he's praying.

"Hello, bug," he says, his voice hoarse. "Wasn't expectin' to see you today."

I hate that nickname.

"Trapper."

Stubble covers his chin and cheeks, new from our last visit. His mustache is as thick as ever, and the hair at his temples has begun to gray. It curls, same as mine, and I wish I had worn my hair in a bun. Tattoos on his neck peek out the top of his jumpsuit. I try never to search his face for glimpses of mine, but I can see it in his crooked smile.

"How's school?" he asks. "You have finals soon, right?"

I lean back and cross my arms. "They're done."

Trapper cracks his neck. "How're Vivian and Wells?"

I find myself looking at him with fresh eyes, like if I try hard enough, I'll find the truth etched into his skin. "They're fine," I say, my voice cracking.

"Good, good." His jaw flexes, and I wonder how long he's planning to wear his Normal Dad mask.

The little boy next to us giggles and claps. "Good job, son! You won!" his father says, kissing his cheek.

"Cute, huh?" I ask, nodding toward them. "A nice family moment. Wonder what that's like."

He blinks. "We can play a game, if you want. I'm sure there's a deck of Uno cards around here someplace."

"I don't want to play Uno with you."

He scratches the back of his head. "I don't want to fight with you, bug," he says. I lick my lips and swallow. "Are you thirsty?" he asks.

"Nope."

He rises from the table and approaches one of the guards, then returns with a can of Coke, my favorite. He sets it on the table in front of me. "I can tell you're thirsty, so just do your old man a favor and drink it."

I roll my eyes but pop the tab anyway. It's icy cold, and it calms my nerves a touch. Trapper sits, leans back, and locks his hands behind his head. I wait for him to say something, but he just looks at me. Finally, I set the can down.

"So?" he asks. "You came here for a reason. Still trying to convince me to give up my rights? I got your letter, by the way. Can't say it didn't feel like a punch to the gut."

"I need you to be honest with me," I say through clenched teeth.

"Honest about what?"

"Honest about what happened to Mom," I say, and his left eye twitches. "I want you to tell me exactly what happened that day. When you woke up, what you ate, where you went, who you talked to."

"I thought you knew it all, bug."

"Just tell me. Please."

He puts his hands back on the table. "Listen, I get that you don't trust me. You've had Wells and Vivian in your ear for ten years, telling you I'm evil. They think the whole goddamn world stops when one of 'em takes a shit. Well, guess what? I got a life, too." He drums his fingers against the table. "But I guess I can see where you're coming from."

"You *guess*?" I ask, then hold my tongue.

"You lost your mom, but I lost my wife and my daughter. My *freedom*."

I dig my fingernails into my palms. Trapper watches me with cool detachment, waiting for a reaction. I won't give him one.

"I heard about Jack Ledbetter." He runs his pointer finger across his throat, and I turn sideways in my seat. "Been ten years since that sham trial. Don't the timing seem a bit convenient?"

"Maybe," I say, unwilling to give any more than that.

His eyes sparkle. "Agreeing with your old man, huh? That's new."

"Your whereabouts on June 25, 2009. That's all I came here for."

"Well, well," he says. "I see you still got no patience, just like when you was knee-high to a grasshopper. You used to whine about wanting your ice cream while I was still scooping it." He scratches his chin. "This Ledbetter thing has me rattled. I've been locked up ten years now for a crime I didn't commit. Someone else did. That someone else is still out there. And now the man who put me behind bars tied a belt around his own neck. He knows something he ain't told nobody."

My face burns, and I clench my teeth together as tightly as I can. I may not remember everything about the day my mother died, but the more I force it, the more I remember other things. I remember Trapper and his temper. I remember the bruises on her body. I remember the fear. It stayed with me, just below the surface, coiled and waiting. His violence matches up with that police report.

A monster with the blue hands. Maybe I really was just a confused girl, my memory warped by the shock of what I saw.

"Tell me about that day, Trapper, or I'm leaving."

He leans back in his chair. "It's the same story I've told you a million times, bug."

"Then you should have no trouble telling it one more time."

He smiles. "Nothing comes for free, right? Growing up in that fancy house, you should know that better than anyone."

"What do you want?"

"I don't want nothing from you, Bett, except for you to stop for a minute and think about my side of things."

"I don't need this," I say, rising from the table.

"I'll tell you everything," he says as I turn toward the door. I freeze. "All the ugly parts, too."

"What's the catch?" I ask, my back still turned to him.

"Sit down and I'll tell you."

I retake my seat, keeping my body angled away from him. He's quiet apart from his breathing.

"I come from nothing," he says after a while. His voice is small, and his green eyes are clear as he speaks. "You ain't never really been around my family, not since you was real little. But I come from nothing. Wells and Vivian couldn't believe that I loved Prudie for anything more than her money, but I did. I still do. I *always* will."

My throat burns, and I breathe out.

"I'm sorry, bug. I ain't trying to upset you."

"Aren't you?" I manage to get out.

He shakes his head, pulls at the neck of his jumpsuit. "I'm nothing in this place. I can't afford a decent attorney. The one the state gave me was a flunky, got arrested for stalking last year. I didn't get a fair trial. Not by a country fucking mile."

"Then why?" I whisper. "*Why* is she gone?"

He looks at the table, hangs his head. "I made a lot of mistakes." When he finally looks up, all traces of the glib, overconfident Trapper have vanished. "I got up early that day, before the sun. I was hungover from the night before. We had a party at our house. We argued about money. We were always arguing about money." He looks down at the table. "I never felt good enough for her. Left her that nasty note. Then I went over to Wells's place, asking for a loan. We were way behind on rent, and I didn't want Prudie to find out I'd lost another job. But he wouldn't listen, said he would take you and

Prudie away from me. I went to the bar for a beer and was driving back home when I got passed by a squad car. Ada was there with you in the front yard, bawling her fucking eyes out. And you...covered in all that blood. I thought you'd been hurt. I didn't realize..." He swallows a few times. "Think about it, bug. I had more motive to kill Wells than your mama."

He goes quiet, and I feel like my eyes are going to pop out of my skull. If money was the motive, then it's true. She didn't have any to give. As long as she chose to stay with my dad, she was cut off. I take another swig of Coke.

"What about the blood? Her blood was all over your clothes."

He shakes his head. "She'd had a nosebleed the night before, and I wore the same pants. It was hardly anything, not the slam-dunk evidence Ledbetter made it out to be."

"Did you do it, Trapper?"

He looks me in the eyes. "You know I didn't."

My scalp prickles. "Did you send someone over there to do it for you?" I don't know where this idea has come from.

He frowns. "Who on earth told you that?"

The monster with the blue hands. "Just answer the question."

He shakes his head. Then a hint of that Trapper gleam returns. "I hear they got two more dead bodies down in Wolf Ridge. Is that really why you're here?"

Just like that, our moment of truth, or whatever that was, is gone.

"What do you know about it?"

"Just what I seen on the news, and what my new lawyer tells me. Blond ladies, right? Stabbed? The creepy smiles?"

I swallow and nod.

"I figured. I seen a reporter saying it might be a copycat, but that ain't true. Whoever killed your mama killed those women, too. And probably that gal, Cherry. Makes my bones itch just thinking about it. Everyone down in Wolf Ridge from Carl Bigsby to your granddaddy thinks I'm a monster who murdered your mom and Cherry. Nah. *Someone* in Wolf Ridge has an impulse control problem, but it ain't me. I can promise you that, though I'm surprised they haven't tried to pin those on me, too."

"Who do you think did it?"

"You've always been so sure it was me," he says, narrowing his eyes. "What the hell is going on to make you doubt yourself? Never have before. You're stubborn, like your old man."

"Ada's back in town," I admit. "She's looking into the murders."

His face clouds. "Your aunt has been nosing around the case for years. When she found out Leo could give me an alibi, she came to see me that same day."

"You *know* about that?"

He nods. "But no one would listen, not even my shit-for-brains lawyer. It gave me hope, and hope is a dangerous thing around here. Thinking there's a chance? Only makes you sink deeper into the darkness."

"How come you never told me about Leo?"

He sighs. "You wouldn't have believed me, bug. You hate being here, and I didn't want to make it worse for you than it already was."

I stare out the window, watching the wind blow through the trees. "There's more," I say. "Ada spoke to Marjorie Ledbetter."

"The widow?" he asks, leaning toward me.

I face him again. "She gave Ada a police interview I did, right after Mom died. But it wasn't the interview they submitted to your lawyer or the court. It was dated a day earlier." I take a deep breath. "In that first interview, I said you weren't there when she died. That some 'monster with blue hands' killed Mom. Jack Ledbetter must've hung on to it all these years."

Trapper closes his eyes, takes a deep breath. I expect him to punch the table or swear. But he just sits there, silent.

"Dad?" I ask, the word sounding strange, foreign. "Say something."

He opens his eyes. "I'll reach out to Ada, get a copy of that report to my lawyer. See if it goes anywhere." He speaks so calmly, it scares me.

"But aren't you upset? All this time, you had *two* alibis. And they lied about it."

Trapper cracks each knuckle, slowly and deliberately. "The wheels of justice move slow, bug, and they often don't move at all for people like me. I ain't stupid enough to think this will change a damn thing. Your grandfather is lucky I'm stuck behind bars. Otherwise, I'd be liable to kill *him*."

"I should go," I say, standing. "My friend is waiting for me."

Trapper stands as well. "Listen, bug, you be careful, you hear? It's not safe in Wolf Ridge. You stick close to home. Don't go out at night. Okay?"

"I'll be careful." I turn to go, and then Trapper says my name.

"I love you, bug," he says.

I walk away, not saying it back. I can't remember the last time I said it, if I ever did.

CHAPTER
Twenty-Seven

Wolf Ridge appears on the horizon, and the muscles in my shoulders knot up. As Eugenia cruises down Market Street, I grip my seat belt as the fountain sprays a fine mist on the hearse. We didn't speak much on the ride home from prison. I mostly stared out the window, hollowed out by my visit.

Trapper McGrath did not kill my mother.

Eugenia turns off the radio, which is mostly static anyway. "Okay, talk to me. You've been catatonic long enough."

I lean my head back against the seat. "Do I have to?"

"No, but you can if you need to."

"Later. Right now, I just want to go home and crawl into my bed."

She's turning onto my street when a police car speeds past us, lights flashing. Eugenia yanks on the wheel and whips back onto the street, following behind. The police car parks in front of Natalie's house, its cherries washing the houses out in pale reds and blues. Eugenia parks a block away as an ambulance zips by. A few neighbors stand in the street, arms crossed, whispering to each other. Lydia's sitting on the front steps. A volunteer EMT kneels in front of her, taping a bandage to her arm. Blood has already started to seep through. Chantal is speaking with her. Andre stands a few feet away with David Dennison, who keeps gesturing at the house and back to Lydia.

"What the hell?" I ask as we approach the crowd, everyone mumbling and whispering. I accidentally trip into someone, who stops me from falling over. It's Brady Adams. "Do you know what happened?" I ask.

"I think she got attacked," Brady says, turning to watch the spectacle. Half the neighborhood is here. Hunter hangs at the back of the crowd. When he catches my eye, he turns and goes into his house.

"Who attacked her?" Eugenia asks.

Brady shrugs, riveted to the scene. "No one knows yet."

The EMT tapes up Lydia's arm as Natalie comes running down the street. "Mom!" she cries.

"I'm okay, baby," Lydia says, wrapping her free arm around Nat. The EMT helps Lydia into the back of the ambulance, and Nat joins her. I move closer to Andre and David, straining to hear them. But Chantal steps in front of me.

"Stay back," she says. "This is a crime scene."

"Is she okay?" I ask. "Did someone attack her? Did you arrest them?"

"That's none of your concern." She pushes me back, and then she shoves stakes in the grass and stretches crime scene tape between them. Andre and David walk to the squad car. David gets in the front seat, and I stand in the road, watching along with everyone else as they drive away.

Eugenia shakes her keys at me. "Let's go to the hospital. Question Lydia about what happened. Hopefully she got a good look at whoever attacked her."

I give her a look. "We can't just bust into her hospital room and start asking questions."

"No, but we can bring her flowers. Come on," she grabs my arm and pulls me down the street.

———

People stare as Eugenia parks the hearse at the hospital in Elmdale, a few miles outside Wolf Ridge. She picks out a shitty bouquet of half-dead daisies at the gift shop, and as we hustle to the nurse's station, Natalie steps off the elevator. Her face is drained of color, her cheeks sunken in.

I forget we hate each other for a moment and almost try to hug her. "I'm so sorry about your mom," I say instead, letting my arms dangle at my sides.

"Here," Eugenia says, thrusting the flowers at her. "We got these for your mom. How is she?"

Nat takes them but doesn't say anything.

"What happened?" I ask.

Natalie's bottom lip quivers. "She said s-some guy came through the back door with a knife. I was over at Madison's house." Her face crumples.

Eugenia and I just stand there. Finally, Eugenia says, "How about a coffee?"

Natalie nods, and the three of us take the elevator to the small cafeteria in the basement. We get three coffees and sit at a table at the back.

Natalie rubs her eyes before taking a drink. "This coffee…," she trails off.

"…tastes like ass," I finish for her.

She nods. "I should probably go back. She was just getting stitched up when I left."

"Is she staying overnight?"

"They want her to, but she refuses."

I smile slightly. "Sounds like something your mom would say."

Nat doesn't smile back. "I'm just so glad David was there," she says, looking up at me then quickly away.

"What was David's part in all this?" Eugenia demands, zeroing in on Natalie. I kick her under the table, but she kicks me back.

"Mom said he'd come over to clean our gutters. She kicked the intruder in the balls and ran into the front yard. Chantal says David must've scared the guy off."

Eugenia and I exchange a look. Natalie chews on her thumbnail, breaking the skin, and then wipes a bubble of blood on her shorts.

"Did she see who he was?" I ask. "Any identifying birthmarks or tattoos or anything?"

"He wore a mask," she says, "so she couldn't see who he was. I better get back." She pushes away from the table and hurries across the cafeteria without another word.

As soon as she's out of the room, Eugenia leans toward me. "It's David, Bett. He dates Melissa, and she dies. He goes to church with Holly, and she dies. He helps Lydia with her gutters, and she gets stabbed. We've got to do something!" A nurse at the table next to us stops chewing her salad and stares at us.

"Calm down," I say, my voice low. "People are listening."

"Right, sorry." She takes a deep breath. "What do we do now?"

"We can't go to the police without any evidence. They'll just blow us off. Maybe they've released Gregory Hornsby." I punch his name into my phone, and a news story pops up. "They're dropping the charges," I say, quickly scanning the story. "Bigsby said new evidence shows Hornsby wasn't in Wolf Ridge at the time of the murders. But he's still under arrest for making a false confession."

"What we really need is some hard evidence against David. Something to take to the police that shows he did it, or at least gives them probable cause to search his home."

"And how do you propose we collect said evidence?"

"We break into his house, obviously," she says.

I shake my head and get up from the table. Eugenia follows me to the elevator. "No way," I tell her. "David doesn't live that far from the diner. Sheila or someone would catch us." My phone buzzes with a call from Granddad, but I ignore it.

She punches the button for the lobby and crosses her arms over her chest. "We go at night when we know David is out of town."

"David is literally always at the diner," I tell her. The doors slide open, and we wait for a woman to step off before getting on. "As far as I know, he doesn't go anywhere or do anything other than work."

"Let's not make assumptions," she cautions as we arrive in the lobby. "Everyone has a hobby, Bett."

"Even serial killers?" I ask.

She gives me a strange look. "They're more passionate about their hobbies than almost anyone."

It takes me a minute to get her meaning, and I shudder. My phone rings again, and this time I answer it. "What?"

"Bettina," he says, his voice falsely cheerful. "Are you forgetting something?"

I frown as we step outside into the humid air. "Forgetting what?"

"Your interview. Your *Harvard* interview."

"Oh shit," I say. "I totally forgot that was today." Between skipping school, going to the prison, and Lydia's attack, it slipped my mind. But I can't tell my grandfather any of this.

"Come home right away. I told Ms. Taylor you had a study group that ran late."

"It might be a few minutes," I say. "I'm not exactly in town."

"Wherever you are, break the speed limit and get home immediately. We'll discuss your punishment later." He hangs up before I can say anything.

"What was that all about?" Eugenia asks, unlocking the hearse. It's the perfect vehicle to transport me to my doom.

"I forgot about my Harvard interview."

"I'll push Bertha as fast as she'll go."

"You named your hearse *Bertha*?"

"You want to talk about hearse names, or you want me to drive?"

"Drive," I say, and slip inside, hoping I make it through this interview alive.

CHAPTER
Twenty-Eight

When I come into the parlor, Grams sits in her rose chair, legs crossed at the ankles, tea in her hand. She's wearing her favorite yellow cardigan and matching skirt. Pearls, naturally. Hair freshly done up at the salon. Granddad perches across from her on the settee. He sips his coffee nervously, looking from me to Ms. Taylor, Harvard class of '99, who sits on one end of the sofa, a leather binder resting open on her lap. Her shoulder-length brown hair has been expertly highlighted with streaks of caramel.

"My apologies for being late," I say, carefully taking a seat on the other end of the sofa and smoothing my skirt demurely. "I was helping a classmate during our study group, and I lost track of time." I look out the window just in time to see Eugenia pulling away in the hearse.

She glances at her watch. "That's fine, it was just a few minutes. You're my only interview this afternoon."

"More coffee, Ms. Taylor?" Granddad asks, leaping up. She pushes her tortoiseshell glasses up her nose and smiles weakly as he takes her full cup into the dining room. Her perfect posture is almost threatening.

Granddad returns with her cup, steam rising, and sets it down on the coffee table. She leaves it. "Now, where were we?" he asks jovially.

Ms. Taylor looks at her binder. "I was about to ask Bett what she was possibly interested in studying at college."

Three sets of eyes retrain themselves on me.

I clear my throat and cross my legs. "The law," I answer, my voice catching. My mouth is so dry I have to peel my tongue off the roof of my mouth. Granddad and I have rehearsed this a hundred times, but I'm nervous.

Ms. Taylor jots something down. "Could you please expand on that?"

I clear my throat again. "My mother was murdered. By my father, or so they say. Anyway, I want to put murderers, rapists, and other bad people in prison. Make the world safer, especially for women."

Granddad shoots me a look, and I shrug.

"I'm so sorry," she says, not missing a beat. She must hear all kinds of sob stories during these interviews. "That must be incredibly difficult for you."

"I was in the house when it happened, but I don't remember much."

She writes down something else before removing her glasses and shifting toward me. Her dark eyes laser in on mine. "Harvard is an incredibly competitive environment with academic rigors and emotional stressors you won't experience anywhere else. Harvard students must be able to think on a new level."

"She'll have no problem with that, I can assure you," Granddad interjects. "She's a straight A honor student. Smart as a whip. She'll be working part-time with me in my law office this summer. There's nothing Bettina Holland can't handle, and she'll make a fine lawyer one day."

Ms. Taylor smiles tersely at him. Then she focuses back on me. "How do you think you'll be able to handle the pressures of Harvard, Bett?"

My temples pound, and all I can think about is Trapper in his jumpsuit. He didn't kill my mom, and Granddad knew that, and I don't know how much longer I can sit here pretending to care about my future when my past has been obliterated, women are dying, and Nat's mom is in the hospital.

"Honestly?" I finally say.

"Yes, please," she says, readying her pen over her binder. "Honesty is what I'm looking for."

I take a deep breath. "I visit my dad in prison every six months, and after those visits, I usually drink, eat a lot of junk food, and sleep. Maybe hang out with the wrong boys. At least, that's how I've been coping lately. Can I handle the stresses of Harvard? I wouldn't know until I got there, but given the current state of my life, I'd have to say no. I wouldn't be able to handle it."

"She's kidding," Granddad says, chuckling lightly with a pained smile on his face. "Sometimes her colorful sense of humor goes a bit too far. Isn't that right, Bett?"

I open my mouth to apologize, to right this runaway train wreck of a college interview, but I can't keep trying to be what they want me to be: the perfect daughter that was taken from them. I'm just Bett, still trying to figure out who I am and how I fit. And lying to a college recruiter isn't going to help anyone, least of all me.

"I'm sorry, Grams, Granddad," I say. "But I have no idea what I really want to do with my life, let alone where I want to go to school—or if I even want to." I look to Ms. Taylor. "I'm sorry I wasted your time."

I stand and leave the room before anyone can respond.

———

Ms. Taylor is long gone, and Granddad paces the floor in front of me.

"I explained to Ms. Taylor that you've not been feeling well as of late, and she agreed to reschedule the interview. You're very lucky, Bettina Jane."

"How am I lucky?"

He stops and stares down at me. "Is this a game to you?"

"No."

"You act like it. Where in God's name were you today? You knew you had your interview."

"I forgot it was today."

"She forgot," he laughs, and begins pacing again.

I clear my throat. "Maybe we should talk about this later, when everyone's cooled down."

He sighs. "This is just like what your mother pulled."

"What do you mean?" I ask.

In the corner, Grams closes her eyes, shaking slightly, and I feel guilty that we're upsetting her. But I had to speak the truth.

Granddad removes his glasses and pinches the skin between his eyes. "Why are you suddenly doubting Harvard, doubting a law career? Isn't that what you've been working toward?"

I shake my head. "It's your dream, not mine. I went along with it because I looked up to you, wanted to make you proud."

"That can't be true, you...," he mutters, trailing off.

"It is, Granddad. You just never listen to me—not really. You're so afraid I'm going to become my mother that you don't *see* me. Did you know I enjoy acting? That I even applied to a summer program? Got in, too, but I declined. I knew you'd never let me go."

Granddad shakes his head. "Bettina Jane!"

"Please," Grams moans. "No more arguing."

Granddad sits down, leans his elbows on his knees. "I want you to be honest with me, Bettina Jane. Just what in God's name has been going on with you lately? Does it have something to do with your father? Or that boy you've been wasting your time with?"

"Xavier?" I ask.

"Is that his name? Well, he doesn't seem like the type of person with which you should be associating. His father used to be our lawn man!"

"So what? There's nothing wrong with that job." I don't tell him that Xavier isn't speaking to me and probably never will again. It's the principle.

"Maybe not. But that boy is *no good* for you. And that Cline girl! She's a strange person to be running around with. People talk."

"Eugenia? She's been a good friend to me. My best friend, really. She's actually supportive, unlike *some* people."

He frowns. "You've got one year left of high school. Just one year. Then college. Don't muck up your entire future for the undertaker's daughter and a guy who's going nowhere."

"Which guy? Xavier or Trapper?"

"Jesus, Bettina Jane. You're going to put me into an early grave."

Grams drops her glass on the rug, and tea soaks into the carpet. Her eyes roll up into her head, and she slumps forward.

Granddad leaps up. "Vivian!" He grabs her to keep her from toppling onto the floor. "Call an ambulance!" he shouts, but my fingers are shaking so badly I can barely dial.

CHAPTER
Twenty-Nine

The emergency room is a blur of white-clad doctors and nurses and beeping machines and bad fluorescent lighting. Granddad and I sit next to each other in scratchy chairs in the waiting room, each slurping on terrible cups of coffee he bought us from a vending machine.

"I did this... didn't I?" I whisper. My headache has grown steadily worse since we waited with her for the paramedics, then drove together in Granddad's car. Every time I blink, I see her eyes roll back and know that this is my fault.

I poison everyone I love.

Granddad puts his coffee down. "Bett, stop that. You did *not* cause this. Don't even say such a thing. She's going to be fine."

"Then why haven't they come out yet to tell us what's wrong?"

"They will," he says. "These things take time, is all. And I'm right here."

I pick up my phone to text Eugenia when a woman in a white coat approaches Granddad. "Are you Mr. Holland?"

"Yes, how's Vivian?"

Granddad and I stand, and he puts his arms around me.

"She's had a very small stroke," the doctor explains. "We're going to run some more tests, but I believe it was a thrombotic stroke. This is a very common type of stroke, where a blood clot forms in one of the arteries that supplies blood to the brain. We've given her a clot-busting drug, which seems to have worked. She's awake and alert if you'd like to see her."

The doctor turns, and Granddad follows. But I can't.

He stops and looks back. "Bettina?"

When we get to her room, I stand just outside the door. Granddad rushes inside, and I can hear Grams's voice, faint but there, reassuring him that she's fine, apologizing for scaring everyone. She asks for me, and Granddad ducks out into the hall. "Bettina? Your grandmother would like to see you."

Stepping into the cold room, my breath leaves me. Grams looks impossibly small in the bed, covered with a blanket, hooked up to machines. I try to move closer to her, but it's like my feet have stopped working. It hits me suddenly that she won't be here forever, that one day my second mother will also die. She might not even know about the hidden police report, or that Trapper's alibi got swept under the rug. Does she know that her daughter's killer is still out there somewhere?

"Bett," she says, her face pale. "I'm so sorry I frightened you."

"Don't apologize to me," I say, wiping away the stupid tears that won't stay put. "I'm the one who ruined my interview today. And I've been stressing you out for weeks. I'm the one who's sorry."

She holds out her arms, and though I don't deserve a hug right now, I lean down anyway, wrapping my arms around her gently, afraid she'll break. She rubs my back in slow circles, like she used to do when I had nightmares as a little kid. She'd sit with me for hours if she needed to, until I fell back asleep.

Granddad pulls a chair over, and the sound of metal scraping linoleum breaks something inside me. Maybe it's too close to the sounds I heard at the prison today, but this room is suddenly way too small with not enough oxygen. "Are you all right?" Grams asks.

"I think I need some water. I'll be right back."

Before I get to the door, she says, "I love you to the moon."

"And back again," I manage to say before hurrying into the hall.

———

R.E.M.'s "Shiny Happy People" blares from the hearse speakers as Eugenia and I cruise through town toward the cemetery. Liam texted me about a party, and I couldn't get out of the hospital fast enough. I texted Granddad from the lobby, saying I was having bad cramps and going home to bed. He replied that he'd be with Grams all night and to get some rest.

It's better if I'm not with her. I just hurt her.

"Why don't your parents let you use their actual car?" I ask, aiming the vents toward my face. The air-conditioning barely blows anything at me. "Don't they trust you?"

"Feel free to walk."

"This song *really* pisses me off," I say, tightening my mom's shawl. "No one is this happy."

She turns down the volume. "You're upset about something." It's not a question. It never is with Eugenia. Most days I like that about her. Not today.

"Whatever."

"Don't be so obtuse. If you're upset, just tell me. Maybe I can help."

I laugh. "I highly doubt you could help me with this. No one can."

"Try me."

I give her the side-eye. "Did your dad go to prison for killing your mom in front of you? Only it turns out, he actually didn't do it? And your testimony put him in prison? And then you blew your college interview and gave your grandmother a stroke?"

"Wait, what?" she asks. "Your grandmother had a *stroke*? When?"

"Earlier this afternoon. They said it was minor, but still. I know it's all my fault."

"We've been driving for fifteen minutes, and you wait this long to tell me?" When I don't answer, she grips the wheel harder. "I'm glad she's okay. No wonder you're in such a bad mood."

I roll my eyes. "Let's just go to this party. I don't want to think anymore tonight, about Grams or anything. I need beer and a couple uneventful hours in the woods. Can you give me that?"

She turns the volume back up, and we don't speak for the rest of the drive. The sun has just begun to fall when we park in the lot and traipse through the trees, past Elizabeth's headstone, to the keg. I take a cup off the stack and pump it full to the brim. "Want one?" I ask her.

"I'm the sober driver."

"One won't kill you."

"Tell that to the drunk drivers who've been laid out in my basement."

I shudder and gulp down half my beer, put off by her lack of tact. We move away from the keg and take stock of who's here. Half the senior class stands together, snapping selfies and crying, pretending they'll keep in touch. A sprinkling of juniors lingers in smaller groups. For a party, it's pretty somber. No music, no fire. I guess two murders will do that. Natalie's standing with Madison and Liam. She catches me looking at her and turns away. A few men stand apart from everyone, watching us and scrolling on their phones. I nudge Eugenia. "Who are they? Parents?"

Eugenia follows my gaze. "I don't recognize them." One of them, a guy with a hoodie and a potbelly, looks at me and then whispers to the others. "But they seem to know *you*," she adds. She's right. They're all watching me now. Probably true-crime podcasters and vloggers who crawled out of their parents' basements to exploit me.

"Losers," I say, before I take another swig of beer, roll my shoulders, and turn my back to the creepy guys. My eyes land on Xavier, sitting alone on a fallen tree trunk, staring into his drink. I almost didn't recognize him at first; his hair has been shorn away.

"Come on, I see Xavier," I say and head back to the keg. I hold my breath as I pump, trying to work up the guts to talk to him.

"But you just had a beer," Eugenia says. "And besides, aren't you two not speaking?"

"Which is why I need another beer."

"You're drinking to alter your mental state."

"Duh." I flick her forehead and finish my beer in one long pull. A couple of junior guys nearby clap for me, and Liam refills my drink.

"Glad you could make it," he says.

"Did you see those old guys?" I ask, and start downing the new one, too.

"Yeah, they tried asking me about the murders. We told them to piss off, but they're still hanging around."

Soon a group of juniors gathers around us, hooting and egging me on. Fresh beers appear, and I make them disappear. I am a void.

"I think you should stop," Eugenia says, grabbing a full cup out of my hands and dumping it on the dirt. A few people boo.

"I was drinking that! Don't be wasteful."

Eugenia shakes her head. "Let's go." She grabs my elbow, but I shake her off.

"Keep your hands off me! You're not my *mom*. She's dead, remember?"

Eugenia doesn't blink. "I said let's go. You're sad. Getting drunk with these people isn't going to help. They're not your friends."

"What would *you* know about it?" I sneer, my voice as hard as the gravestone I stumble into. "You've never *had* friends, remember?"

"*Bett*," Eugenia says, stepping closer.

The men hold their phones toward us, probably filming. "*Eugenia*," I say, turning away from them. "You don't know anything about me. Not really. And honestly, what do I know about you? Other than playing detective, we don't have anything in common."

Eugenia glares at me. "You're drunk, Bett. Stop talking before you say something you'll regret."

"I have a *million* regrets," I say. "If I piss you off, it isn't one of them."

I swear someone in the crowd whispers my dad's name, and suddenly I can feel my mom hugging me, can taste the cake Granddad fed me at her funeral, can smell the sweat of the prison. Just as I'm about to fall, an arm wraps around my waist, and Liam leans down. "You okay?"

"I will be," I gasp. "As soon as I get another drink."

"She's had enough!" Eugenia says. "She's going home."

"You can leave, Eugenia! Go hang out with your parents in the morgue, or whatever it is you do at night!"

Eugenia stares at me, eyes hard, unreadable as a statue. She blinks, and a single tear rolls down her cheek. She doesn't try to hide it or wipe it away before she turns and leaves.

"What was that about?" Liam asks.

My stomach churns. "Just unloading some dead weight." I shake him off and weave toward the fallen tree. Xavier pulls a silver flask out of the pocket of his hoodie. He unscrews the lid and takes a pull as I sit next to him.

"Can I have some?"

He shrugs, but hands me the flask. "Suit yourself."

The gin burns down my throat like pine needles. "Disgusting," I say, shuddering. The rest of the crowd begins to blur together, faceless and cold. Someone says Holly's name, and a few girls start crying again. "I thought you weren't talking to me anymore."

He takes the flask. "I'm not. You sat next to me."

I try reaching for the flask again, but he holds it away. "I don't want you to be mad at me," I say, pretty sure I'm slurring my words now.

"Lucky for you, I won't be around much longer," he says as he tightens the lid. "I'm leaving next week."

My mind spins. "Leaving for where?"

"Military school. My parents are really pissed about me flunking a bunch of classes. Starts in two weeks."

"Where's the school?"

"Charlotte." He says it like he couldn't care less about the school. About me.

I look into Xavier's face, at his impossibly blue eyes. "You know what? It's for the best."

"Cold." He puts the flask back in his pocket and stalks off into the crowd.

Two figures break free from the trees and weave toward me. "You're Bett, right?"

It's Xavier's stoner friends, Dave and Jax. I cross my arms over my chest, hoping they'll take the hint and leave me alone. They pass a joint back and forth, and Dave blows smoke toward me. "Still too good for us, huh?" He nudges my leg with his worn-out leather boot.

I stand. "I was just heading home."

"We can take you," Jax says, holding up a pair of keys. He moves in closer, and the horizon bobs up and down, like I'm adrift at sea. "You need someone to help you." He smells my neck.

"Please," I croak, smashing my eyes shut, trying to make the world hold still.

The blood.

Her broken eyes.

"She said please," Jax says, and something wet moves across my ear. Dave's tongue, I think.

But all I can see is Grams collapsing, the way her body went limp, lifeless in a second. Maybe it would be better for everyone if I just disappeared. If I could just slowly dissolve into the dirt, particles and cells, one with the earth. I could give something back, leave the worst parts behind.

My stomach cramps and my pulse drums and my mouth dries out, and I can't help but feel all the sorrow in Wolf Ridge is somehow my fault.

I am a dangerous place.

Bright lights break through the trees, and someone shouts, "Cops!"

Then everything explodes, bodies running in every direction, beer cups dropped to the ground. "I feel sick," I say as I slump into Dave's arms. My mouth fills with spit, and I keep swallowing it down. My stomach seizes, and then I throw up, all over his jacket, his jeans, his ugly boots. He shoves me away.

And I'm falling endlessly down into the dirt.

Disappearing.

Just like she did.

Hands grip my arm, and Hunter helps me out of the woods before easing me into the back of his car, somehow evading Andre and Chantal.

"Why are you helping me?" I slur, remembering his place on Eugenia's murder board. Maybe I'm about to end up under a dumpster, too, with hateful words carved into my face.

He looks over his shoulder at me, his face a blur. "Because I wish someone could have helped Holly. And even though you weren't friends anymore, I know you do, too."

I've thrown up out his window twice by the time he pulls into my driveway. "I am so sorry," I tell him, trying and failing to grip the handle well enough to open the door.

He gets out and opens my door, helping me onto the driveway. I teeter in my high boots, so not ready, or sober enough, to go inside that house.

My grandparents are Sunday brunches and fresh-cut flowers, pleasant smiles and rainy afternoons spent reading.

They are not me: drunk in a driveway, mascara smeared, speckled in their own vomit.

CHAPTER
Thirty

Eugenia's reading on her front porch when I arrive the next morning. Granddad called from the hospital; I lied and said I had "womanly problems" so he'd let me stay home. Periods freak him out, which I knew would end the conversation. My only real problem is a pounding hangover. That, and possibly a ruined friendship with Eugenia. When she spots me, she puts down her book and sighs. "It lives," she says.

"Har har."

"What are you doing here?" she asks. "I don't recall inviting you over."

"First, I want to apologize. I was an incredibly giant asshole," I begin, walking halfway up the porch steps.

"Which time?" she asks. "Last night at the party? Or the time you made fun of my poem in front of the entire class? Or the myriad of times before that?"

"*All* of them," I say. "You've been a really good friend to me—the best friend I've ever had, to be honest—and I haven't always been decent to you. If you can't forgive me, I understand, but I needed to say it."

She looks down at her worn copy of *Frankenstein*, then back up at me. "It's never been easy for me to make friends. People think I look funny, dress weird, say the wrong things. Living here doesn't help. But it seemed like you finally saw past all that. Like you saw *me*."

I take a deep breath and let it out. Let it all go. "I *did*, Eugenia. I do. I really like who you are. You're smart, and well-read, and *different*. You take no shit from anyone, especially not from me, and you say what you mean. You're also not a total fuckup like I am. I admire you."

Tears slip from her eyes, and I think maybe we're about to have a moment. But then Eugenia does something I'd never expect: she throws her head back and screams. A brutal, throaty scream.

"Eugenia?" I ask, trying to keep my voice even and calm. "What, uh…what was that?"

She deflates. "Last night you said we didn't really know each other."

"I said a lot of shit last night."

"But you're right," she says, training her eyes on mine. "I haven't been completely up front with you about why solving these murders means so much to me."

"Isn't it like you said? Women have to look out for other women?"

She wipes her eyes. "I really meant that. But it's also because I failed someone. In a way, I killed her."

"Whoa, hold up." I climb the rest of the way onto the porch and sit next to her. "Please explain because the Eugenia Cline I know is *not* a killer."

She takes a deep breath. "Do you remember a while back, that woman in town who died? She fell down the stairs?"

"Yeah, kind of," I reply. I remember Grams and Granddad discussing it one morning over breakfast, how it was such a tragedy. I think she'd gone to school with my mom.

"I met her once, before she died." Eugenia looks at her front door. "She was here, with some guy. I think his mom or grandmother had passed, and they were here to plan the funeral. I remember it was summer, superhot, and our air-conditioning wasn't working very well.

"I came downstairs to sneak a Popsicle from the kitchen. My parents had shown them into the coffin showroom and left them there. They do that, to give people space. Anyway, I got my treat, and as I was passing by to go back to my room, I heard something. A slap and a thud."

"The man hit her, didn't he?" I ask, memories of Trapper's violence always at the back of my mind.

She nods. "He came stalking out of the room, nearly ran me down, and went outside. The woman, she was on the floor. She got up slowly, told me nothing had happened, not to make a fuss, to keep it quiet. She had blood coming out of her nose, but she wouldn't stop smiling at me. Like she was trying not to scare me."

"And did you?" I ask. "Keep her secret, I mean?"

"I wanted to tell my parents, but every time I tried to, the words got lost. And they were so busy with the arrangements. Either way, I didn't say a thing. At the funeral, she seemed fine. She smiled at me and gave me a peppermint candy, and I made myself forget what I'd seen.

"And then," she continues, her breathing growing shallow, "a few months later, I brought my dad something to the basement. I don't remember what, but I caught a glimpse of a body. It was that same woman, Bett."

"The one who fell down the stairs?" I ask.

"Yes, only that's not what really happened. That man who'd hit her killed her. I knew it the second I saw her on the table. Dead, because I didn't stand up for her. I didn't do what was right." She closes her eyes, chin quivering, and I can see how hard she's trying to keep it together, to keep herself from feeling.

"Eugenia, it's not your fault what happened. You were just a little girl."

She won't look at me. Instead, she crosses her arms and stares straight ahead. Like she's looking back to that day with the woman. Maybe she's playing it out differently, telling her parents what happened. I've done the same a million times.

"Eugenia, listen to me," I say again. "You weren't there. You didn't make it happen. Even if you had told your parents, she might still have died the same way. And you can't make it unhappen."

"No. But maybe I can still save you."

"Save *me*?" I ask. "I don't need saving. I'm fine."

"You scared me last night, Bett. The way you were drinking and pushing me away. You have other friends." She picks up her book again. "But I don't. And I don't want to lose you."

"You're *not* going to lose me. Where is this coming from all of a sudden?"

She grabs my hand, squeezing harder than I knew she was capable of with those tiny bird hands. "I think you're the killer's next target, Bett. Ever since Ada gave you that police report, it's become clear. Whoever hurt your mom is out there. First, they killed your mom's doppelganger. Then, someone closer to you. Someone you saw every day who looked a *lot* like you."

"And you think I'm the next logical victim," I say, my ears starting to ring. I feel stupid for not realizing it sooner, but she's right.

"We need proof, Bett, and we can't wait any longer. I went into the diner early this morning, and David's going camping this weekend with some friends. He'll be gone Saturday morning through Sunday afternoon. That's our window. We stop him before he hurts you or anyone else."

"This weekend is prom," I say absentmindedly. "Which I'm banned from."

"Which makes it even better. No one will be around, and no one will be expecting to see you there. We can slip in and out. The case will be solved by this time next week....I promise."

CHAPTER
Thirty-One

Prom is a big deal in Wolf Ridge. This year's theme is Paris, and the prom committee managed to hire a string quartet and rent lights glimmering with Swarovski crystals. And the whole thing is dedicated to the memory of Holly Walters.

At least, that's what I've heard. I'm sitting on a bench on Market Street with Eugenia, making sure the promgoers see us together as their limos and jeeps glide past. I nudge her, and she hands me her coffee. It's still warm. A white limo stops in front of the nice Italian restaurant, brakes squealing, and we watch as guys in rented tuxes and girls in glittering gowns spill out onto the sidewalk. Madison's wearing a black two-piece dress that shows off her slim waist. She hangs on Liam's arm, and Natalie and Hunter are with them, too, all in black.

"I'm amazed they're able to smile," I say, handing back the mug. A half-empty box of donuts rests between us. My grandparents think I'm spending the night at her house.

Eugenia takes a long drink. "Are you disappointed you didn't go? I'm pretty sure Liam wanted to ask you."

I shoot her a look. "No way. We've got more important things to do tonight than a pointless rite of passage."

"How's your grandmother doing?" she asks. "My mom sent flowers."

I haven't been back to see Grams in the hospital. I told Granddad I still had period cramps when he left for the hospital this morning. I just can't look at Grams, not until I've done everything I can to earn her love back.

Not until I've righted all these wrongs.

———

At midnight we sneak out of Eugenia's house, her backpack filled with tools and weapons, and slink through town toward Rose Street. The prom ended at eleven, and everyone should be at Natalie's house by now for the after-party. I guess Lydia okayed it to keep everyone safe and together. A tiny part of me feels like I'm missing out.

Our phones are charged and on silent; Eugenia even brought her Taser, just in case. We're wearing black, hair pulled into buns.

David's neighborhood is quiet when we arrive, and we move along the side of his house. There's a door at the back, but it's locked. "Wait," I whisper. "Do we even know which floor he lives on?"

"He's on the first," she replies. "Let's try the front door." I follow her back through the weeds and overgrown lilies and up onto the porch. She puts on gloves and twists the knob. It opens. "I told you criminals make mistakes." She smiles and slips inside. I follow, locking the door behind us.

David's house is hotter than a cow's balls, and it smells like sweat and pine needles. The hallway is a hazy gray, and a digital clock on a table up ahead says a quarter after midnight. "Should we use our flashlights?" I ask.

"Better not. A neighbor could see and get suspicious."

"So where do we start?"

"The kitchen, I guess." A doorway to our right leads into a cramped kitchen. The window above the sink is bare, and moonlight brightens the white linoleum. I start opening drawers. They're filled with silverware and plastic lids, old batteries and receipts. Eugenia drops down and searches under the sink.

"Find anything?" I ask.

"Just bleach and dish soap and other junk."

I keep pulling open drawers, looking for a long glint of metal. The knife he used to kill Melissa and Holly. The police never found it, so there's a chance David brought it back home. He's probably washed it by now, but that doesn't matter. Only I can't find anything but a butter knife anywhere in his kitchen.

"Where are his steak knives? Knives for chopping?" I ask. "It's *weird* he has none. The man cooks for a living."

Eugenia closes a cabinet. "He probably dumped it somewhere else."

"Maybe at the diner?"

"Could be. But we can't go there tonight. Let's keep looking here." We slowly move out of the kitchen, losing the moonlight, and into an open room. The shapes of furniture and a TV appear in the darkness.

"Seriously, I can't see for shit in here," I say as I go to the couch closest to me. I run my hand along the cushions, afraid of what I might find.

Eugenia bumps into something, and it crashes on the floor. "Crap," she whispers. "I think it was a lamp."

We both stand still, listening for footsteps above us. I try to slow my breathing, but I can't. My heart is up inside my throat, and I close my eyes.

After a while, I say, "I think we're okay. But be more careful."

After we search the bathroom—which holds nothing more than some soap, shampoo, and the smell of mildew—we move into the room at the end of a narrow hallway. David's bedroom. I close the door behind us, and then I close his blinds. "We need to use our flashlights."

"Fine, but keep the lights pointed down, just in case," Eugenia warns.

I click on my light, and it shines down on shaggy brown carpet. Dirty T-shirts lay forgotten on the floor. Eugenia shines her light on an ugly brown dresser and opens one of the drawers. "Yuck, his boxers," she says, gamely digging through them anyway.

I move toward his unmade bed. Plain bedspread, one small pillow. David's life is starting to make me feel sad…until I remember he's likely a serial killer who took my mom from me. I heave up one corner of the mattress and aim my flashlight. There's something there. I pick it up and shine my light on a photograph of David and my mother from high school. They're sitting in the backyard of Magnolia House, smiling, with their arms around each other.

"Holy shit," I mutter, as Eugenia takes it from me.

"This isn't evidence of murder, per se, but it may be evidence of obsession." She sets the photograph face down on his dresser. "You all right?"

I take a deep breath. "I'm good. Let's keep looking."

Eugenia returns to the dresser, and I open the closet doors. The hangers inside hold mostly T-shirts, a couple of sweatshirts. Basic boring guy clothes. A shelf above has a few boxes, so I take them down and open them. They don't have much inside, just old baseball cards, some Teenage Mutant Ninja Turtles action figures, and a dried-up corsage that turns to dust in my hands. I put everything away as I found it, and then I push the clothes apart to check the floor. His shoes are actually lined up in a neat row, which seems out of character based on the rest of his apartment. There's a lone shoe box pushed up against the wall, so I pull it out. Inside is one shoe: a pink satin stiletto.

"Eugenia," I say, my voice trembling. "You need to see this." She hurries across the room and shines her light on the shoe.

"Is that Cherry's missing shoe?"

I nod, my hands trembling. "I...I think this might be what we've been looking for."

"And these," she says, holding up a pair of blue riding gloves. "The interview you gave to Bigsby, about the 'monster with blue hands.' He might have been wearing something like these when he killed your mom...maybe even when he killed Cherry, Melissa, and Holly."

"I need to sit," I say, sinking onto the floor.

I knew when we came here, we might find terrible things. But this is just all too much. Eugenia takes photos of all the evidence before carefully placing everything back where we found it. Our plan is to give the photos to Andre.

"I think we should go," she says. "Don't want to push our luck."

"But we still don't have anything to definitively tie him to Melissa's or Holly's murder."

"I think this is enough to convince Bigsby to start looking seriously at David Dennison."

"You're right," I say, and Eugenia helps me up. We shut off our flashlights and place them in her bag, and she opens the bedroom door. As we move into the hallway, something clicks at the front door. It starts to open, and we practically trip over each other as we scurry back into the bedroom. I close the door softly. "What are we gonna do?" I ask.

"The window!" Eugenia climbs onto the bed and draws up the blinds.

"Is somebody here?" I can hear David through the door.

"Hurry!" I hiss, looking from Eugenia to the door and back to her. "He's coming!"

"The damn latch is painted shut," she grunts, but suddenly the window is lifting, and a breeze wraps around the room. Eugenia punches out the screen, drops her backpack out the window, and climbs out after it. I'm halfway through the window, balancing on my stomach, when I hear David enter.

"Hey!" he shouts, grabbing hold of my leg. "What are you doing in here?"

"He's got me!" I scream at Eugenia. She grabs hold of both my hands and pulls as hard as she can. But David's stronger, and her hands are slipping out of mine. I kick my free foot backward as hard as I can. The kick lands, and David swears, dropping my leg. I scramble the rest of the way and land next to her in the dirt, falling hard on my tailbone. Eugenia's already on her feet and pulling me up when David sticks his head out the window.

"Bett?" he says. His face is all bloody.

Eugenia pulls her Taser out of her bag and gives him a shot in the neck. He falls back into the house. "Run!" she says, and we take off down the alley.

The streetlights paint the road in swatches of orange, and our shadows grow out ahead of us, our movements choppy. We bust onto Market Street; all the businesses are dark and closed.

"Nat's!" I shout, and we take off down her street, gasping for air.

CHAPTER
Thirty-Two

We hear the party before we see the house. Music thumps, and then her house comes into view. The windows are all lit up, packed with people moving around. Cars line each side of the street.

Eugenia and I stop in her front yard, looking back. There's no sign of David. "We should go in," I say, bent over and trying to catch my breath. "He won't follow us, not with so many people inside."

"I think this might be scarier than breaking into David's place," she mutters breathlessly, but walks up the sidewalk anyway to the front steps. I give her a look before I push open the front door. Heat rolls outside, and there's so much glitter on the floor this place could double for a crafting store. As we hurry inside, I look behind us, but there's no one following.

"We'll be safe here for now." I wipe the sweat from my hairline. "Let's just try to blend in and act like everything's normal."

A few people have noticed the girls dressed all in black and out of breath. I stand up tall and thrust my way into Nat's living room regardless, Eugenia on my arm. The furniture is pushed against the walls, and the carpet is gone. They always had the softest white carpet. Once, Nat spilled her grape juice on it, and Lydia didn't even get mad. She just laughed and moved an ottoman to cover it. I'm kind of sad it's gone and wonder what else has changed in my absence.

Eugenia hovers at my side. "Now what?" she asks. "People are *staring*."

We drift through layers of taffeta and silk and hair spray fumes. The guys have all shed their coats and bow ties, and are laughing too loudly, taking up too much space. The girls snap a million selfies, trying too hard to turn this night into something more than it is.

Carefully, we manage to slip into the kitchen for water. Someone's set up a game of beer pong on the table. Natalie and Madison stand together on one end, across from Brady and Hunter. Natalie's ball bounces toward a cup and misses.

Natalie watches as I get a glass from the cupboard and fill it with water. Eugenia glugs the whole thing. "Do people even really *like* beer?" she whispers. "It tastes like warm piss."

Brady's next shot goes in, and he whoops. "Drink, Baker!" Natalie forces a smile, fishes the ball from a cup, and drinks it.

Liam comes into the kitchen just as she finishes her beer. "I thought you gave up drinking, Nat," he laughs. Natalie sets the cup down and looks away.

"That night in the alley?" Brady sneers. "God, she was a mess."

"Be nice," Madison snaps. "Nat, what are they talking about?" She's wearing so much makeup her face looks plastic, but her eyes are all red.

"We stopped for late-night Chinese last week and found Nat stumbling around in the alley like she'd just downed a bottle of Everclear," Brady jokes. "She could barely form words."

I watch Nat. She keeps her chin dropped toward her chest, her hand fluttering with her wrist corsage.

"Ease up," I say, and everyone looks at me. "We've all had our moments when we drank too much." I offer a small smile, but Nat turns and leaves the room without another word.

"Didn't know you were here." Madison looks at me penetratingly. "I need a new partner. You want to play?"

"Ask Eugenia," I say, and follow Natalie out of the kitchen.

I don't see her, so I go down the hall to her room, knocking once before I open her door. It's dark, and I flick on her desk lamp. Her walls, once covered in posters of her favorite singers and movies, are bare. Taking deep breaths, I open the window for some fresh air. It's still way too humid outside, but the stale air in here is hard to breathe. There's almost a chemical layer to it.

On the dresser next to the window is a black ring. It sparks something in my memory, because…*it looks like Holly's.* I pick it up to look closer when the door opens and Natalie steps inside.

"What are you *doing* in here?" she asks. When she notices me holding the ring, she snatches it away. *"Don't touch that!"*

"I'm sorry," I say, shocked. "I was looking for you. You seem…"

"She left it at our sleepover. At Madison's." Natalie turns the ring over in her hand, slips it on—then yanks it off and shoves it in a drawer.

"I'm so sorry, Nat. I can't imagine what this has been like for you. Actually, I guess I can. Still, I'm really sorry about Holly."

She sits on her bed. "Can you leave? I need a minute."

"Sure, no problem." At the door, I look back. Natalie's slouched over, staring out the window, her prom dress almost too big on her. As I close her door behind me, Lydia turns down the hall. I freeze, until I remember she gave this party her blessing and isn't going to get us all charged with underage drinking. At least I hope she isn't.

"Bett," she says dryly as she moves toward me.

"What are you doing home?"

She gestures at her shirt, which looks like it's been splattered with blood. I swallow.

"Some drunk woman spilled her daiquiri all over me. I'm here for a quick change, then back for the next tour. Business has been crazy lately."

As she hustles by, the smell of rum wafts off her. She opens the door to the basement, I assume to toss it into the wash, and I wander back into the living room. Eugenia's still in the kitchen, backpack on the floor as she throws a perfect arc shot that forces Brady to drink. I give her a thumbs up, and she shrugs, which in Eugenia-speak means she's fine. Maybe even having fun.

All the adrenaline from our break-in at David's is gone, and I'm left feeling heavy and tired. I just want to go home. Eugenia and I will have to speak with Andre first thing tomorrow, not Bigsby. Maybe we can catch him at home. He's the only one I trust anymore in this town. And if Andre won't listen, I'll go to Ada. She'll make sure the information gets out there.

As I pull out my phone to check in with Granddad, Lydia leaves out the front door, wearing the same stained top. I try to shrug it off, but something gnaws at me. Why come all the way home to change and then leave in the same ratty clothes?

I stick my head in the kitchen to grab Eugenia, but she's *actually* smiling. She deserves to have some fun for once, so I leave her to her beer pong, hurry down the hall, and slip into the basement unnoticed.

The stairs creak as I descend into the dank, dark space. There's no light switch at the top of the stairs, which I always found annoying. On the last stair, I reach around the wall and flick on the light. Nat and I used to hang out here sometimes, first playing hide-and-seek and later her Ouija board. It's pretty much the same. Exposed ceiling stuffed with pipes and cobwebs. A washer and dryer leaning in one corner. Dirty windows papered over. Their old air hockey table is gone, an ugly brown stain on the concrete in its place. I'm not surprised; the fan barely worked, and our games usually ended in frustration as the puck stalled out in the middle of the table. Still, it's just another sign our past is gone. Those little girls don't exist anymore.

Sadness settles into my bones as I move slowly toward the washing machine. There's a box of detergent sitting on a shelf above it. I look inside, and it's full. When I pull the knob on the machine water spurts out, so the machine's working. Why did Lydia come down here at all if not to wash her shirt? Maybe she had an emergency at the bar and had to hurry back. I check my phone again; no signal down here. I shove it back in my pocket and face the open expanse of the room.

I've got that strange feeling again, like I did when I found Melissa. But it's been a weird night—a weird few weeks—and I'm exhausted.

No good can come of snooping around Lydia Baker's basement.

Still, my eyes travel the space again, and I inch closer to the stain on the floor. It could be oil, maybe paint. It's swirled around, like someone tried to wipe it away. No. It's nothing. I'm not thinking straight.

I go back to the stairs, ready to end this day. When I put my hand on the railing, something soft brushes against it, probably a spiderweb. I yank my hand away and check. Leaning in closer, whatever touched me comes into terrifying focus:

Hair. Blond hair, crusted in blood, stuck on a small nail.

The same color as Holly's hair.

"Shit." I flick the light off and feel my way up the stairs in the dark. It's fine, it *has* to be. It has to—

When I open the door, a silhouette blocks out the hallway light. Before I can ask them to move out of my way, a shock of electricity blasts into my chest, and I'm falling backward, nothing but air behind me.

CHAPTER
Thirty-Three

My ears ring, and the back of my head throbs. When I gently probe it with my fingers, they come away bloody. The room is dark.

I blink a few times until the night comes back to me: I'm in Nat's basement. Footsteps and thumps of music come from above. The stairs slowly come into focus. When I push up onto my elbows, things go wobbly. I lie back down, hoping I don't have a concussion.

Closing my eyes, I take deep breaths, willing myself to calm down and drag my ass back upstairs, find Eugenia, and get the hell out of this house. My chest hurts, and I try to remember what happened. Did someone jab me with something? Did I electrocute myself somehow?

Something shifts in the darkness off to my right. Feet, then legs, materialize out of the gloom. A person, towering over me.

"Bettina?" Lydia asks, still in her stained top. "Are you all right?"

"My head hurts," I murmur, relief washing over me. "I must've tripped and fell."

She doesn't try to help me up. "What are you doing down here?"

"Looking for Natalie," I lie. "Thought she came down here."

She kneels next to me, and at first I think she's going to help me. But then she leans closer and whispers, "Don't lie to me."

Cold prickles my entire body.

"I'm s-sorry. I shouldn't have come down here."

"That's right, you shouldn't have. You made it clear months ago my daughter's friendship means nothing to you, so you no longer have free reign in our home. Understood?"

I nod quickly. "I understand."

"Good." She stands and turns on the lights. The brightness hurts my eyes, makes my head pound even more. I struggle to sit up, and then Lydia pushes down on my shoulder. "Wait a minute," she says. "I can't let you move. Not if you're seriously injured."

"I'm bleeding," I say. "I need a bandage or some ice."

She goes over to the laundry shelf and brings back a paper towel, which I press to the back of my head. "This will have to do for now," she says. I don't question why she won't let me get up, just hold the towel to my head.

"I won't bother anyone," I say. "I can go out through the back if that's what you're worried about. I don't want to ruin Nat's night. She deserves to have some fun."

She shakes her head, sighing. "You must think I'm pretty stupid."

"I don't—"

She holds up a hand, and I clamp my mouth shut. "You've been down here. You've seen everything. You really think I can let you leave *now*?"

"But I haven't seen anything," I say, trying not to look at the stained floor, the hair on the railing. I think of Eugenia upstairs, of our evidence that's suddenly making less sense than it did an hour ago.

Holly's ring in Nat's room.

Nausea ripples through my body, and I swallow it away.

Suddenly the door at the top of the stairs opens. "Mom?" Natalie closes the door and hurries down the stairs. "What's going on?" She's changed out of her dress and into jeans and a T-shirt. She's wearing Holly's ring again.

"Nat," I say, managing to sit up.

"Leave her," Lydia warns, her voice cold. She moves between us, so that Natalie has to lean to one side to see me. I stare at her, pleading, trying to send her a psychic message. Something's not right with her mother.

We're not safe here.

"What happened?" Nat asks.

"I fell," I say, trying to sound calm. "You know me, so clumsy. Your mom was just helping me."

Lydia takes Nat's elbow and drags her to the other side of the basement, speaking in hushed tones. Nat looks over at me, but Lydia squeezes Nat's face in her hands and jerks her head forward. I can't hear what they're saying. Something is passed between them. Then Natalie comes back to where I'm sitting and holds out a hand. Her eyes are red.

"Oh, thank God," I whisper as I struggle to stand. "Your mom is being seriously weird tonight." The room spins a bit, and Nat steadies me until it passes. When I try to move toward the stairs, Nat pulls me back. "What are you doing?" I ask as I stumble.

Nat starts to softly cry. "I'm so sorry, Bett," she whispers.

"For what?" I ask, and that's when she zaps me with a Taser.

CHAPTER Thirty-Four

My eyelids are plastered shut, and it hurts to open them. I must have lost consciousness again after Nat zapped me.

Nat. Natalie Baker. How is this happening?

I'm still in the basement; it's dark again. No music from upstairs. My hands are tied behind my back.

"Hello?" I say, my voice wobbly. No answer. I open my eyes as wide as I can, trying to pick up any shapes or scraps of light, but it's like trying to look through murky water. I rise up onto my knees, then stand. No one tries to stop me.

Maybe I really am all alone down here.

My heart ticks up as I shuffle a few steps forward. I *think* the stairs are straight ahead. I have to be close now. I ease a foot out in front of me....

Something creaks, and then hands shove me on the shoulders so hard, I fall onto my back. My right shoulder screams, like maybe it's popped out of the socket. All the air rushes from my chest, and I gulp and choke, trying and failing to breathe.

"*Sit still.*" It's Lydia's voice, somewhere in the dark. I catch a bit of air, sucking it in greedily, practically hyperventilating. "And don't bother yelling for help; everyone's gone home. No one will hear you."

Something flickers, and a small camping light blazes yellow. Lydia holds it over me, wearing a pair of blue gloves, the kind you wash dishes with.

The monster with the blue hands.

My whole body suddenly feels like it's filled with concrete.

It can't be. Lydia wouldn't hurt anyone. My shoulder burns, and I try to adjust myself to take some pressure off it.

She kneels next to me. "I really wish you could have left well enough alone, Bett."

"Leave *what* alone?"

"Trust me when I say this hurts me more than it hurts you." Her hands wrap around my neck and begin to squeeze. I thrash my legs, trying to buck her off, but she's much stronger than she looks.

"It'll be better this way. No more suffering, and I can save my bar." Her breath smells like stale coffee and liquor. "I love him, Bett. Always have. I'd do anything for that man. Anything he needs or wants. Anything he asks."

It takes me a second to realize who she's talking about:

My father.

"She had everything I wanted, and she never appreciated it. She was beautiful and thin and perfect, everything Wolf Ridge expects a good woman to be. And she treated Trapper like a pauper, when he was a poet. Couldn't she see that?"

I keep kicking my legs, but my head hurts, her grip tightens, and I'm seeing stars. She's clamped her eyes shut, and soon my vision dims, too.

"A poet," she repeats, her face blurring, gray seeping in around the edges. Her voice sounds far away now. "He was there for me when no one else was. He *saw* me. He *loved* me. I'd do anything for him. He values loyalty. Most don't."

Suddenly the pressure lifts, and I gasp for air, opening my eyes.

Lydia has moved back against the wall, watching me. She has a knife in her hand. She's breathing heavily, her eyes wet. I can't tell if she's winded or afraid. Maybe both.

I'm shaking so hard my feet keep thudding against the cold concrete. My mind can't seem to piece together what I'm seeing or hearing. It *can't* be true.

"When your mom died, Bigsby and your grandfather spared no expense. You would have thought Princess Diana had died! Quite different from Cherry's murder. Did you know Cherry was pregnant?"

My stomach heaves, and I'm sick down my neck and the front of my shirt. I don't want to hear anything else she has to say. I want to go home.

"Trapper was already dating your mother. He *couldn't* have a bastard child. I didn't need to be asked twice."

A coldness seeps through my bones as her words settle into me, their meaning. "He really asked you…?" I can't finish the sentence.

"I hear the judgment in your voice. But your father was my savior! My daddy left when I was still a baby, and Mama had man after man in and out of our house. Some of them liked me a little too much. She kicked me out when I was fifteen, like it was my fault.

"And then I met Trapper at a party. His sultry voice, the beautiful things he was saying…it was like coming alive for the first time. We were rapt, all of us! He could have had any woman in that room. But he chose *me*. He gave me a place to stay, a shoulder to cry on. And he saved me, again and again. And I was there for him, however he needed me."

Pieces of my conversation with Trapper at prison come back to me. I had asked him if he sent someone else to hurt my mom. He never answered.

But Lydia just did.

"Why?" I gasp. But no sound comes out. I can't find my breath. Lydia's eyes are like two dark holes, zeroed in on mine. She is the monster with the blue hands.

"She was going to leave him, take her inheritance! We *depended* on that money, or at least the promise of it. We're not all born with silver spoons up our asses."

I clench my jaws, trying not to cry. But I'm shaking so badly now I can't help it.

She traces the knife along her inner arm. "I was *never* good enough for anyone in this town. Those perfect girls with perfect faces don't know how good they have it. Girls like *you* and Holly Walters and Melissa Atkins. How protected you are. How sheltered. You just look down at girls like me and my Natalie. But your daddy didn't."

"Nat's my friend," I say, which makes her laugh. I hope Eugenia got away, that she's somewhere safe.

"Natalie never saw it, but Holly tortured her, always poking fun at her weight or her face or her clothes. And Melissa looked *so* much like Prudie. *Exactly* like Prudie. So I took them both away, just like he asked me to. Two women—that's what he wanted. Two women done the same way Prudie and Cherry were. And now his lawyer can file an appeal. He'll be out, and we can finally be together."

"No," I say, my voice shaking. "You can't do that. He can't…"

"It's too late, sweetheart. And now my tour is making a killing. Don't you see? Everyone loves a good murder mystery! They love beautiful dead women! And I'm a master storyteller, Bett. The money we'll make from *your* death will set us up for life. Book deals, shows, movies."

"Those were real people you killed, Lydia, not characters in a story! And now you've dragged Nat into this?" I think back to what Brady said in the kitchen: Natalie stumbling behind the Chinese restaurant. Drunk, so drunk…so miserable…

Did she help with any of this?

Lydia points the knife at me. "I'm teaching her how the world works. Kill or be killed."

My eyes dart around the basement as I try to think of something to say, something that will convince her not to end me. "He's not worth it," I blurt out.

She cocks her head to the side. "*What* did you say?"

"He's using you to do his dirty work. And now Natalie's life is ruined, too."

A bead of blood bubbles up from her inner arm.

"What's to stop him from killing you once he gets out?" I go on, afraid to stop. "Or turning you in to the cops?"

The knife's still pointed at me, but she doesn't move any closer. "He won't. He wouldn't."

"Was sending him to prison part of your plan? Or did you mess it up, Lydia? He'll turn on you in a *heartbeat* to stay out of jail."

The knife tip droops a fraction.

"I won't take the fall for this," she mutters. But for the first time tonight, she sounds uncertain. "Natalie needs a mother. I won't abandon her the way my mama did me. Trapper will take care of us, like always. He promised."

"You need to stop him from getting out of prison. My grandfather can help you."

Lydia rushes forward and jabs the knife toward me, and I try to slither backward. "And I'm just supposed to believe you'll let Trapper rot in prison the rest of his life when you know he's innocent?"

"He's not innocent!" I shout. "He ordered you to kill those women! He brainwashed you, used your love for him to make you do terrible things! He's a murderer! He shouldn't ever get out!"

Her eyes go unfocused, like she's seeing something that isn't there. "It'll be tragic, the news of your death. But in a way, it'll also be poetic. Almost…beautiful. And just so very *great* for business."

She kneels at my left side and holds the knife to my neck. I hold my breath, afraid to move. "A mother has to protect her child," she murmurs, her breath steamy against my face. "I can't just let you go. You know that."

The knife begins to pierce my skin, and wetness runs down my neck.

I whimper. "I'm Trapper's daughter. Please don't do this, Lydia. I'm a part of him."

She hesitates, and I realize this is my only shot.

I slam my forehead into her face as hard as I can.

Her nose cracks, and when she leans away, I roll to my right, my shoulder screaming in pain. As I scramble to stand, a sharp pain tears through the back of my leg. I fall onto my knees, drag myself until I hit the wall. Flickers of light explode around me, and I'm about to pass out.

Blood drips down Lydia's face, staining her teeth red. "You should have left it alone," she snarls. "Why couldn't you just leave it alone?"

Suddenly the basement door swings open. Natalie stands in the doorway.

"*Nat, please!*" I shout, trying to stand.

"Stay upstairs!" Lydia commands. "You don't want to be down here for this."

Nat thunders down the stairs and stops in front of her mom. She holds out a hand. "Give me the knife, Mom."

"Move out of my way, Natalie. I need to finish this. Just go to bed like I asked. Be a good girl."

"Let me do it, Mom."

Lydia scoffs. "You don't have the nerve, baby girl. Let Mama take care of this."

"I'm ready," she says. "Haven't I helped you before? I moved a body for you. And Bettina Jane has been *horrible* to me."

They stare at each other. After a beat Lydia places the knife in her hand.

"Prove it, then."

Nat slowly turns and comes toward where I lay on the floor. "Nat, please, you don't have to do this," I beg.

She bends down and whispers, *"Just play along."* Then she takes the knife and jabs it into my stomach—not very deep—and quickly pulls it back. I suck in a breath.

Red blossoms all over my T-shirt.

"See, Mom," she says, turning around. "And you said I couldn't do it."

Lydia shakes her head. "Chest, Natalie. Three to the chest. You know better."

Nat kneels down.

"Where should we put her when it's over?" Lydia asks as Natalie aims the knife over my chest and—again—makes a shallow stab, flooding my shirt with superficial blood. I almost pass out from the pain. "I was thinking her mother's grave. The headlines alone will shake the true-crime world."

"Yeah, Mom, great idea! Why don't you let me finish up down here? Let me focus."

Lydia gestures at me. "One more, or it'll take forever for her to bleed out."

"I'll do it. Don't you trust me, Mama?"

"I do, you know that. I can see you're ready." She kisses Nat's cheek, looks back at me once more, and goes upstairs.

CHAPTER
Thirty-Five

Once the door closes, Natalie rushes behind me, and I wait for the knife to sink into my body again. But then she cuts whatever's holding my wrists together. "Natalie, what the hell—"

"*Quiet*," she hisses.

My wrists have been rubbed raw. "Nat. Is your mom really *killing* people?"

Natalie looks at the knife she's still holding. "I can't talk about it. Please don't make me." She suddenly lurches away and throws up on the floor. I wince and cover my nose, trying not to smell her sick. She spits and wipes her mouth. "We have to wait until she finishes her wine and passes out in bed. Then I can get you out."

"This is crazy, Natalie. You've been helping her? Did you hurt Holly?"

Nat gulps back a sob. "No, I swear I didn't hurt anyone!"

"But you've been helping her cover it up, haven't you?" She doesn't answer, but I don't need her to. "You could have come to me. I would have helped you."

"No one can help me now." She wipes her eyes and moves toward the stairs. She tilts her head, listening, her eyes huge in her gaunt face. She's like a walking skeleton, and I wish I'd recognized that she needed help. Real help.

Natalie's another girl my father's killed, spiritually. And all without getting his hands dirty. *Fucking coward.*

"She's still moving around up there. We need to wait." Nat paces, walking toward the washing machine and back again. She avoids stepping on the brown stain.

"Is there another way out?" I ask after a while. "One of the windows?"

She shakes her head. "She nailed those shut from the outside weeks ago, and she'd hear the glass break."

I try not to imagine Holly trapped down here, begging Lydia to stop.

"We could try?" I ask.

She shrugs, and I move to the closest window. I peel off the newspaper taped to it and try to pull it open. But Nat's right; it won't budge. "We could break it quietly, maybe with fabric or towels to muffle the sound. You're skinny enough to fit through. You could go for help," I say, looking back. Nat's sunk onto the floor now, crying. The knife lies next to her.

I sit by her. "This isn't your fault," I say, putting my arm around her. She's lost so much weight I can feel every bone in her back. "Our parents are sick. This is on *them*."

She shakes her head. "I could have done something—anything. But I was too afraid of her! And she's all I have." She's crying so hard now I can barely understand her. I eye the knife, then slowly pick it up. Natalie either doesn't notice or doesn't care.

We wait for a long time. Upstairs, everything is silent. Lydia must be asleep.

"I'm leaving now," I say gently. "I'm going to go to the police. I won't tell them your part in this."

She looks up. "Why?"

"Because you were my best friend for a long time."

She wipes her nose. "No, Bett. I won't let you do that. I can't keep these lies anymore. I don't care what happens to me. I just need this to be over. I'm coming with you."

"You sure?"

She nods. "I'm sure."

Knife in hand, I move to the stairs. I don't seem to be bleeding as much as I was at first. The first stair groans when I step on it, and I try the next more slowly. Still squeaky. Each of them are.

The hallway upstairs is dark and quiet. Lydia's bedroom door is shut. I look back at Nat, who puts a finger over her mouth. We walk slowly toward the living room and round the corner.

As I put my hand on the front door handle, Nat groans and slumps against the wall. I turn around as Lydia jabs at me with Eugenia's Taser. I jump back, accidentally dropping the knife, which clatters to the floor next to a trampled corsage.

Lydia dips and comes up with the knife, pointing it at me. "I *knew* she wouldn't be able to finish this. Poor thing."

Behind her, a figure appears in the doorway to the kitchen.

A figure I have never been more grateful to see.

"I called the police," Eugenia says loudly. She aims a baseball bat at Lydia. "Drop the knife, or I will not hesitate to bash your brains in."

Lydia glares. "You wouldn't dare."

Without hesitation, Eugenia winds back and swings.

Lydia screams as the bones in her wrist crunch against the wall, and the knife goes flying.

She holds her wrist against her chest, and then suddenly she's rushing at me, faster than Eugenia can swing again, screaming like a banshee, her face twisted in anger.

My father's anger.

I rear back and punch her square in the nose—harder than I hit Holly—and she drops to the ground. "That's for my mother!" I scream, then kick her in the ribs as hard as I can. "And that's for me!"

"We need to get out of here, Bett," Eugenia says.

"Not without Nat," I say, who's still a mess on the floor. Wincing, I reach for her and pull her up. Her eyes flutter, and we stumble outside as blue-and-red lights flash against the house and the sirens grow louder.

Nat looks at me, and I can see now that she is utterly broken. I reach for her hand, and she holds on to me so hard.

But I feel nothing at all.

Or everything at once. It's hard to tell the difference sometimes.

CHAPTER
Thirty-Six

Andre brings me a cup of coffee. I'm seated at his desk at the police station, wrapped up in a scratchy gray blanket. Eugenia sits next to me. The sun is just starting to come up, and streams of light filter through dusty window blinds.

"I put in some cream and sugar," he says. "I hope that's okay."

"Thank you, Andre." My hands shake as I bring the paper cup to my lips. The paramedic bandaged me up in Nat's front yard, but I refused to go to the hospital. They were superficial wounds, but at least the pain lets me know my heart is still beating. That I'm not dead.

Eugenia sips coffee in the chair next to me, unwilling to leave my side. She left the party with everyone else after Lydia told her I'd already gone home. But something nagged at her, and when she discovered her Taser was missing, she came back.

David sits at Chantal's desk, giving his statement. He says something about Lydia burning her clothes and some blue rubber gloves the afternoon of my mom's murder, but I tune the rest out. Lydia used to take me and Nat for ice cream almost every day in the summer. She braided my hair. Showed me how to use tampons. She listened when I needed a mother's perspective.

Maybe it was subconscious guilt over what she'd done.

She's locked up somewhere in the building. And Natalie's life is ruined. My father ruined it. *I* ruined it. All I wanted was to stop a killer and prove my father was guilty so I could move on. But by bringing Lydia's crimes to the light, I may have set him free.

"Where's Natalie?" I ask.

"They took her to the hospital," Andre says. "She was having some kind of panic attack."

"It's not your fault," Eugenia says, reading my mind. "Lydia hurt your mom, *and* she hurt you. She deserves to be punished."

"But Natalie—" I choke out.

"We'll be there for her," Eugenia says. "However we can."

The door bursts open, and Granddad strides to Andre's desk. "What is going on?" he barks in Andre's face. Eugenia's parents enter just behind him. They kneel next to their daughter and wrap their arms around her.

"Calm down," Andre says. "Everyone is fine, but Bett has been attacked."

"By what?" Granddad asks. "An animal?"

Andre hesitates. "Lydia Baker."

"Lydia Baker?" Granddad looks at me for the first time. "Are you all right, Bett?" He touches my sore shoulder, gently like I could disintegrate. "You should be at the hospital."

"She has superficial wounds on her head, stomach, chest, and leg, but she refused to go the hospital," Andre answers for me. "We're holding Lydia in the back."

"Good, good," Granddad says, focusing on Andre. "Why would Lydia *do* such a thing?"

I set my coffee on Andre's desk. "Because she killed my mom, Melissa, and Holly. Cherry Hobbs, too," I say. "And we figured it out."

Granddad looks down at me. "That's not funny, Bettina Jane."

"She's being serious," Eugenia says. "And everyone around here better start listening to what she has to say."

I shrug off the blanket and stand to face him, wincing from the pain. "Lydia admitted it to me. She's been in love with Trapper for years. That's why she killed them. He *ordered* her to."

He scoffs. "I can't believe that. Lydia would never…"

"She admitted everything," I say, my voice cold.

The back doors open, and Bigsby comes striding in. "What in God's good name is going on?" he demands.

I look him dead in the eyes. "Lydia Baker killed my mother, Cherry Hobbs, Melissa Atkins, and Holly Walters. And tonight, she tried to kill me, too. You *knew* Trapper didn't kill my mom, at least not by his own hands. You knew it the first time you interviewed me."

He shakes his head. "You were a confused, frightened child. Not exactly a reliable witness. The guilty man is right where he belongs, and I'll do whatever it takes to keep him there until the day he dies. Ain't that right, Wells?"

Granddad rubs his hands over his face. "Trapper is guilty," he says unconvincingly.

Bigsby nods. "Exactly. We did it all by the book."

Chantal rises from her desk. "Chief," she says, "you might want to listen to what Mr. Dennison has to say."

David looks at me, then at the chief. "She burned her clothes the day of Prudie's murder," he says. "I remember I went to her house around four, and she had a fire going in the backyard. Burned her jeans, black hoodie, and some blue rubber gloves." He hangs his head. "It always bothered me, how she didn't seem all that upset or surprised Prudie had been killed. But I told myself it was nothing. Women just don't do evil stuff like that. Or at least that's what I thought."

Bigsby scoffs. "That don't mean nothing."

"I think she stabbed herself the other day," David goes on. "I didn't see anyone creeping around her house."

"I'm so sorry, David," I say, my voice catching. He gives me a sad smile.

I face Granddad. "Don't you get it now? Lydia's the monster with the blue hands. She killed my mom. Your daughter."

Granddad drops into a nearby folding chair, unwilling to meet my eyes. "Please, Bett," he says, his voice trembling. "We always thought it was him. How could it have been anyone else?"

"But it wasn't just him, Granddad. He's been pulling Lydia's strings for years, even from prison. And now more women are dead."

He buries his face in his hands.

The room spins a little, and I sit back in my chair. No one says anything. What else is there to say? I may have gotten what I wanted—just not what I need, whatever that is.

CHAPTER
Thirty-Seven

When I get to the hospital, Ada is curled up in a chair next to Grams's bed, snoring softly. Grams is awake, wearing her pink nightgown and filing her nails as early morning light trickles through the window. A half-eaten plate of eggs sits on the table next to her, and her eyes light up when I appear in the doorway.

"Bett!" she says. "I'm so glad you're here." She scoots over in the bed and pulls back the sheet, and I gently crawl in next to her. Once I'm covered, my body crumbles. She smooths my hair and kisses my forehead, tightens her arms around me, and I finally let myself fall apart. Maybe for the first time ever.

"Your grandfather told me everything," she says after a while.

I look into her eyes; they're so much clearer than they've been in a long time. "He did? Are you upset?"

"Relieved," she says. "Relieved that you're safe, and that we can all stop pretending."

"Pretending what?"

"That we're not hurting. That being angry or pretending it never happened will take away our pain. I loved my Prudence, and I always will. I want to honor her life, not hide from it anymore."

"Grams, I don't even know where to start," I say. I feel filled with lead, I'm so tired.

"Why don't you rest for now, sweetheart. I'm not going anywhere."

So I close my eyes and fall asleep next to her.

⌒

The next day, Eugenia and I agree to meet at Sheila's for breakfast.

When I get there, I lean against the building to wait for her. The sun is liquid yellow in the sky, already heating up the first day of summer break. The muscles in my neck and shoulders are pulling so hard I can barely look down at my hands. They still shake, so I ball them into fists. A rusted-out Buick parks in front of a house down the block, and a man gets out, slurping a coffee as he slowly walks up the sidewalk and goes inside. I wonder what his story is, if he's just gotten off a night shift at one of the mines or was out partying all night.

We are all mysteries.

Eugenia turns the corner, dressed in a black sundress, a stack of papers tucked up under one arm. She looks perfectly normal, like nothing out of the ordinary happened at the prom after-party.

"You look awful," she says, not to be rude, but to acknowledge what I went through.

"Thank you," I say. And I mean it. I earned the circles under my eyes, the scars and the scrapes, too. I nod toward the papers. "What do you have there? Your manifesto?"

She shrugs, suddenly shy. "Kind of? It's the beginning of my novel."

"I thought you didn't want anyone to read it?"

"That was before someone tried to kill you. Here," she says, almost shoving the stack into my arms. "Read it for yourself."

The first page lists only the title and her name: DEAD GIRLS TALKING BY EUGENIA W. CLINE.

"What's it about?" I ask.

"A couple of girls in a small town who solve crimes."

"It's about us?" My eyes get wet, but I don't try to wipe it away.

"Kind of. You'll see. Now let's eat. My body is close to cannibalizing itself."

As soon as we step inside the diner, Sheila barrels around the counter and pulls us into a crushing hug. "I cannot imagine the shit you girls went through the other night," she says. "I am so sorry this town failed you so badly."

"Swear jar," I joke.

"I have a better idea," Sheila says. "Breakfast is on me, for the rest of summer."

We tuck ourselves into a table at the back. "You want to talk about it?" Eugenia asks, reading over her menu.

"Not today. Right now, I want to read this masterpiece." She rolls her eyes, but a smile tugs at her mouth as I dig into Chapter One.

EPILOGUE
Four
Months Later

Ada had sent my original police interview to Trapper's lawyer before Lydia went all Charles Manson and the Family on me after prom. But the police couldn't find any hard proof that Trapper ordered the murders. Just my word against his. And Lydia still refuses to admit Trapper played any role. She's in his clutches, maybe forever.

Granddad worked on the case all summer, along with everyone at his law office, trying to keep him in prison. But police found Lydia's DNA on Melissa's and Holly's bodies. Holly's blood was also on the basement floor. They also retested blood evidence from my mom's case: a few drops on the sheets that Jack Ledbetter also withheld from Trapper's lawyer. It was Lydia's blood. Cherry Hobbs's family won't let her body be exhumed for testing, so her case remains unsolved, even with Lydia's confession to me. (The pink shoe we found in David's closet was part of an old Halloween costume; it didn't match Cherry's.)

Today my father is walking out of prison a free man, his record wiped clean.

He used women to hurt women and got away with it.

Just like that. Just like they always do.

Ada, Eugenia, and I wait at the far end of the prison's parking lot, sitting on the hood of the Rolls. (I knew Granddad would never sell it.) Trapper's scheduled to be released today, and I need to witness it.

"You ready for this?" Eugenia asks. She wouldn't take no for an answer when she asked if I wanted her to come along today.

"As ready as a girl can be when her guilty-as-hell dad gets out of prison."

Only two days ago I said goodbye to Natalie. She left for New York to live with her aunt and uncle. She'll finish high school there, get counseling, and then who knows. Natalie came home the day of Melissa's murder to find Lydia scrubbing blood out of their living room carpet. Melissa's wallet was on their couch. Lydia told her it was self-defense, that Melissa flew into a rage, that she had no choice but to stab her. And Natalie covered for her, even planting the wallet in Xavier's truck. Helped cover for Holly, too.

Grams and Granddad offered to let Natalie live with them, but Nat said Wolf Ridge doesn't feel like home anymore. I don't blame her.

It doesn't often feel like home to me, either.

I rescheduled my Harvard interview for next week. I don't know if I want to be a lawyer. If I learned nothing else these past few months, it's that other people's expectations and perceptions aren't my burdens to carry, and that justice doesn't always find us.

I am more than what happened to my mother that June morning over a decade ago. The rest of the world may never see me as anything more than a story to be told, a character on a podcast or in a documentary, someone to dissect over cheap beers and greasy fries on a Friday night. But I finally see myself as more than that. And that's been liberating as hell.

"How about you?" I ask Ada. "Are you ready for this?"

She rented an apartment downtown for the foreseeable future, working on her podcast and writing a new book. We've had a few family dinners and brunches together at Magnolia House, and I'm glad Grams and Granddad are making an effort. The best part of Ada living in Wolf Ridge are her stories about my mom, all the adventures they had together and how much she doted on me as a kid. Even my grandparents have started talking about my mom again. She's no longer just a ghost. She's becoming real.

"I'll never be ready," Ada says. "That man had me convinced he was innocent. I'll make certain he never knows a day's peace again."

I point to the building. "The door's opening." A guard steps out first, holding the door. Trapper moves slowly outside, shielding his eyes from the sun. He's wearing jeans and a plain white T-shirt, and carrying a small brown bag. An older woman in a baggy sweatshirt shuffles toward him. That must be his mother. My grandmother. She pats his back, but they don't embrace. He lights up a cigarette, tilts his head back, and releases the smoke.

Trapper scans the parking lot, his head stopping when it faces me. He stands motionless.

I sit up straighter. I want him to know I see him for exactly what he is.

He drops something to the ground and gets into a van with the woman. The engine sputters as it leaves the parking lot.

He's out.

I can't believe they let him out.

Climbing off the car, I drift to where he just stood. The faint smell of smoke lingers. The sun glints off something on the sidewalk. It's a matchbook—SHEILA'S DINER.

The blood.

Her broken eyes.

I kick the matchbook into the grass. He'll make a mistake eventually, brag to the wrong man, cross the wrong woman. I slip on my sunglasses and walk back to the car. "Should we follow him?" Eugenia asks. "I could probably hack his phone, too, if he ever gets one."

The van has almost disappeared down the road, not much more than a speck. He's had a stranglehold on me since I was six years old. I don't want to carry his shit anymore.

"I've got a better idea," I say. "Let's live our lives. Sound good?"

I can tell Eugenia's itching to tail him. But she nods.

"Hey, Eugenia?"

"Bett?"

"You're my best friend. You know that, right?"

She grins. "And you're mine."

We climb into the Rolls and head in the opposite direction, planning to stop for ice cream on our way home.

I never look back.

Megan Cooley Peterson is an author, editor, and coffee drinker. As a teenager, Megan was part of a repressive, cult-like doomsday church that didn't like to be questioned. She questioned anyway. Megan has written about her experience in Bustle, highlighting how it helped shape *The Liar's Daughter*, her first young adult novel. The author of more than 80 nonfiction books for children, she has written on a wide variety of topics, including dinosaurs, sharks, urban legends, and haunted objects. Megan lives in Minnesota with her husband and daughter. Learn more at megancooleypeterson.com or connect on Twitter @meganncpeterson or Instagram @megancooleypeterson.

Acknowledgments

When I was a little girl, I dreamed of becoming a writer who lived in Maine. My backyard would be on a cliff facing the sea, and I would sit outside with my typewriter and write novels. Well, I may not be Stephen King living in Maine, but my writing dream has come true. And it would not be a reality without the loving support of my family and friends.

My family lost a bright light in 2021. My mom, Lori Rae Lundhagen Cooley, was funny, sensitive, and always there for the people she loved, no matter the cost to her. She was my favorite person to sit on the porch with, drink coffee, and talk about anything and everything. (Also, thank you for typing up my fifth grade Hawaii report for me when I forgot it was due the next morning!) I carry you with me.

Thank you to my husband, Dale, and our precious daughter, Molly. The love I have for the two of you can never be fully expressed in words. You are my home.

To my dad, Randy, and my sister, Adrien. We're finding our way together each day, and your excitement for this new book means so much to me. To my sister-in-law, Samantha, you are a breath of fresh air.

Thank you to all my lovely friends, who always believe in me even when I don't. You know who you are. And an extra special thanks to my friend Cheyenne Campbell, who reads all of my stuff and is a constant cheerleader.

Writing a book can be a solitary endeavor, but publishing a book takes a team! I have so many people to thank for helping me bring it fully to life. To Mora Couch, thank you for your keen editorial insight and your unending love of these bright, fierce female characters. Team Eugenia for life! This is our second book together, and I couldn't be prouder. I'd like to thank the entire team at Holiday House for all their hard work, and zeebythesea_ for their stunning cover illustration. And thank you to the lawyers who so graciously answered my questions about custody laws in North Carolina.

To Amy Giuffrida, my wonderful agent. Thank you for your constant support, impeccable communication, and for answering all my worried emails and messages. I cannot wait to see what else we can do together! And thank you to the incredibly talented authors of the A-Team! Your support, advice, and fun chats keep me going.

Last but not least, I have to thank you, dear reader. The story you hold in your hand no longer belongs to me. It belongs to you.